FATED TO THE WOLF PRINCE

The Hunted Omegas

APRIL L. MOON

Book Cover by Llewellyn Designs.

Edited by Linda Ingmanson.

First edition 2024.

❀ Created with Vellum

ONE

Brielle

My lab was my safe place. All the familiar rows of shiny beakers, medical testing equipment—well loved, if a little dated—and my desk, shoved off to the side and so buried under brightly colored Post-its and scientific journals that the dented surface of the wood hadn't been seen in ages. It was quiet, serene, and—

"Oh my God, Brielle!" Leigh's urgent tone as she burst through my lab door—without knocking, as usual—shattered my blissful concentration. I spun around, turning my back to the bank of machinery to take in her outraged appearance. She was in her exercise gear, blonde hair falling out of a messy bun, and her cheeks were hot red. "You're never going to believe this! Please tell me you checked your pack mail this morning?"

"Umm, no. I visited Mr. Coffee and came straight to my lab to check the results of last night's test run."

"Of course you did," she snarled as Shay, the much quieter leg of our best-friend trio, knocked softly and pushed through the door to stand behind her.

"Don't snap at her, Leigh. It's not her fault."

Leigh spun on Shay, eyes narrowed. "Don't act like you're

happy about this—you won't even talk to any of the men in the pack! This is an outrage! A travesty! A violation of our twenty-first century suffragette rights! It's, it's—"

"A mandate from the high alpha," Shay finished succinctly, though a deep flush stained her cheeks from Leigh's frank assessment.

"A mandate? What does it say?" I stepped forward anxiously. Mandates were never good news, and they always shook things up. *I've been shaken enough in my twenty-seven years of life, thanks.* I liked my little lab and my best friends and my sleepy, backwater-Texas pack.

"It says that shifters are cavemen who think they can drag us around by our hair at a whim! Well, I won't stand for it. Alpha Todd is about to get his pelt shaved, and I expect you two hussies to hold him down while I use the clippers, capiche?"

Her nostrils flared as she looked back and forth between me and Shay.

"Can I actually see the mandate, please?" I addressed the question to Shay, since she was keeping a calm head. She silently proffered the letter clutched in her hands.

The paper was thick and creamy, heavier than expected—almost like a fancy wedding invitation. The high alpha's seal was stamped on it with dripping purple wax. I unfolded the letter, and my hands started to shake as I read the first few lines.

By decree of High Alpha Kosta, son of Konstantin, son of Kasmiro, ruler of the nine great packs, a great pack gathering has been called. The alphas of each pack, along with their seconds and thirds, are hereby ordered to report to Pack Blackwater grounds within two weeks of the date of this summons. They shall accompany all unmated pack mates over the age of twenty, who are to participate in a series of matching activities.

The wolf shifter bloodlines have been weakened in recent centuries, with our numbers perilously in decline. This gathering is necessary to find the true mates that have been denied to so many by the global nature of the world today. This gathering will usher us into the future of pack life by ensuring the continuation of our species for centuries to come.

"*All* unmated pack mates? Worldwide." *Holy hell in a hand-basket.* "And where is Pack Blackwater territory? I've never even heard of it." I passed the paper back to Shay, not bothering to read the rest right now. Leigh's head looked like it was about to explode, she was so livid.

"Oh, that would be Kane's new territory in Alaska. You know, Kosta's *son*. Nepotism much? Basically, this is one big old matchmaking effort so alpha daddy dearest gets his pride-and-joy prince mated off right away, to keep his *own* bloodline strong. Pah! Why don't they throw in the ODL too? Make us all good and miserable." She threw her hands up and started pacing back and forth in the *much* too small entryway.

"Leigh! The ODL, really? We're not omegas. We're safe from them. And there's no point confusing the issue."

Leigh waved away Shay's chastisement, not put off from her ranting in the least.

"I mean, at least he's keeping it fair. All the single guys have to come too," I offered, trying to appease her in some way, even as my mind was reeling. I had to go to Alaska and meet... every unmated male wolf in the high alpha's territories. My hands wouldn't stop shaking, so I picked up my coffee cup. I took a small sip. It was already cold, but it was something to keep my hands busy.

"Fair, *sure*. You really think that old daddy-o is going to be fine with us picking someone else if we match with the prince? *Fated mates*. You can't force that! You find your mate when you're supposed to, not when some pompous asshole alpha waves his furry tail at everyone!"

She gestured wildly with her hands while she talked, putting the familiar piles of Post-its at the edge of my desk in grave danger.

"Leigh, it's going to be all right. The mating signs don't lie. If you don't spark for the prince, you won't have to deal with it." Shay's tone was quiet but firm. I loved that girl; she was always so steady.

"It's just ridiculous! It's the twenty-first century. I'll mate who I damn well please, and anyone who doesn't like it can go bite a tree!" She stopped pacing and leaned back against the office door, her shoulders visibly deflating.

"This is about Marcus, isn't it?" I asked softly.

"No, of course not," she huffed, but looked guilty.

"It's okay to be disappointed that he found a true mate, Leigh. You were in love with him."

"I am *not* disappointed, okay? I'm happy for him. True mate trumps all, and we all know it. It just... yeah, it sucks that I'm back where I started, and he's off and mated and his wife is already pregnant with their first pup." Her voice cracked, so I abandoned my coffee cup to wrap her in a hug.

Shay joined us from the other side, and we made a bestie sandwich. Wolves craved touch, and we could no more let her ride through this pain alone than she could bear it alone.

She lowered her forehead and rested it between ours. "I'm sorry, guys. I swore I wasn't going to get upset. I swore it, and yet here I am, the idiot who caught feelings and can't let go, even though the writing has long been on the wall. It's... it's starting to feel like it's *never* going to be me, you know?"

"Not to bring logic to an emotional party, but of the three of us, you're absolutely most likely to get matched. You're one of the strongest she-wolves in the pack, you're outgoing, and people love you. I'm the *actual weakest* wolf in the whole pack. Nobody's going to match with me, but I'm okay with that. I'll cheer you two on, and then we can all come home to Texas, and my one true love." I waggled my eyebrows, and they both groaned.

"You've got to stop calling this lab your one true love. It's weird, even for us." Leigh rolled her eyes at my stupid joke, but she wasn't looking as miserable anymore. So, mission accomplished.

"Besides, just because you're a lower designation in our pack doesn't mean you'll be the weakest from *all* the packs. Every pack has a psi, not just ours. I'm sure you'll find someone, if your wolf is ready." Shay squeezed my hand before stepping back.

My wolf. Sure, she was *raring* to come out and find me a match. Not.

I wasn't only the weakest wolf in the whole pack—the psi, only one step above an omega, and those were no longer allowed to exist—but I could barely shift. It was humiliating, and I was sure it was going to come up during all the compatibility testing. More often than not, I skipped the full-moon pack runs because there was no point. Maybe four times a year, my wolf came out to play, and she was the literal runt of the litter. I was smaller, weaker, and I could only hold the shift for about ten minutes before I blacked out. And that was *before* I woke up naked and human. I was a real catch by wolf standards.

I shuddered at the thought of *every unmated male wolf in the world* seeing what a loser I was. Definitely staying married to my lab.

"Come on, let's all go grab breakfast together. I'm sure everyone's going to be up and talking about this," Leigh suggested. With one last look of longing at my machines, I flipped off the lights to my lab and locked the door on my way out.

The results would be there after breakfast with my pack.

TWO

Kane

The board splintered and snapped in half beneath my bloody knuckles, but I didn't hesitate. "Another!" I barked at my top enforcer and second-in-command, Gael.

He pulled a fresh board from the stack without comment and braced himself for the next hit. I reared back and snapped my fist through it. Just like the dozen before it, it was hollow comfort for my raging anger.

My damn, meddlesome, didn't-know-when-to-quit father... I fell back with a snarl before Gael could pull another board from the stack, and planted my hands on my hips so I could pace. I couldn't sit still, or I was going to start punching holes in the side of my barn, and I'd just built the damn thing. I couldn't afford repairs right now.

Not with a quarter of the wolf population of the world descending on us within two weeks.

"Why does he think this is a good idea? One giant mating mart isn't going to result in anything but bloodshed. That many unmated males in one place, with all those pheromones... It's going to be chaotic, and people are going to get hurt. Why would he do this?" I was mostly talking to myself, but Reed answered nonetheless, from his position leaning casually against one of the barn's support beams.

"Perhaps because you're in your thirties, and he's tired of waiting for you to woo and bite a woman on your own, hmm?"

I growled at him in response. My wolf pressed to the forefront, searching for the danger causing my rage. When all he found was our most trusted pack mates in an otherwise empty barn, he curled up with an annoyed huff. *You too, buddy. I'm not ready to be mated yet, and you're going to have to deal.* He didn't deign that worthy of a response, dropping off into sleep. Though he did flick his tail at me as if flipping me the bird before closing his eyes. *She-wolf-hungry bastard.*

My wolf had been delighted when I'd gotten the call from my father that morning declaring my pack grounds the site of the first all-pack gathering in centuries. The idea of all those eligible she-wolves had sent him howling and yipping with glee. Me, on the other hand, not so much.

"Regardless of why"—Gael gave Reed a pointed *not*-helping look—"we've got a lot of work to get done, and he said to start expecting people in as little as one week. Where are we going to put everyone? We've got some rooms in the lodge, sure, but only one bunkhouse has been completed. If we put the entire pack on it, we could advance the schedule, and have the second one done for sure, and the third dried in, if nothing else..."

I groaned, still too mad to focus on the details, even though the final decision had to be mine. That was the deal with being Alpha; you got all the power, you got all the responsibility. It wasn't nearly as fun as it was cracked up to be. Forcing myself to calm, I closed my eyes for a moment and drew in a few deep breaths through my nose. The familiar scents of sawdust, earth, and spruce flooded my senses, bringing me a few inches back from the ledge. The overbearing, domineering, meddling—

Stop, Kane. Focus.

I shook my head to clear it and gave him a decision. "We

pull everyone except Marise and Neo, because we need them free to do food preparation as well. Gracelyn is obviously unavailable, given the pregnancy. Everyone else can pitch in. Accelerate the second bunkhouse, make every room a double, and if the third bunkhouse isn't done, that can be where the guys bunk, and the early arrivals can pitch in before the festivities start. We can also put people up in here, if needed. It wouldn't be the first time any of us have slept wild."

"Sounds like a plan, Alpha." Gael ducked his head in acknowledgment and excused himself from the barn.

That only left me and Reed, my third.

"Do you want to talk about it?"

"No," I said, already back to pacing. I ran my fingers through my messy hair for what felt like the tenth time in ten minutes.

"It's not going to be so bad. The other Alphas will know who their hotheads are, and we'll do our best to keep everyone busy. Gracelyn is enjoying her bed-rest duties of activity planner. That was smart, by the way—give her something to do up front so she feels important, even if she can't be up and about."

Gracelyn was our only pregnant she-wolf, and Reed's cousin. Sweet as a lamb, until you ticked her off. Then she knew how to use her fangs.

"Yes, well, I can't have her hurting herself, can I? Adam would try to take my head off."

He chuckled, the sound darkly amused. "He is even more overprotective now."

I sighed and finally stopped pacing. "I don't blame the man. We lose more of our women to birthing than any war or disease has ever taken. It's no wonder our numbers dwindle when the pregnancies are so hard. If I were in his shoes, I'd be a wreck on four paws."

"When."

"What?"

"*When* you're in his shoes. You're not getting out of this gathering unmated. The sooner you accept that, the better. Your old man is on a mission to see you mated and paternal, stat. You know the ruling line has to be secure, and he is not going to leave you be until it is."

I growled again, annoyed by his logic. Thinking of myself in Adam's shoes left me sick to my stomach. Sure, I was Alpha and responsible for the well-being of my pack, and I loved them all. But a pregnant mate was a whole different level of worry. I had control in some situations, but in most, my pack mates were free to live their lives and make their own decisions.

Putting the woman I loved in *danger* by the sheer fact of being with her, the natural progression from marriage into parenthood, to starting our own little pack... it horrified me. The thought of mating with a woman, impregnating her, and losing her and the baby in one fell swoop... It was a good thing the mate bond would kill me alongside them, because I'd go feral otherwise. The thought left me paralyzed with fear.

No, I wasn't ready. And no amount of meddling from my father would make me ready a minute sooner. My wolf let out an annoyed huff at my line of thinking and began pacing. He didn't agree, but he'd have to learn to deal right along with my father.

THREE

Brielle

Twelve days later

The plane ride to Alaska was mostly uneventful. Shay and I read books, while Leigh downed all the tiny bottles of alcohol the flight attendant would give her. Drinking for a wolf was kind of pointless since our fast metabolisms burned off the alcohol so quickly, we rarely felt any effects. Most of us didn't bother. If my pack mates wanted a buzz, they'd get furry and go racing through the forest. It wasn't really an option for me, but I was comfortable with my quiet, studious life.

Today, however, was an exception. Leigh was afraid of flying, so she'd shelled out all her pennies to stay slightly buzzed the whole flight. When we landed in Anchorage, we then boarded a rental van and started the ten-hour drive north to the Blackwater pack's territory. Leigh was so happy to be back on solid ground, she wouldn't stop singing until she passed out *three hours later*.

That left Shay and me with eight of our pack's males and no buffer. You see, Leigh might have been loud and rambunctious, but she was the perfect bestie for our otherwise quiet trio. She kept everybody looking left, so they never worried about what Shay and I were doing on the right. Perfection.

But now she was snoring softly, blonde head propped against the van's window and a small drool spot forming against the glass. It was tangible, the feeling of too many eyes on my skin as I pretended to read my paranormal romance. Had I read the same paragraph three times in a row? Yes. Did I know what it said yet? No. Was that going to stop me from going for the fourth read? Not in the slightest.

I still wasn't eager to engage. The Alpha and his first two wolves rode in the front, and they were all quiet. But the other five males were grumbling among themselves, a fact I was doing my dead-level best to ignore.

"It's wrong, taking our she-wolves. I know a few of us might find mates, but what if we don't? We'll never get a chance if they take all our women. We're a small enough pack as it is, without the oh-high-and-mighty one deciding his *pup* needs first dibs on all the unmated she-wolves."

That was Dante, one of the older unmated males in our pack. He was at least two hundred, but I didn't know his exact age. It made sense from his perspective to be annoyed about possibly losing an eligible female to a younger wolf when he still hadn't found his own mate, but I found it shocking that the men were concerned about losing *us*.

"Well, we won't give him first dibs. I'm sure there'll be opportunities to meet some fine ladies outside scheduled hours. He might be required to behave, but that doesn't mean the five of us can't do a little extracurricular meeting and greeting," Ricky said, his tone dripping with innuendo and his grin devious.

I shifted in my seat, uneasy at the idea of our pack planning to break the rules before we'd even arrived. This was the high alpha's event. I didn't imagine he was the sort of man you'd want to get on the wrong side of. He was *the* most dominant wolf in the northern hemisphere, possibly the world. I risked a glance over at Shay. She was still flipping pages in her paperback, head tucked down, but her eyebrows had completely disappeared beneath her bangs. I turned back to my e-reader, ignoring the words on the page as the men continued to discuss their plans for *extracurricular activities*.

Jonesy broke in from the front seat next. "Yeah, and did you hear the rumor that you're expected to be mated at the next full moon if the mating signs show up? Can you believe that? I'm all down for sniffing some tail, but I have no interest in getting shackled yet. I've got a long time before I'm ready to deal with rug rats and a mate bond." He was the Alpha's third, but he was unmated and apparently had strong opinions about the purpose of the gathering, as well, if his eye roll was anything to go by.

I hadn't heard anything about a timeline for the mating to take place, but unease grew in my stomach as the drive continued. It wasn't possible to get a false match for your fated mate, but that didn't make the person any less of a stranger. I found myself hoping suddenly that what I'd told Leigh the very first day was true, and that I didn't get matched. I wanted to go home to Texas, to my little lab and my study of shifter medicine.

I was only allowed to pursue it because our pack was so small. It was frowned upon in general to study the differences between wolf shifters and humans. If the research was discovered, it could put our entire species under the microscope for power-hungry human scientists. I knew the risks, but it was my one rebellion, my refusal to choose a more "appropriate" career. I wanted to know why my parents died, and I wanted to know what flaw in the wolf shifter genes had allowed a sickness to take my mom down so long before her time. I didn't care what anyone else thought about it.

"With an attitude like that, the ladies will be lucky to have you," Leigh slurred, half-asleep as she adjusted her position over to Shay's shoulder instead of the window. "Pipe down, will you? Trying to get my beauty rest, here."

"Yes, pipe down, all of you," Alpha Todd said from the driver's seat. "And anyone bringing the high alpha's wrath down on this pack will be dealing with *me*, are we clear? I expect you to be good representatives of the Johnson City pack."

"Yes, Alpha," the men all grumbled, but fell blessedly silent after that.

MY NECK HURT, my calves were cramping, and I smelled like van. Really, it was the perfect first impression for the milling crowd of wolves when we stepped off the van at midnight. At least my hair looked good. When Leigh had woken up, she was bored and decided that we all needed fancy, intricate braids in our hair. She had double French braids—it was all I knew how to do—Shay had gotten a Dutch crown with tendrils of her brunette locks artfully framing her face. Mine was a composition of many smaller braids tapering down and woven into a loose mermaid braid over my shoulder. It had taken two hours, and I was pretty sure I'd have to leave them in permanently, based on how attached Leigh now was to her masterpiece.

The air was fresh and clean with a tinge of cold that burned my delicate nose, even though it was May. It was wonderful to stretch after so many hours stuffed in the twelve-passenger van with only two short bathroom breaks along the way. My wolf was oddly present with me, probably due to the excitement and presence of so many other wolves. I mentally stroked a hand down her silvery back. It was a welcome change from her usual silence, and I hoped she was able to stay with me for a while.

The Alpha's men unloaded the bags, and in moments, I was juggling two pull suitcases, my duffel full of lab notes, and blood-draw tubes slung over my shoulder. It wasn't perfect, having to find a local lab or freeze them until I got home, but I was hoping I could get a wider array of willing wolves here to give me samples for my testing. In fact, once I'd realized how much this little trip could advance my research, I'd actually gotten kind of excited.

There was no shot in hell of me getting matched, but this? *This* was a benefit I could get excited about. More blood samples meant a wider array of data to compare and search for anomalies against my own. It could move me years ahead of schedule on my research, but I had to figure out a way to get the wolves here to volunteer. I knew that would be no easy feat.

Leigh was almost as loaded down as I was, but Shay traveled light, with only one midsized rolling suitcase and a backpack slung over one shoulder, so she rolled one of my suitcases for me. We wandered together toward a clipboard-holding wolf in a suit who read off names and room assignments for the line forming ahead of us. My head was spinning with possibilities, so I didn't notice when the line moved until Shay prodded quietly.

"Brielle, we're next." The soft-spoken words were barely audible over the sounds of the milling wolves talking and laughing, but I was used to it and attuned to Shay's voice.

We stepped forward together, and as usual, Leigh took charge for our group.

"Johnson City pack, Leigh Barnes, Shay Woodlawn, and Brielle Masters. The males of our pack are over there, as well." She waved vaguely at the van, where the guys were showing off and doing handstands, for some odd reason. Oh wait, a gaggle of she-wolves one van over. Spotted the reason. With an eye roll, I turned my attention back to the suited man. He was eyeing me oddly, and I straightened my spine. Had I missed a question? A quick glance at Leigh's and Shay's expressions told me no.

Surely news of my weaknesses hadn't preceded me, right? I couldn't imagine my Alpha would want to spread that news a second sooner than necessary. The man took a longer than usual drag of air in through his nose, then shook his head and dropped his eyes to the clipboard.

"All right, Leigh, you are in room two-oh-eight, with a... Shailene. Is that your full name?" The man, Reed, according to his name tag, cast his eyes back and forth between me and Shay, waiting for confirmation.

She nodded silently, so he ticked her off on the list. "I'll make a note that your preferred nickname is Shay, so there won't be any confusion. Now, Brielle, you'll be in room two-oh-nine, directly across the hall, and bunking with Cherry from the Omaha pack. I believe her pack came in yesterday morning, so she may already be asleep, but she knows to expect you."

"Okay, thank you." I gave him a polite smile, but he was still looking at me strangely.

"Which way is our dorm?" Leigh cut in, and the man pulled his gaze from mine slowly, like it took effort.

"I'll have one of our wolves escort you." He peered over his shoulder and scanned the crowd, looking for someone specific. "Gael!" His shout wasn't louder than necessary, but it was laced with power and a hint of an alpha bark, which made my wolf whine and shake her head. This man was too dominant to be holding a clipboard, whoever he was. I'd wager he could give our Alpha a run for his money, easy. Was he one of the high alpha's men? Either that or our pack was even weaker than I thought.

A tall, broadly muscled man with intense green eyes jogged over from where he'd been talking to an even taller—good gravy, what was he, six-*five*?—brooding alpha wolf. The brooding alpha scowled at Reed, and then his eyes flicked dismissively over the three of us. But when they landed on me, they locked on like a missile. He was utterly, undeniably gorgeous, and everything I never knew I'd wanted in a man. Dark hair trimmed close to his head but a little longer on top, sharp cheekbones, and a straight nose. Tan skin from a life spent outdoors was paired with muscles that looked like they came from hard physical labor. His dominance was so thick in the air, I could taste the sharp tang of it from here. I got a faint impression of citrus and something spicy, though that was absurd even for a shifter nose at this distance.

Strangely enough, my wolf wasn't whining as she had at Reed. The dark haired wolf and I stared at each other across the dark field, and she rose shakily to her feet, pacing forward, agitated for some reason. There was energy, pure and brilliant, blazing across the field between us, even though it was dark except for the half-moon. My wolf howled and pressed forward against my control, shocking me into stillness. I was barely breathing as I stared at the handsome stranger. As I watched, his eyes began to glow bright green, his own wolf peeking through in response to mine.

Gael skidded to a stop next to us, on high alert, and I hurriedly dropped my gaze from the handsome, intimidating alpha across the field. I glanced up quickly and took in Gael's thick eyebrows, the scar on his cheek that bisected his stubble and ended abruptly on his throat. His tight, black T-shirt and black cargo pants made me guess security, or maybe even someone's enforcer. Though why they'd need security to escort us to our dorms was beyond me. Surely the area was safe, if they'd brought us all here?

"How can I help, Reed?"

The two shared a long, lingering look before Reed bobbed his head in our direction. Mental communication? Maybe they were pack mates. "Can you please escort these three to rooms two-oh-eight and two-oh-nine?"

"Absolutely. Ladies, this way."

He turned and marched off through the milling wolves, not

taking the time to make sure we followed. Reed gave us a finger wave in dismissal, then turned his attention to the group of wolves behind us. I snuck a quick glance toward the alpha, but was nearly rolled over by a wave of disappointment when I found him gone. *It's for the best, Brielle. Get your head out of your tail.*

"Was that weird, or was it just me?" I whispered to Leigh and Shay as we half trotted behind Gael to keep up. Luckily, he was tall and easy to spot, or else we'd have lost him in the bustle.

"Definitely weird. Hottie McHotterson had total eyes for you, babe."

"Uh, no way. Did you feel how dominant he was? My wolf didn't like it."

Leigh snorted, shaking her head. "Your wolf? She barely comes out to play. Don't blame intimidation on her. That's hardly fair to the poor girl."

"I'm serious, Leigh! She's been alert ever since we stepped off the bus."

"Huh, well, that's probably a good thing. So many wolves might be able to pull her out of her shell. Maybe she needs a stronger alpha?"

Our conversation came to an abrupt end as Gael opened the door to a massive, log-cabin-style lodge. The place towered at least two stories up, with beautiful dormers cut into a green tin roof. The double front doors were painted a matching green, making the place feel natural and like it blended into the forest. If it wasn't a country mansion, anyway.

We trailed up the front steps one by one, and Gael dropped the door to help with our bags.

"Sorry, I should have thought to carry those for you. Geez, what have you got in this one, rocks?"

"No, not rocks," I said, indignant.

Leigh laughed, not bothering to cover her smirk. "Did you pack a whole bag of lab equipment? Why am I not surprised."

"Hey, I'm ninety-percent sure that your entire second bag is shoes. Lay off." I leveled her with a pointed glare.

"Shoes are necessary. Lab equipment—"

"Is *also* necessary," I argued.

"Uh-huh. Because we'll have so much free time for you to work while we're here courting hot wolves." She leaned her forearm up onto Gael's bicep and gave him a wink. "Like this fella here. What's your story, hot stuff?"

My cheeks burned at her blatant flirtation, and I wasn't even the one making a show of things.

The man's eyebrows nearly flew off his face as he gently removed her arm from his shoulder with two long fingers. "No story worth telling, princess. Now, if we've got everything together, I'll show you to your rooms. I'll find somebody to help bring the extra bags upstairs, you can leave them here." He gestured to the base of the staircase, which gracefully curved up and up into the giant lodge.

The interior was every bit as beautiful as the exterior when we stepped inside. Furnishings were a little sparse – there were only a few chairs here and there along the front wall, tucked beside the windows out to the porch. But the craftsmanship was impeccable. Exposed beams, burnished floors, and a soft off-white paint on the walls, provided the perfect backdrop for a gorgeous mural of two howling wolves. They were side by side, the smaller wolf tucked against the larger one's shoulder, as if they were mates.

Gael grabbed Leigh's shoe suitcase and one of mine from Shay, then jogged up the stairs like it was nothing. I was torn for a moment, but ultimately decided to leave my suitcase full of clothes at the bottom of the stairs. I could get more clothes, but it would be very hard to procure the test vials and lab notes in an area as remote as this. Somehow, I doubted my usual two-day shipping back home would apply here.

As quickly as I could, I hurried after the three of them, pushing thoughts of the beautiful stranger out of my mind. I would never be strong enough to mate a wolf like him, even if I knew I'd dream of those eyes, brilliantly glowing and calling to my wolf, as soon as my head hit the pillow.

FOUR

Kane

My wolf was losing his damn mind, and I had to get out of here or I was going to embarrass myself. When Gael slid to a stop next to Reed and I temporarily lost sight of the mystery woman, I managed to wrest back my usually unshakable control long enough to jog away toward the back of the dormitories. It was dark and quiet, with none of the hustle and bustle of the wolves arriving and greeting old friends at the front. As soon as I rounded the corner, I stopped, leaning my forearms against the rough-hewn exterior and dropping my forehead to my fists.

Deep breaths in and out began to settle my wolf, though he was *so* restless. That woman—whoever she was—had set him off. I don't know how long it took for me to regain my composure, but when I straightened and turned around, Reed and Gael were both standing in front of me, looks of concern etched into their faces.

"What?" I growled, even though I knew *exactly* what. Through the pack bond, they'd felt my wolf demanding control, and me quietly fighting him back into submission ever since.

"That's what I'd like to know," Reed said, voice deceptively mild. He must have passed off his check-in duties, because his clipboard was nowhere to be seen.

"You nearly lost it right in the middle of the crowd, man. I can't remember you losing it since we were teenagers. What triggered you?" Gael asked.

My shoulders were tight, heat prickling between my shoulder blades as I stared back at them and considered what to say. Finally, I settled on the truth.

"The woman. One of the ones you were checking in. Our wolves... noticed each other. But mine panicked, for some reason, and started demanding that we go to her, *protect* her. Which is ridiculous, because there's not a predator in two hundred miles dumb enough to approach this many wolves." They didn't bother asking which of the three women, because they already knew. I growled in frustration and ran my palms back and forth over my shorn hair. I wanted to punch a mountain-high stack of boards, but that wouldn't fix this. Because my wolf? My wolf wanted to follow her scent trail, track her down, and *protect*.

It was utterly ridiculous.

They exchanged a knowing look, and I snarled. "Spit it out! Don't stand there looking smug!"

"I think you just found your mate, brother. Congratulations." Gael was the first to speak, his grin so wide, it threatened to split his face in half.

"No, there's *no way*. There has to be another explanation."

Reed tucked both of his hands down into his suit-pants pockets and rocked back on the heels of his too-shiny dress shoes. "She felt it too, Kane. She looked like she'd seen a ghost, and her eyes glowed until Gael snapped her out of it. They're brown, by the way. Like ice crystals coating a pine branch."

A growl tore out of my chest, my wolf angry again that our

friend, pack mate, *blood brother*, knew more about her than we did.

"Do you think you'd be reacting this strongly for any other reason? Did you sense that she was in trouble in some way? Maybe pack problems? We could investigate," Gael offered, holding up a hand in the universal gesture for *settle down, you hotheaded dipstick.*

I turned my back on them for a moment, closing my eyes and trying to focus on the question. Could that have been it? I was a very dominant alpha. I protected the females and young of my pack fiercely, and we had a zero-tolerance policy for abuse. My wolf would have reacted that strongly to any she-wolf in danger, except...

When I let the memory flow back through me, it wasn't anger from my wolf. The memory of her smooth, soft-looking skin and gorgeous, thick brunette braid under the moonlight froze me in place. Desire burned through me, thick and hot, and I felt my pants tighten uncomfortably in physical reaction to the memory. I bit back a groan. My wolf wanted her. And if I stopped lying to myself for more than three seconds, I would have to admit that I wanted her too.

I wanted her under me, to trail kisses over her bare skin, a sheen of sweat making her glow as we moved together under the moonlight, on a soft bed of leaves out in the forest. To make her scream my name in ecstasy as I sank my teeth into her neck, leaving behind a mating—

"No! *No.*" I spun on my heels, glaring at my two best friends as I tried to force the heated image out of my mind. "She is *not* my mate. It's not possible. She isn't nearly dominant enough to be an alpha mate. The she-wolves in our pack aren't bad, but even they'd run roughshod over a wolf as weak as that. It was something else, and I don't want to hear another word about it from either of you. Are we clear?"

"Crystal," Reed said drily.

The soft sound of grass crunching caught my attention, and my eyes snapped to the corner of the building. Had someone been eavesdropping on that conversation? Gael had the same reaction, and a snarl fell from his curled lips. He took off after whoever it was. When I rounded the front of the dormitory, I nearly ran into the back of him where he'd stopped dead in his tracks.

"Who was it?" I asked, but he didn't have to answer, as my next breath drew in a heady, impossible-to-miss scent of delicate jasmine and ripe, sweet apple. *Mate.*

FIVE

Brielle

Humiliation, burning and miserable, nearly ate me alive as I ran full-tilt through the front door of our dormitory, and streaked back up the stairs toward my room. My roommate hadn't been there when Gael dropped us off, but after fifteen minutes of waiting, I'd come back down to grab my own suitcase. Of course, it hadn't been there. So I'd wandered out front, looking for Gael—and heard his voice coming from the back of the building.

What I'd heard after that nearly broke me. The man, Kane, thought I was his mate? And he *didn't want me* because I was too weak?

All my worst fears were confirmed in that one moment, and I didn't stop to think, just bolted. I was going to take a shower hot enough to burn away the embarrassment of this awful encounter, and then never make eye contact with the man again as long as I lived. He thought I was his mate? He had another thing coming. I didn't want a mate at all, let alone a pompous one who cared more about *designation* than a person's character. He could take his mate bond and stuff it, right up his egotistical arse.

I slammed the door to my room shut, flipped the lock, and shoved open the bathroom door. The big, beautiful tiles and the gleaming bathroom fixtures were blurred by my tears as I wrenched open the glass shower stall door and cranked the water all the way to hot. I was going to scrub the memory of his hurtful words right out of my skin, if that's what it took to forget his dismissive, hateful tone. I stripped off my van-scented clothes and kicked them into a pile, then rested my forehead against the crystal-clear glass door, letting my eyes flutter closed while I waited on the water to heat.

At least no one else knew. I would never speak a word of it, not even to Leigh and Shay. There was no need to spread my humiliation around, and surely he'd be avoiding me, so, no harm, no foul. *No mate either.*

An insistent knock at the outer door pulled me from my self-righteous anger. It was probably my roommate. Didn't she have a key? I pushed the bathroom door closed, so our first meeting wouldn't be with me buck naked. The room began filling with steam as another persistent knock pounded on the door. With a groan, I grabbed one of the fluffy white towels from the floating shelf on the wall, and wrapped it around myself. It covered *mostly* everything, but I had a little more junk in the trunk than the average wolf, and there was a slit over my thigh that I couldn't get closed.

Maybe she'd lost her key. I stomped across the room, trying to force down my annoyance in favor of a friendly smile I really wasn't feeling. I'd let her in, say hello, and then lock myself in the bathroom. We could get acquainted tomorrow. When I snatched the door open, it wasn't a she-wolf on the other side, but *Kane*. The one who not only thought I was his mate after one glance, but who'd also immediately dismissed and rejected me. Standing there, looking hotter than sin, while I was in—

I felt the blood drain from my face as we locked eyes, and then his dropped to skim down over my towel-clad form. The look was as potent as a physical caress, and I hated my traitor body as goose bumps appeared on my skin everywhere his gaze trailed over me. After a moment, his attention snapped back up to my face, and we stood there in heavy silence.

My anger began to build, shoving away the desire that he'd pulled up from my belly with his blatant perusal. I took a step back and slammed the door as hard as I could. But rather than a satisfying *thwack* into the frame like I'd expected, he stopped the door with lightning-fast reflexes, fingers wrapping around the edge and pushing it carefully back open.

I bit my bottom lip as it swung wide, revealing his thundercloud expression. He wasn't snarling—yet—but he was *pissed*. His anger and dominance hung thick in the air, and this close, I could smell his addictive scent—orange and cinnamon, like a delicious, glazed gingerbread cookie. My mouth was watering, which was absolutely the wrong reaction to a pissed-off alpha. Why wasn't I freaking out right now, or, I don't know—dissolving into a puddle of psi-wolf goo on the floor at his feet? A question for another time, when he wasn't looking at me like he wanted to set me on fire for breathing.

"Why were you eavesdropping on our conversation?" There was a hint of a growl to his question, and I bristled at the insinuation that I was somehow in the wrong.

"Excuse me? Are you kidding me right now?" I took an angry step forward, the back of my arm nearly brushing his chest where I clutched my towel tighter—crap, I was still naked—to cover my boobs. "Gael was supposed to find someone to help bring up one of my bags, and when it wasn't here, I went down looking for it. I heard his voice and walked around to *ask him where my bag was*."

He lifted a single eyebrow—skeptical of my story, no doubt—even though it was true. We wouldn't worry about the part where I'd sagged against the building, more distraught than I had a right to be about his frank and unkind assessment before I'd bolted.

"I'm sorry you had to overhear that."

I rocked back on my heels, shocked that he wasn't fighting me, angry, accusing... He was just going to apologize? When he was the one who'd said the mean things to begin with?

What was probably meant to appease my temper only stoked it higher.

I stepped forward and surprised myself with the growl edging my words. "Yes, poor weak woman, too beneath you to be considered as a true mate. I couldn't possibly handle being told you don't think we're compatible. Well, listen here, buddy—I don't want to be *your* mate either! So, stay away from me, and everything will be just fine." I had taken an unconscious step forward, but didn't realize it until his eyes lit with amusement, and he dropped his gaze down to take in my arm, pressed tightly against his T-shirt-clad chest.

Suddenly flustered at the heat radiating off him, I took a pointed step back inside the room, not dropping my glare.

"What's your name, little wolf?"

The words were barely more than a low rumble, so why did they hit me like a streak of liquid heat straight to my core?

I pursed my lips, stubbornly refusing to answer. Then he stepped forward, crowding into my personal space. He was close enough that the little hairs on the back of my arm brushed him, but nothing more. Not *true* contact. So why was my arm tingling like I'd stuck my finger in a light socket? Flustered again, I tipped my head back, looking up at his softening expression as he studied my face like he wanted to memorize it.

No, he doesn't want you! He thinks you're weak and unsuitable!

The little voice in the back of my head was still screaming at me, but when he lifted a large, tanned hand and offered it to me, palm up, my breath caught in my throat. My own hand floated up without my permission, hesitating briefly before sinking slowly down to brush against his waiting palm.

As soon as my fingertips brushed his calloused skin, I felt it. *Heat.* It exploded through me, feeling like a thousand stars bursting, flooding my veins at once. I gasped, pressing down into the sensation, and clasping his palm against my own.

He grunted, rocking back slightly on his heels, as we stood there like idiots, holding hands and staring into each other's eyes.

"Hey, Brielle, what— Oh. Well, *hello there*, Mr. Tall, Dark, and Delicious. What's your name?" Leigh's flirtatious voice sent a prickle of unease through me, and I barely bit back a snarl at my best friend. When he stepped back and turned to answer her, he dropped my palm, and I felt the loss like a physical wound.

"Kane."

The single word fell from his lips, but it didn't click until I heard Shay's soft gasp from behind Leigh.

Kane. I knew that name, even though I hadn't placed it earlier in my anger. Kane, Kane...

The high alpha's son.

Oh, Goddess.

SIX

Kane

Brielle. The name sounded like sunshine and the ocean breeze, crisp and perfect, something I wanted to caress and savor on my tongue. It fit her, and it was burned into my memory right along with her facial expression when our skin touched for the first time. Pure, unadulterated bliss.

I'd felt the same, but had been unable to tear my eyes from her face, this complete stranger who had already sunk her claws straight into my heart.

How? How was it possible to feel such a soul-deep connection to a complete stranger? Yet I could no more deny it than I could my lungs their next breath. She... she was mine. My mate. But how could she be, when she'd never have the strength to lead a pack by my side? When I dropped her hand to face the curious she-wolf across the hall, reality had rushed right back in, souring the moment and my stomach along with it.

"Kane," I answered her, though I felt the need to run straight into the woods and shift so I could sink into that animal oblivion. Become nothing more than paws and fur and fangs and claws, digging deep scratches into the earth as I pushed myself faster than my human body could ever go. *Soon*, I quieted the beast inside on instinct, though he was oddly calm given all that had just happened... content, even.

"Well, well, well... you are quite a specimen. And, Brielle, why are you wearing a towel? Inviting the studs home already? I'm proud." The she-wolf gave Brielle an exaggerated wink, and she blushed profusely, the red creeping up her neck to her cheeks. "I'm Leigh. Nice to meet you." She stepped forward boldly, ignorant to the earth-shattering moment her friend and I had just shared. It felt wrong, pressing my palm to hers in a handshake, but it would be rude of me to reject the offer of friendship.

When she gripped my hand, I felt nothing, but froze when an aggressive growl ripped from Brielle's throat. I dropped Leigh's hand immediately and spun back toward Brielle.

She slapped a hand over her mouth, clearly shocked at her own reaction. Without another word, she slammed and locked the door. My wolf hearing had no trouble picking up her footsteps running to the back of the room, and the slam of the bathroom door a moment later. When I turned back, Leigh and her silent friend were both staring at me, slack-jawed.

"You... you two are mates? And here I thought it was going to be Mr. Suit from check-in. You're not *at all* her type, but I ship it." She grinned, the expression somehow lascivious rather than friendly.

"Please keep this to yourself," I said, adding a hint of alpha command to the words.

She frowned as she felt the compulsion, but didn't argue. *Couldn't* argue, and I felt like a jackass. But... I also wasn't ready for all and sundry to know, and I didn't think Brielle would be either. I needed time to process. *And run*, my wolf added, on his feet and prowling now that Brielle had hidden away from us.

"Have a good night," I murmured and took my leave, the

feeling of their eyes still burning my back as I reached the stairs and jogged down.

I RAN, and I ran, and I ran. Trees blended together, melding into one endless mass of color at the edges of my vision, their unique scents coalescing into one beautiful melody of *wilderness*. It was where I was most comfortable, and I relished letting go, leaving the responsibility of being the high alpha's heir behind. If I didn't, It would crush me.

My wolf and I were a strong team, and I was grateful to have his sharper side when I needed to make tough decisions. He'd never steered me wrong, which was why his fixating on Brielle as our mate was so unexpected. She was wholly unsuitable, soft and pliant and intoxicating, yes; but even standing an inch from her, I could barely feel her wolf. She had one. Reed had seen her eyes light from within back at the clearing.

My wolf growled at the thought, still hating that Reed had something of our mate that we didn't, even something as simple as the first glimpse of her wolf's eyes.

Soon, I reassured him, and he ran faster before skidding around a tree and heading down a mountain, arrowing straight for the rivers' confluence. The mighty Yukon and the Tanana cradled our territory, and the place where they met had a kind of power that no other did in this area. I hadn't realized how far we'd run, but I could no more mistake the smell of that place than the smell of my own cabin.

My paws dug in as we ran downhill, sinking farther into the earth as my front paws bore my weight down. It wasn't long before the rushing water grew louder and the trees broke, revealing the surging waters. It was home, in a way. And a power cradle. I didn't know how or why, but I could sense it just the same. I'd often wondered if this was what drew me here to build a pack of my own. I slowed to a stop, tongue lolling, at the river's edge. This place soothed me, it always had, and so long as my pack called Alaska home, I knew it always would.

I lay down on the bank, belly flush against the cool, damp earth, and rested my head on my paws, thinking over the whirlwind events of the last two weeks. Most of them brought a strong sense of pride from my wolf. We'd pulled together as a pack and knocked out the construction of two huge dormitories in a short amount of time. We'd been handed the huge challenge of hosting this event for the packs, and we'd delivered. It was an honor, and an obligation of enormous proportions. We weren't done yet, of course, but I was damn proud of my wolves.

And then I thought about today. The influx of pack after pack from all over, squeaking in before the final deadline. Most were unmemorable, blending into a blur of faces and scents. There was one that concerned me—the Russo pack, from Virginia. They'd been giving my father a hard time for decades, constantly challenging his leadership. The fact that they'd shown up a day early and with twelve male wolves with grins on sent my internal alarms jangling. If anyone were to try something, it would be them.

Gael agreed, and he was keeping a close eye on their pack members. He could handle it, but I'd be staying on my toes as well. I had no doubts they'd try something, but we'd be ready.

The Northern Territories pack was equally large, but their only threat was some overly aggressive she-wolves. They'd been eye-fucking me since they stepped out of their transport vans, but I could ignore that. The males of their pack were old and long-since mated, and the females were the daughters of the pack leadership, hungry for my title more than who I was as a person.

Then, at the culmination of it all, was Brielle.

Brielle.

Even her name had my wolf sitting up, letting out a short

whine on the bank that disappeared into the misty void above the rivers. He wanted her, wanted to bite her, claim her. Right now, with no waiting. He didn't have the man's compunctions about getting to know someone, or how her lack of strength would affect pack dynamics.

She is strong, my wolf growled, startling me. He rarely bothered to form words. Our connection was soul-deep, and I understood him well even without words. A simple fact of an intertwined lifetime.

She is not. She is psi. And a psi can hardly rule over alpha she-wolves.

He snarled, and leapt to his feet, not deigning to respond. Instead, we turned and raced back up the steep bank, arrowing toward the tree line as if a grizzly was after us, but I knew, even if he wouldn't speak again.

He was running back to our mate.

WE WERE close to the pack headquarters when the distinct feeling of unease ran through the pack bonds, sparking my awareness. It was Reed, and the tug on the bonds left no doubts that whatever the problem was, it was urgent. My wolf kicked our speed up another notch without question. Reed was my blood brother. If he needed us, we ran like the wind.

We wove between trees, dodging limbs and leaping over downed deadfall with the ease of a predator on a hunt, kicking up dirt as we flew past obstacles. Reed was waiting for us when we rounded the corner of the main lodge and skidded to a stop to avoid hitting him. He had a pair of gray sweatpants in hand, so I quickly changed back. He didn't beat around the bush as he passed me the pants.

"The ODL is here."

My head snapped up, shocked. "What? Why would they be?

We don't have any omegas here. These are all adult wolves, of age to be mated. The ODL does their foul work when wolves are babies."

"I know, and I told them that, but they're refusing to leave."

I snarled, irritated at the snag in our otherwise smooth execution. My father could be here at any time—he wouldn't tell me when, because that would ruin his fun of surprising me, but I knew it would be soon—and I wasn't going to have the Omega Defense League hanging around, causing a scene.

"Where are they?"

"I had them escorted to your office. Didn't figure we wanted them stinking up the hallways." He sneered, and I shared his opinion. The Omega Defense League was a necessary part of life, or so we were told. If you asked me, they were relics of a bygone era and a waste of good wolf kind.

"Let's go. The sooner we get them out of here, the better."

"Couldn't agree more, Alpha, but they wouldn't leave unless they spoke to you."

I growled, not surprised, but highly irritated.

I stormed through the mostly quiet halls, my anger simmering hotter the closer I got to my office. It was necessary at every birth to allow a member of the Omega Defense League to come and test the child for omega powers. But with every wolf being tested and found not to be omega at birth, there was no call whatsoever for them to be here, unless they were after Gracelyn's baby, who wasn't due for another month, at least.

Besides, it turned my stomach, what they did. Killing innocent babies just because one of their designation had turned bad hundreds of years ago? It all seemed like a bad myth. Omegas were reputed to have special powers, strong enough to shift the dynamics of even a whole pack. Most were said to have gentle effects: healing, fertility, persuasion. Until Narcissa.

Narcissa was the first and only omega to ever have the power of war, and she used it to gather to her the strongest, most bloodthirsty wolves the world had ever seen. Then she went on a mission to find her fated mate, and none would do besides Bran Cadogan. High alpha of all Europe at the time. When she mated him, her plots expanded past one band of angry wolves and suddenly encompassed a continent.

But that was a myth from the past, and the three odious ODL representatives in front of me were a *right now* problem.

A lesser fae, a shifter—lynx, by the cat-piss reek of him—and a vampire, each wearing polished silver armor stamped with the interlocking ODL insignia. They stared imperiously down their noses at Gael as I shoved the office door open, letting it bounce off the wall. Gael was leaning forward, both palms planted wide on my desk, glowering back.

"To what do I owe the displeasure?" I refrained from snarling, but didn't soften my glare. The lynx stepped forward, ducking his head briefly in a show of respect.

"Alpha Kane, we are here to investigate a report of omega magic. We will be as efficient as possible, but due process must be followed any time a report is filed."

"I want to see the report," Gael said. He was standing at my side now, arms crossed over his chest, but no less domineering for the shift in pose.

The lynx flinched back from the alpha bark pushing the words and held up both hands. "My comrade will be happy to provide it." He waved for the vampire, who strolled forward in a lazy way that pissed me off. I growled, lifting just one side of my lip as he dropped the paper to my desk rather than placing it in Gael's outstretched hand. Rude, smug bloodsucker. *Bastard.*

Gael ignored the slight, picking up the paper and scanning it before passing it to me. What I saw made me growl louder.

Anonymous tip: Omega magic sensed at the Pack Blackwater gathering.

"That's it? This is why you've stormed into my office in the middle of the night, with nothing to go on and no children to be assessed?"

"I wouldn't say *no* children," the lesser fae drawled from his post against the wall, looking bored. "My senses tell me there is one, unborn. The mother seems to be in distress, which can be an early sign of omega energies."

Reed lunge-stepped forward angrily, an unusual break in self-control for him. We were all on edge tonight, and these fools weren't helping. Gracelyn was his cousin. Of course he'd take offense at them sniffing around her and her pup.

I placed a hand on his shoulder, urging him to back down. I had this well in hand.

"As you're aware, due process is to be notified within three days of birth. Our pregnant mother is not due for at least a month. Therefore, you've arrived regrettably early. As you yourself have already stated, there is only *one* child on the premises. And unless you've failed spectacularly to fulfill your stated purpose... there couldn't possibly be any adult omega energies here. Now, you'll see yourselves out, and remember not to step foot onto my territory again unless summoned." I held up a hand toward the door, a clear dismissal.

The vampire bristled, but none of them moved for the door. A red haze teased the edges of my vision at their blatant disrespect, and my wolf pushed to the forefront. The lynx shifter cringed back, clearly affected by my dominance and ire, but stubbornly didn't budge.

It was the fae who dared speak again, defying my orders. "Normally, you are correct, sir, but with a report of any kind, we have two weeks to investigate any potential omega—"

The door to my office slammed open, revealing my father, face twisted in a snarl as he stalked forward. The fact that he was graying at the temples did nothing to lessen his terrifying presence, and even after five centuries of life, he was in prime physical condition. His dominance dwarfed mine, a fact my wolf bristled against.

"What is the meaning of this?" The words were ice-cold and calm, and even I took a half step back at the unspoken threat in them.

The lynx crumpled to the floor under his gaze, but the fae and the vampire stood frozen, as if clutched in his fist.

"Speak!" he barked again, this time laced with full power, and words tried to spew forth out of my own mouth. Only the fact that the order wasn't directed at me personally allowed me to keep them in.

The vampire grimaced as words poured out against his will. "We are investigating a report of omega energies. We will be here for two weeks, as per the Interspecies Governing Council's writ. We have provided a copy of the report and will take our leave for the night."

My father took another menacing step forward. "You can do your cowardly sniffing from a distance, but if you touch one hair on a single wolf's head under my protection, I'll end you, council be damned. Leave."

The fae reached down, scooped up the quivering lynx under one arm, and hauled him out behind the vampire, who'd used his supernatural speed to bolt out the door so fast, he seemed to vanish. My father's second, Dimitri, shoved the door shut on their heels with one booted foot.

"Sergei will see that they leave the borders of your land. I sensed them and posted him at the door. One day, we will be rid of the ODL entirely, and their foul ways." He strode forward and dropped easily into one of my guest chairs across from my desk. "Sit. Tell me what's going on."

SEVEN

Kane

I took my seat reluctantly, something about my father's swooping in and booting the intruders from my office leaving me feeling like a chastised child, not a powerful alpha in my own right. I knew it wasn't fair to think that way—he was leader of all wolves, after all. Of course he was stronger than I, with my one pack.

It still rankled, the feeling like someone running their hand the wrong way up my wolf's back, and I did my best to shove aside my wounded pride as I faced him across the hand-carved cedar desk.

"They've shown up with a bogus anonymous tip, and they're sniffing around our one pregnant she-wolf."

Reed stiffened near imperceptibly at Gael's words, and a murderous light glinted in my father's eyes. We took women's maternal safety seriously, as it was deeply personal to us. For Reed, it didn't get more personal than his only cousin's first pup.

"I assume you've already got an idea of who submitted this tip?"

"We suspect the Russo pack, but we have no proof yet,"

Gael answered, his tone professional. I appreciated that he didn't go straight for the pitchforks as my first enforcer, but it also underlined that I needed to pull back my own judgments until there were facts on the table. It wouldn't do to be shown as dealing unfairly with any of the packs under our family's control, and I had to be forever cognizant of that. The joys of being alpha son of the high alpha. All the power you could ever want, in a tight, tight muzzle of fairness. My wolf rumbled in my mind, annoyed at the man-made distinction. He saw things so simply. Tear the throats out of any and all threats, then run through the woods howling with glee. Simple; easy to remember.

"I take it you've already got a plan in place to get that proof? I'd love a reason to take a strip out of their hides." My father's grin was vicious, and I couldn't blame him. They'd been a kink in his tail for decades.

"I've got two of my best men on rotation, keeping an eye on them at all times. My men know to stay unobtrusive, but stay close enough that they can stop them if they get up to anything dangerous," Gael confirmed.

"Hassling Gracelyn when she's this close to her due date isn't *dangerous* enough for you?" Reed snarled, an uncharacteristic lapse in control. He was worried for his cousin.

"You know that's not true, Reed," I placated, standing and laying a hand on his shoulder. He stilled at my touch, but the tension in his shoulders was enough to snap a lesser wolf in half. "Gael is being smart. He's not being blinded by the obvious threat and is keeping an eye open for the wolf that waits in darkness. You wouldn't want him to miss something when we don't have the facts, would you?"

"No, Alpha," he said, dropping his head and rubbing his eyes with the heel of his hand. He was exhausted and worried. My wolf sensed it from the pack bond, but even if he hadn't, I could see it in the lines of his face. "Apologies, Gael." He grimaced toward our friend and blood brother, who waved him away.

"Not necessary."

I gave his shoulder a small squeeze. "Go rest, both of you. We've got a long day tomorrow, and not enough dark hours left between now and then."

They both gave quick nods in deference to my station, then left the office. My father stood slowly, appraising the exchange with those ever-calculating steely eyes of his. To my surprise, he also headed for the door, but paused at the last moment with his hand on the knob.

"You're a good Alpha, son. Seeing to the needs of your people. But remember that as Alpha, you have to make the hard decisions, even when you don't want to." He pinned me with one last inscrutable gaze, then left the room, his man at his heels.

With the ominous reminder echoing in my head, I flicked off the light and headed for my own bed. The one where I definitely wasn't going to have dirty dreams about Brielle keeping me up all night.

EIGHT

Brielle

The milling crowd of wolves the next morning was more than I'd ever seen in one place, and I knew without a doubt the memory of this day would be burned into my senses for as long as I lived, even if I'd slept like utter poo. The scent of pine and the sharp tang of excitement mixed with a low undertone of bitter anxiety hung like a cloud over the group, with occasional snarls ripping through the air as one wolf or another got too excited and was immediately rounded upon by his Alpha. It was enough to rip me fully out of the dreams that had left me tortured and sweating, tangled in the sheets, wishing they were Kane's hot, hard body.

No one wanted to be humiliated in front of High Alpha Kosta, and he was presiding over this gathering that started in—I peeked down at my watch—thirty seconds. Excited whispers rolled through the crowd like a wave, and I looked up. An older but still fit wolf had stepped onto the stage. He was graying at the temples, but otherwise, there was no way to differentiate him from any other male wolf walking the grounds. Then it hit me.

Raw, unfiltered, crushing alpha dominance.

My knees started to shake, and my palms started to sweat. I leaned my shoulder into Shay's on my left, and she looked up at me, concerned, before quickly looping an arm around my shoulders in support. She flicked Leigh's arm on my other side, who was avidly watching the proceedings with a heated glint in her eyes. When she looked down, I could practically feel her frown, but she also looped an arm around my waist, bolstering me between my two friends in a sandwich of protection.

My wolf reveled in the touch, and I marveled for the umpteenth time since we'd arrived at how *forward* she was. It was... new and unusual, but I liked the feel of her, even if I didn't know what to do with her yet. I worried, though, that it was a reaction to so many wolves in one place, and that she'd fade back into distant quiescence when we headed home to Texas.

She whined in my head, trying to tell me something, but I didn't know what. The high alpha took center stage, lifting a hand halfway in a steadying wave to the crowd of clamoring werewolves in both a welcoming and calming gesture, but my eyes were dragged away like magnets toward the left side of the stage, where a line of other alpha wolves waited.

Two, I'd never seen before. They had severe buzz cuts, pale, olive-tinted skin, and midnight-black hair. Their eyes were coldly surveying the group, and I knew instinctively that these were Kosta's men. I let my gaze skitter past them, lest they lock eyes with me and see it as a challenge.

Yeah, right. I'm a weakling from Texas who can barely challenge a sidewalk without falling down. I'm not challenging anybody. One look from them and I'd flop over and faint like a friggin' goat.

They landed on another cluster of alphas right at the edge of the stage. If you weren't paying attention, you might have thought the five of them were together, but I could nearly see the separations in the air. *Not pack.* The little division screamed between the two steel-eyed alphas and the three I recognized: Gael, Reed, and Kane.

Mate. My wolf rumbled, and I was shocked when a soft rumbling sound echoed in my own chest. I couldn't take my eyes off Kane, and as the tiny sound buzzed through me, his eyes snapped to mine, causing heat to bloom in my core and slowly suffuse my body like tea steeping under the hot sun of his gaze.

He can't hear that. Surely not? There's so much noise here.

But even as I denied it to myself, his eyes began to glow green, and he took a half step forward. Gael's hand on his shoulder stopped him, with a terse look toward Kosta, who had just opened his mouth to address the crowd.

There was no microphone, no fancy sound system or megaphone to carry his voice, but the words reached us all nonetheless, laced with irrefutable power that sent my knees back to shaking, even though my pack mates were still holding me tight.

Ugh, I hate alphas.

"Greetings, pack!"

"Greetings, Alpha!" We responded as one, some of us with less enthusiasm than others. Even Shay, who was perpetually silent in the presence of men, whispered the words at my side, as if they were pulled out against her will.

"It pleases me greatly to see you all here, together. For what is the strength of the wolf but pack? The connection is greater than any other, save one: that of mates. The true bond that ties our souls together, intertwining one life with another. The moon Goddess's own blessing to her most treasured creation. For it was her own wisdom that saw wolves, saw how we connected, and entwined the spirit of man and wolf. And it was her gift to us that we do not have simple marriage like humans. No, she knew that we could and should foster a bond so deep that not even death can render it in twain."

I shivered, my whole body beginning to shake at the words, and I could no more keep my eyes from Kane than I could keep my lungs from drawing my next breath. His eyes were already boring into me, and the connection from across the crowd was like a physical caress, sweeping from my neck, tingling past my breasts, and lighting up my sex. My core clenched, and I soaked my panties, despite the distance between us. I should have felt humiliated, but all I wanted was more. *More of him, STAT*.

The high alpha had continued speaking while we had our moment, and Leigh's pinch to the back of my arm snapped me out of the lust-filled haze I'd fallen into.

"—and that is why we will begin simply. Everyone will report to the barn, where tables have been set up. We'll work in hour-long blocks, doing what the humans call speed dating. You will have five minutes with each possible match, and at the end, you will exchange a handshake. We know that physical contact is the simplest, most direct way to confirm a mate match, but let me be clear: no further physical contact is permitted. Alphas, you are expected to control your wolves, and I expect decency and respect from each of you."

He leveled a shrewd gaze on the crowd, stopping here and there to narrow his eyes. "The woman you are lusting after right now may be another's mate, and you will not disrespect her by being more forward. A handshake, and no more. If you feel that you have found your true mate, please notify the alpha group monitoring the room, and you will both be taken aside and registered so that you may explore the connection in a safe manner. My son's people have created a schedule, and it is posted at the barn. Well met, and may many true matches be found this week." He lifted a hand again in that half-wave, half-settle-down gesture, and then exited the stage. The male wolves around us cheered so loudly, the dominant pheromones rose like a wave. I felt myself beginning to sag under the pressure as some let loose with howls, and a few even shifted right there in the clearing, unable to contain their wolves at the possibility.

"We've got to get her out of here!" Leigh hissed and began to elbow people and stomp on feet to make a path out of the oppressive crowd. I couldn't think, couldn't help, merely hung there, overwhelmed and humiliated at my reaction to so many dominant wolves in one place. It was a blessing that our home pack was so small.

Though it was growing, I thought idly as Leigh and Shay hauled me free of the crowd, earning a glare from Alpha Todd. We'd had four pairs mated in the last year, a huge boon and why we had such a small group for this trip.

Once we broke free of the throng of surging wolf bodies, my legs began to steady, and I was able to suck in some lungfuls of fresh air as my friends deposited me on a bench made of half a massive log, cut and cradled between two quarter logs to stop it rolling away.

"What was that?" Leigh asked, dropping into a crouch so she could get eye level with me. "Are you okay? Do you need to eat something, or was it just too much alpha juice in too little space?"

I snorted weakly at *alpha juice*, but it wasn't truly a laughing matter. We were scheduled to be here for three weeks, and I couldn't go weak at the knees every time we were gathered together, or dinner was going to get real unpleasant, real fast.

"I don't know, but I think it was just... too much. The scents, the energy... I—" Tears welled in my eyes, humiliation and shame burning through me. "I'm so sor—"

"You had better not be about to apologize to us, Bri-belle. You listen here, and you listen good. We are sisters, and we take care of each other. Period. We're going to stick close together, and if you need out, you say the word. Capiche?"

Leigh's stern face told me she wasn't kidding, so I choked the apology back down.

"Capiche," I whispered, though the apology weighed heavy in the back of my throat, wanting to burst free. I hated my weakness, hated that none of the rules of *normal* wolves seemed to apply to me, to my family line.

"We have ten minutes, Leigh. Let's get some coffee into her before the speed dating starts."

"Good idea. When in doubt, caffeinate." She fist-bumped Shay, then both of them looped arms around me again and hauled me to my feet. "We've got hotties to stun, and we can't do it without the proper amount of liquid enthusiasm."

TWELVE MINUTES and the most enormous cup of to-go coffee we could find in the dining hall later, the three of us stood just inside the barn doorway, looking at the posted instruction sheets.

Hour One: Women will remain in assigned seats, men will rotate.

Fifteen-Minute Break

Hour Two: Men will remain in assigned seats, women will rotate

Fifteen-Minute Break

Catching the gist, I scanned down to see the list of assigned seats and let out a relieved breath when I saw that we weren't right next to each other, but the three of us were at least all in the same row.

"We're in row seven," I announced, pointing to our names.

"Let's get this show on the rizzy!" Leigh clapped and rubbed both of our shoulders before leading us past the first few rows, where nervous wolves milled, most of the females already sitting, chatting with their neighbors. Shay's seat was closest, so she sat between a fiery, pint-sized redhead and a dark, lovely brunette with deep brown skin and a foot of height on her. A few seats later was Leigh, but she turned to me before sitting.

"Do you want me to walk you to your seat first?"

I hated the worried look in her eyes when she should be focusing on herself and finding her own mate. Leigh was too generous for her own good, and despite the pain she'd been through in the last six months of her long-term boyfriend finding *his* true mate and leaving her, she was still focusing on me and not on her chance to find the love she'd been after since her teen years.

"No," I said, trying to infuse every bit of backbone I possessed into the word. "Don't worry about me, okay? This is a room full of hot, single men looking for their forever love. You focus on you, and the *hotties*," I used her word with relish, "about to fall in love with you, okay?" I gave her hand a determined squeeze. "I'm going to be like three seats over. If I faint, you'll be first to know."

"No joking about fainting," she growled, pointing an accusing finger at me.

"Pssh, I'm going to be fine. Bored, but fine."

With a sharp nod, she took her seat, and I hurried the last few tables over to my assigned number and sank gratefully into the cushioned chair. The few minutes before the start time felt like eternity as I looked around the room, taking in the soaring, rough-hewn ceiling beams, oversized windows, and sawdust floors. This really was a barn, and not the fancy, million-dollar rustic wedding kind. It had the faint scent of oil, mixed with the sawdust beneath my shoes and the rich earth and pine that permeated everything here.

My butt had barely touched the seat when a stream of men started pouring in through the big, open barn doors. My nerves ratcheted up, sending anxious butterflies careening around my belly like drunken sailors. Was Kane going to be in this group of men? I bit my lip, scanning all the unfamiliar faces. I did see the men from our own pack who I recognized, and the few who spotted me gave polite nods, but their eyes were wide and eager for other, new females. It might have stung if I weren't avidly looking for someone else too.

There, toward the back.

He wasn't in the crowd, mingling, but he stood just outside the far door, scanning the gathering, lingering here and there on another wolf before moving on.

Protective. Alpha. My wolf rumbled inside, and I rubbed hard at the spot dead center of my chest where the sound wanted to escape. Her feelings added to mine were leaving me flustered and split. I was annoyed with Kane. Sure, there was a physical pull, but also he was a pompous, overbearing ass with a whole lot of over-the-top ego. We weren't going to talk about how that translated into panty-melting, heart-stopping, palm-sweat-inducing energy.

No, definitely not. His eyes reached the row where I sat, and I pointedly looked down at the small wooden table in front of me. It was simple, wide planks cut from rough-edged boards, but made with care. I could swear I felt Kane's eyes burning tracks down the side of my face, but stubbornly refused to look back up.

A she-wolf, heavily pregnant and reclining in a big, cushioned chair with an anxious-looking male at her side, blew a whistle. Everyone froze, and I resisted the urge to make a joke in the resulting silence about Pavlov's dogs.

Barely.

A small argument broke out between the she-wolf and her mate, but in the end, she stayed seated with a huff and accepted the megaphone that he passed her.

"Hello, hello, everyone! We're so glad you're here, and you're going to have so much fun the next few weeks!" She waved enthusiastically, and I instantly liked her. She was vivacious, and the wide smile on her face was genuine. Her ankles may have been puffy—my trained doctor's eye clocked it from across the room and made a mental note to introduce myself after the activity and ask if she'd tried any ginger compresses—but her spirit was high.

"My name is Gracelyn, and I am the organizer of all the activities this week. If you have any questions at all, you can come and see me—" A snarl ripped from her mate's throat, and she gave him a pointed look over the top of the megaphone, before amending her statement. "You can come see one of my assistants." She waved over to four volunteers, each wearing a whistle of their own, like we were at some sort of twisted singles summer camp. "And my *assistants* will notify me if needed. Now, today is speed dating, to get some basic compatibility flowing, but there is so much more coming. Just you wait! And for any true mates that are identified and confirmed by the Alphas, I'm working on some fun, secluded activities to let you get to know your one true love, in style."

Her eyes sparkled as she looked down at the clipboard in her lap. "Okay, the order is posted on the wall, and men, you'll be rotating to the left this hour. Ladies, please stay seated. We'll blow the whistle every five minutes to let you know it's time to shake hands and move on. Ready, set... Go! Meet your true loves!" She grinned as she passed the megaphone back to her mate, who handed it to one of her many volunteers. I tracked Kane with single-minded focus as he approached the line of tables in front of me, until a broad chest blocked him from view.

When I looked up, a smiling Gael was standing in front of me. He'd been next to Kane, but I never saw him move. Heat filled my cheeks, and I waved for him to take the seat in front of me.

He pulled it out and sat with a brief smile. "Good morning, Brielle, how are you?" he asked politely, though the smile hadn't reached his eyes.

"I'm okay. I admit, though, I'm surprised to see you here. It seemed you three were running things, not participating."

He chuckled, the sound a low rumble in his chest as he dropped his wide, tanned hands on the table between us. "Even we don't get excused from the high alpha's scheming. If he says everyone unmated, we say yes, sir."

"Ahh, well, I guess he couldn't excuse just a handful of you, then, could he?"

"No, he wouldn't. He wants us all mated and making little wolf pups."

I chuckled at the thought and couldn't help my gaze wandering over to Gracelyn, the heavily pregnant she-wolf. I couldn't imagine myself mated, let alone pregnant and beaming. *One problem at a time, Brielle.*

"So, tell me about yourself. How was the trip?" Gael broke the ice, and I was grateful that I didn't have to think too hard.

"It was good, but long. I enjoy flying for the most part, but Leigh's a big chicken, so she tries her best to stay tipsy."

His eyebrows shot up, and he glanced a few seats over, where Leigh was leaning forward, showing off her cleavage in a low-cut tank top to a shaggy-haired, blond wolf. They'd make very blond babies together who could be on surfer magazines.

He snorted, and I realized belatedly that I'd said the last bit out loud. "Sorry. What about you? Are you local, or...?"

He nodded. "Yes, we've lived here for two years. Mostly it's quiet. We've been trying to build good pack infrastructure, so we started with the lodge and clearing some nice hiking trails. We've also got some wolves in community-outreach positions, so we can ensure we keep up a good reputation with the locals."

"Community outreach, that's smart. What do you consider to be—"

A sharp, shrill whistle cut me off midsentence. "Oh, well, then," I stammered to a stop.

He gave me a brief smile and stuck out his hand dutifully. No sooner did my palm graze his than he winced and pulled it back. I barely even felt the warmth of skin on skin, and I couldn't help but frown.

"Gael, why—"

"I'd better get a move on. Your next wolf is already waiting." He nodded and left abruptly, leaving me confused. Why hadn't he wanted to touch me? It was literally the whole point of this exercise, and... My brain went into a full spiral. Did he find me so repulsive, he couldn't even bear a *handshake*?

I knew as a psi I would be an undesirable mate for a strong alpha, but it still hurt. I was just a person. My intestines were trying to tie themselves into a knot, but I shoved the embarrassment and confusion down as the next male wolf sat.

He was shorter and narrower than Gael, with a thinner face, but very kind eyes. When I sucked in a steadying breath, the scent of clean linen and something medicinal and herby washed over me that I couldn't place. Nothing that compared to Kane's intoxicating cinnamon-orange scent, but not offensive either.

"Hi there, I'm Xander. What's your name?"

"Hi, Xander, I'm Brielle." I forced a smile, and pushed thoughts of Gael's oddness out of my mind. If I spent my time worrying about Kane's pack and its idiosyncrasies, I'd be here all dadgum day.

"Beautiful name for a beautiful woman. I'm from Washington. How about yourself?"

THE HOUR PASSED in a swiftly churning blur of faces, each handsome in its own right. First was Xander, then Ober, a surfer dude who was, amusingly, scared of the ocean—James, Brett, Steven—I met them all, and I'd be hard-pressed to pick them out of a lineup, besides the quick mental snapshots I was trying desperately to take.

It seemed to be a divine law that there were no ugly shifters, though none of the men I met called to me like Kane, the next row over and tantalizingly out of reach for the whole hour. I did not let myself look his way again, though my wolf sulked at the back of my mind, unwilling to so much as sniff any of the men who clasped hands with me, one after the other after the other. Finally, Gracelyn let out two short, sharp whistles to signal the end of the hour and the beginning of a fifteen-minute break. I breathed a short sigh of relief and shook hands with the handsome shifter across from me—Kevin? I thought it was Kevin.

"It was lovely speaking with you, Brielle. I'd be interested to take you kayaking, if ever you've got some free time."

"Umm, sure. Let's see if they give us any free time." I forced a chuckle, and held out my hand. His fingers wrapped around mine carefully but firmly, just the right amount of pressure to invoke a feeling of friendly familiarity, but just as with all the others—save Gael, who wouldn't deign to touch me—there were no fireworks and no spark. I could see the disappointment in his eyes, and couldn't help but wonder what was wrong with me, that I *didn't* feel disappointed?

I pushed back my chair, glad to stretch my legs, and met Leigh's eyes. She jerked her head to the side, and I quickly made my excuses to Kevin and followed her over to get Shay, who looked withdrawn and pale.

"Shay, are you okay? What's wrong?"

She just shook her head, refusing to speak or meet our eyes, keeping them fixed on her hands, clasped in her lap.

"Come on, sweetie, you need some fresh air." Leigh reached for her arm to help her up and out of her seat, but she flinched back and closed her eyes. Leigh froze, and I dropped down onto my heels so I could look up at her.

"Shay, look at me, please."

She blew out a long breath through her nose before finally opening her eyes again.

"It's just me and Leigh. I'm completely over this and ready to get some pheromone-free air. How about you?"

She gave me the smallest of nods, but wouldn't hold my gaze.

"Okay, when you're ready, we'll get out of here for a few. But we won't touch you, okay?"

She nodded again and pushed unsteadily to her feet. She wouldn't unclasp her hands, even to brace herself on the table. She walked woodenly between us as we exited the barn and made a beeline for the waiting refreshment tables, and my heart ached for her.

She hadn't shared what had happened to her to end up in foster care, but as a wolf, it was incredibly rare. All we knew was that when she'd joined our pack, she was a scared, silent teen who would cower if any man approached her and could barely handle human contact, even from the pack's females. I suspected abuse or human trafficking, but I didn't know, and she'd never volunteered the information, even as we grew closer and she came to trust us over the years.

When illness took my mother a year after Shay joined the pack, she had been firmly by my side, silently supportive, and we'd been best friends ever since. Even Leigh, who couldn't be more opposite with her need to talk a mile a minute and love of flirting with the unmated males, would defend her tooth and nail. We were bonded, and there was no two ways about it.

The whole situation made me feel like the worst friend. I had been so wrapped up in my weird situation-ship with Kane that I hadn't begun to think about how Shay would handle all the forced time with so many men.

The shell of my best friend standing in front of me, though, pushed everything else out of my mind.

I tapped Leigh on the back of the arm while we waited in line for lemonades. She looked over Shay's head at me, so I leaned in to speak quietly.

"I'm going to ask Gracelyn if we can switch around and stay together for the next few rounds. It might not help, but... I don't want to leave her alone like this."

"Good idea. We'll meet you back there with drinks before the next whistle."

"Thanks." I squeezed the back of her arm, then jog-walked back to the barn we'd just exited. So focused was I on Shay's predicament, the warning growl of Gracelyn's mate didn't sink in until he stepped in front of me, eyes low and threatening.

"Oh! Hi, I'm so sorry, I didn't mean to startle you." I held up both hands in my best calming gesture. "I was just hoping to speak with Gracelyn for a moment—my friend, she... she isn't doing so well, and I was hoping we could shift the seating for the next round..." The growl didn't stop or ease up, so I changed tacks. "Also, I noticed that Gracelyn's ankles were a bit puffy and wanted to make sure she was aware of ginger compresses, which can really alleviate swelling and make her more comfortable at the end of the pregnancy."

The growls ceased immediately, and he spun to face Gracelyn, pulling me forward by the sleeve.

"Hi!" she said brightly, leaning forward awkwardly in her recliner. I noticed on closer inspection that the dirt was disturbed underneath, as if it had puffed out when someone plopped it down here, possibly with her already in it.

"Hi, Gracelyn. I just wanted to ask—" Her mate growled. "I, uh, just wanted to tell you *first* about ginger, which can do really great things for swelling. It's pregnancy safe and offers a boost to the lymphatic system. Also, my friend isn't doing so well with this activity, and I wanted to make sure if it was okay if we all stayed together for the rest of the rounds?" I spewed the words so fast, she looked confused, then accusingly at her mate.

"Adam, take a walk."

"Absolutely not."

"Adam, *take a walk*." The steel in her spine was impressive, staring down a physically imposing, dominant wolf from her seated position. He wasn't alpha, but he was at least gamma, and I could feel the annoyance rolling off him strongly enough that I wanted to take a step back.

He narrowed his eyes at her, but reluctantly gestured over two female volunteers who were waiting in the wings. When he stepped away, he was rubbing his palm over the back of his hair in frustration.

She fixed a smile on me, waving an apologetic hand after her mate. "Sorry about that. He's overprotective, with the baby and all, but it's gotten worse since I've had to be on bed rest. I made them carry me out here, because I didn't want to miss all the fun." She hugged her clipboard to her chest, then glanced me up and down. "But, I know you didn't come over here to hear about my woes! What can I do for you—seat change?"

I frowned, trying to process her light-speed information sharing. She and Leigh really would get along. "Who put you on bed rest? That's quite unusual for a wolf to need it, though I can see you have the swelling. Do you mind? I've been studying medicine for quite a while, and I'm our pack's healer back in Texas."

She waved for me to do as I wanted. "You're unmated and already the healer? That's impressive. Usually the healer has to be mated. How'd you swing that?"

I shrugged a shoulder blithely as I felt along her ankle. "Small pack, so not many options when Dee and Zeke were ready to retire." Definitely puffy, and the indents weren't filling in nearly as quickly as I'd have liked. "I am happy to speak to your healer, but I'd like to see you on a regimen of ginger and red raspberry leaf starting immediately, and I think light walking starting tomorrow would be good for you. When are you due?"

"A month, give or take." She wobbled one hand, resting the

other gently over her swollen belly. "And after we're done, I can introduce you to Doc. He's crotchety, but he's got every kind of thing in the infirmary."

Doc sounded like the perfect person to start with, and explain my research to. Win-win. "Excellent. I'll come back after the event. Speaking of which—"

"You and your friend can stay together. I noticed she was struggling, and it's no problem. We want this to go well for everyone." Her warm smile was genuine and pulled out a matching one from me.

"Thank you, Gracelyn, I appreciate it."

"Of course. You better get a move on, though. Ninety seconds!" She gave three short blasts on the whistle, warning everyone to take their places, so I hustled over to Shay and Leigh.

We had a long day ahead of us still.

NINE

Kane

I ground my teeth, and counted to ten as the woman across from me continued talking about her twin sister's second set of twin girls. I'm sure they were lovely, but if I looked up, I was going to see her very ample cleavage practically spilling out of her lacy, see-through top, and at the moment, it just didn't appeal. There was only one woman's cleavage I was interested in, and the she-wolf it belonged to wanted nothing to do with me.

Granted, I'd earned that.

But watching her across the room, exchanging pleasantries with man after man, was starting to grate. She hadn't done more than shake hands, the same as I'd been forced to do over and over all morning, but each time her hand touched another man's, my wolf snarled. So loudly, in fact, that Gael and Reed were both feeling it down the pack bonds. When Gael had been about to shake her hand this morning, my wolf had snarled *so* loudly, he'd winced and tried to avoid the contact. Now she probably thought my pack mate was a jerk, but... I wasn't mad about that.

I wanted all her affection, all her attention. It was royally unfair, I was an ass, and I didn't see a damn thing I could do about it.

I could no more stop wanting her than I could stop breathing; but I also couldn't see a way forward in which she was fit to lead alpha females. It was our very nature, to follow the strong and protect the weak. She deserved my protection, yes. But she didn't deserve to lead.

It grated, but it was the way of the packs. I forced my eyes up when the stream of words stopped, pointedly ignoring the blatant display of her chest and fixing my attention on her face. The she-wolf in front of me might have been pretty, if I were capable of seeing anyone else that way now. But I wasn't, and her lips were pursed angrily. They couldn't compare to Brielle's, which were a soft pink invitation across the room, and completely, wholly unavailable.

Shoot. Had she asked me a question when I'd been counting?

"Are you even listening?"

"My apologies, did I miss a question?" I pushed all the contrition I had into my voice, but she still wasn't appeased, shoving her chair back and standing, arms crossed, before the whistle even blew.

She glared angrily across the crowd, eyeing her next match and pointedly ignoring me. Thankfully, within a few seconds, Gracelyn blew her little dictator's whistle, and I proffered a hand. She was reluctant, but she shook it anyway, digging in her nails a bit *too* hard.

"It was nice talking with you, Kaley," I murmured, already glancing over her shoulder to see who Brielle was shaking hands with.

"It's Kylie, you asshole. I'll be notifying my Alpha of your rude behavior."

I couldn't argue, and didn't try as she walked off, already

beaming a megawatt smile at the wolf to my left. I was ninety-percent sure that she'd told me she was a member of the Northern Territories Pack, which tracked. They were the most aggressive she-wolves I'd encountered so far. Yet for all her offense at my behavior, she'd come to meet me reeking of their Alpha wolf, Vance.

The next she-wolf walked up, and I could smell the fear rolling off her, the emotion a sharp, sour smell polluting her normal... daisy? Petunia? I couldn't tell. It was floral and sour, and I had to resist the urge to sneeze. At least that I could blame on allergies.

"Hello, I'm Alpha Kane. It's nice to meet you," I said.

She quivered, but didn't respond.

"And you are?" I inclined my head, attempting to get an answer, but the poor, nervous woman bolted straight for the door, not looking back.

I could feel Reed's amused cackle over the pack bond, and I cut my eyes his way in annoyance. He was only a few seats away from his turn with Brielle, and I had to bite back a jealous glare. It wasn't his fault. I'd made sure one of my men was on her row for every turn. I hadn't made it myself, but they were the next best thing. *So long as they didn't touch her.* My wolf's hackles rose, and for a moment, I mistook the sudden motion as a reaction to the idea of my pack mates touching my mate. *Not our mate, calm down.*

Of course, my eyes rolled back to Brielle like stubborn magnets, pulled to her like the planets are pulled toward the sun. Constantly, irrevocably. And what I saw made my muscles feel like molten lead, hot and burning and ready to lunge. Shane Russo. Brielle had just approached his table, and he was smiling at her, leaning forward and motioning to the seat with a barely hidden leer.

I growled, low in my throat, unable to control the sound. His eyes flicked my way briefly—we were all wolves; no one within a fifty-foot radius was unaware I was angry, despite the low volume—and I saw a glint of interest and, dare I say, *glee* spark in their unholy depths as he turned his full attention back on Brielle.

Mine! Not his! my wolf demanded, pacing angrily for a second before clawing at the ground and sending dirt flying everywhere. It took all my will, my many years of practiced control, not to shift on the spot. I realized after a few rounds of deep breaths that my fingernails had shifted to claws, and I was digging holes into the wood table in front of me with how hard I was clutching it.

Forcing my hands off the defenseless table, I sucked in a deep lungful of the timid female's waning sour petunia scent, but it did nothing, absolutely nothing, for my wolf.

Or my calm.

Because *she* wasn't my mate.

Brielle was. And the time I'd spent denying it? Her weakness, the fact that she pushed me away, the fact that it was too soon... the fact that I wasn't damn well *ready* for a mate yet?

None of it mattered. Because what my wolf knew, I could no longer deny when I could feel it down in the marrow of my bones.

She. Was. Mine.

My wolf flung back his head and howled at my agreement.

A tinkling laugh filled the room, dragging my attention back to Brielle. Her back was to me, but I could see her shoulders shaking lightly and the cocky smile on Russo's face. My hands began to shake as the acceptance rolled through me like a wave of burning awareness. Her scent. Her proximity.

I stayed in my seat, riveted by the sight of her, even from behind when she wasn't aware I existed. Her gorgeous, shining, russet hair. The delicate line of her neck.

My fangs descended, the urge to mark her lush, perfect skin

and claim her a physical *need*. One that I could absolutely, under *no circumstances*, give in to. Here, in a public hall.

I was going to white-knuckle it through this activity and ask to speak with her like a civilized man, not a feral rogue. *We already had one of those to deal with. I couldn't become the second.*

That thought sobered me slightly, allowing my claws to finally retract. Reed's brother Dirge had suddenly gone feral two summers back. Nobody knew why, as he'd stayed in fur this entire time and wouldn't let anyone near him—in human or wolf form—despite Reed's monthly attempts to communicate with him.

I was too powerful to get anywhere *near* that ledge. With as much dominance as I had... I could wipe out entire towns. In the modern world, that would be a disaster the likes of which had never been seen before. Dirge was only kept close by the presence of another, more dominant wolf. If I lost it...

I shook the thought from my head. I would deal with this, with her, *today*.

Gracelyn blew a short blast on her whistle to signal the end of this round, and I stood, grateful for a reprieve. It wasn't ideal watching Brielle work her way down a line of other men, but at least she'd be away from the Russo mutt.

A strawberry-blonde she-wolf in a long, billowy skirt approached my table, and it took everything in my power to offer her a passable smile.

"Hi, Alpha Kane. I'm Bianca. It's nice to meet you." She stuck out her hand for a shake first, and a small part of me admired her directness. She wasn't my mate, but she'd be a good match for another dominant male here, I had no doubt. Perhaps I'd mention her to Reed. He needed someone to take his sharp edges off.

A gasp, soft as a whisper, sent my hackles rising and my teeth baring as I looked past Bianca to where Brielle had stood to leave Shane's table.

They'd had to shake hands—it was part of the exercise—but he'd taken it a step further. When he'd come around the table for the shake and she'd offered her palm, he'd used it to drag her against his chest. She was wide-eyed and raised her hands as if to push herself back off him, but she didn't make it that far before my wolf tore himself out of my skin.

TEN

Brielle

There was a brief tearing sound, then the hall filled with snarls, and a blur of fur and glinting teeth came barreling straight toward me. No, not toward me—toward *him*, Shane. He had crossed about twelve lines when instead of just accepting the amicable handshake required for the activity, he'd snatched me into his chest.

His scent was all wrong, my wolf's hackles were raised, and before I could even begin to think of how to politely extricate myself—or impolitely, because *what an asshole*—Kane was rocketing our way. Shane shoved me ruthlessly to the side, and I stumbled, almost falling were it not for Reed appearing in front of me with preternatural speed. He righted me with the barest of touches under my elbows, then spun us so that his towering frame was between me and the now *two* snarling, circling wolves in the aisle. Gael was by his side a half second later, the two of them an impenetrable shield.

But I didn't want to be shielded. I wanted to see what the hell was going on. I peered like a child between their massive, muscle-corded arms, getting a glimpse of a steel-gray wolf with eyes that were flat rage, and an even bigger one circling him, lips peeled back to show off an impressive display of fangs. The larger wolf was Kane. My wolf recognized him and howled her approval of his strength and dominance.

In wolf form, he was as tall as my shoulders, utterly massive, his coat a gorgeous mix of colors. He was a dark wolf, with black over most of his face and back, and soft striations of brown and silver shot throughout. His fur was thick and shiny, and some part of my brain wanted me to walk up and sink my fingers in and squinch it in my hands. I just knew he'd be soft under my touch, though nothing about him was soft right now, and that was an utterly *insane* reaction.

I should be freaking out. These two males were fighting—over me, for some reason—like complete idiots.

My runaway thought train was derailed when Shane decided it was time to stop messing around and leapt toward Kane's flank. Kane spun effortlessly out of the way and lunged low, snapping deadly jaws at Shane's exposed underbelly.

He missed by inches, and I caught my breath. There wasn't much that could kill a shifter. We healed so fast, it would take a lot for either of these two to do serious damage, but a total evisceration? That would do it, unless emergency surgery was involved to stabilize the wolf until his natural healing abilities took over. Even a shifter couldn't handle losing all the blood in his body *that* quickly. So why was Kane going for his gut over such a small thing?

I hadn't wanted a hug, no—but I also didn't want to watch the idiot get *gutted* in front of me. I stood on my tiptoes, but couldn't get anywhere near the tops of my self-appointed guards' shoulders. *Stupid, freakishly tall wolf-men.*

The two began snapping and clawing more in earnest, circling closer and closer, like two halves of a twisted, angry puzzle, and Shane let out a loud yelp when Kane connected with his back leg, drawing blood and eliciting a vicious crunching sound that made me cringe. That was at least one broken bone—maybe shattered.

That was *enough*. This had to end before somebody went for the throat. I was not going to be responsible for anybody dying.

Especially not Kane, though it seemed he had a solid upper hand.

I elbowed Gael to try to get a gap I could push through, but he held fast with a grunt, and didn't even spare me a glance. So, instead of trying to budge Reed, I made a split-second decision and bolted to the side, darting around Reed's far elbow and straight into the fray.

Their twin growls had no effect on me, their dominance rolling off me like rain off a good slicker—I'd process that later—and I flung myself between Kane and Shane, holding up my hands to stop them. Kane barked, the sound a clear alpha command that made my hands shake. Even without a pack bond for him to convey words, the message was *crystal* friggin' clear.

Move.

He wanted to finish the fight. And I could see it too. Kane with a bloodied muzzle standing over Shane's limp body as his eyes turned glassy, and his blood soaked into the sawdust-covered floors while I tried fruitlessly to stabilize him and put his intestines back into his body.

Yeah, no. I wasn't signing on for that. I'd felt no connection whatsoever to Shane, so this fight was utterly pointless, and killing a shifter over it was beyond comprehension.

I held fast against Kane's command, even though my legs wanted to run straight for the barn doors, and not stop until I hit my sweet, sweet Texan home turf. I leveled a glare on each of them, making very dangerous eye contact in the process.

"There is no reason to fight like this. I'm fine, and I'm right here. Both of you need to shift back, so Shane's wounds can heal, and we can all put this behind us."

Neither stopped their endless circling, like sharks who'd scented blood in the water, and a wave of irrational anger nearly bowled me over.

They were just going to ignore me? *Hell naw.*

"Stop!" I snarled the words, and both of them froze as if stuck in a block of ice. "This ends now." Kane was the first to regain motion, and as he stalked slowly toward me, my knees started shaking too. What was wrong with me? More importantly, how the heck was I, a bottom-of-the-barrel psi, holding eye contact with a dominant alpha?

His eyes glowed a greenish hazel and bored into mine with… was that a hint of respect? It was hard to read emotions on a wolf's face.

He stalked in front of me, brushing hard against my torso as he put himself between me and Shane, who still hadn't moved a muscle. The contact had me rocking on my heels to stay upright, and my hands sank into his thick fur on reflex.

Goddess, he was *soft*. Powerful, muscular, and so dominant, being this close to him made the hairs on my arms stand on end. But standing there with my hands buried in his fur, as he put himself between me and the wolf he considered a threat? It was heady, and I wanted to wrap myself around him like a cat in heat.

Basically, I'd punched a one-way ticket to crazy town right alongside these two testosterone-riddled males. Joy.

Kane drew himself up to his full height and towered over Shane. As soon as their eyes met, it was as if whatever spell held Shane frozen dissolved, and the steel-gray wolf crumpled to the ground under the power in Kane's eyes.

The darker wolf's lips were pulled back in a ferocious threat, saliva dripping from the wicked canines onto Shane's snout. The seconds stretched long and tense, and I held my breath as Shane made his decision.

If he didn't submit, I had no doubt that Kane would rip his throat out, right here, and right now.

The only other wound I likely couldn't fix on a wolf. I balled my hands into fists, probably pulling some of Kane's hair, but he didn't flinch, his whole focus on Shane.

Finally, *finally*, Shane bent his head back, averting his eyes and baring his neck to Kane.

Kane barked one more time, and forced Shane's shift back into human flesh. I closed my eyes at the horrid sounds he made—it hurt like the devil's own sunburn shifting with a broken bone, or so I'd been told by other shifters I'd treated back home—and I didn't envy him one bit.

It was only a few seconds, though, and then his pack mates were surging forward, surrounding his naked form, and hoisting him up under the arms to carry him from the barn.

Kane stood sentry, with Gael and Reed coming to stand on either side of us, but I averted my eyes, not intent on ogling Shane's naked backside as they carried him off to lick his wounds in private. Though, the gathered crowd didn't seem to have the same compunctions, and the whispers started up before he'd even cleared the double barn doors. Reed passed Kane a pair of sweatpants, and I swear there were several disappointed groans from women in the crowd.

Nausea rolled through me with the force of a tsunami, and I must have moaned or something, because Kane's wolf snapped his head around to stare at me.

"I have to get out of here," I croaked out before bolting for the exit too. I was going to throw up if I didn't get some air. Water. Something.

"Brielle, wait!" Leigh's shout was lost to the crowd, and I didn't slow—I couldn't, or else I was going to toss my cookies right there for the whole crowd to see. Hopefully, she and Shay would find me, after I got my stomach under control.

I clutched my belly and ran, blindly unaware of the different outbuildings I passed, focused only on getting back to my dorm room. It wasn't much, but it was the closest my wolf had to a den while we were here, and my wolf instinctively wanted the safety that only holing up behind a locked door could bring.

Charging through the front door of the dorms, I didn't slow as I hit the stairs, at least until I hit the top. A spearing pain lanced through my belly, and I doubled over, clutching it harder. What was wrong with me? Was this the consequence of going toe to toe with an alpha? It felt like my body was trying to tear itself apart from the inside.

As soon as I could breathe again, I hunch-ran the rest of the way down the hall to my door. My hands shook as I tried to unlock it, and fumbled the keys.

Tears flooded my eyes as they clanked to the wood floor, the weight of everything that had happened today crashing in on me all at once. But before I could try to retrieve them, a masculine hand was there, scooping them up, and lifting me up against his chest.

"It's okay, I've got you. You're safe." The words were a soothing murmur against my hair. With my next breath, Kane's scent washed over me in a beautiful blur of cinnamon-orange, and my whole body turned to putty in his arms.

ELEVEN

Brielle

What was it about his scent that drove my wolf wild with need? She was pacing again, pushing hard to come out to play, which was so far beyond unusual.

He effortlessly opened the door with one hand, cradling me against his chest like I weighed nothing with the other. *That is definitely not true, which means he is hella strong.* Before he could swing it shut, though, Leigh's hand slapped against the wood, stopping it on its hinges.

"Hold on there, buddy. I get that you're head honcho around here, but that right there is *my girl*, and if you hurt her, I will rip the hairy balls right off your body with my bare hands, you feel me? We are a trio, and we're not leaving." Shay was behind her, shoulders hunched with ill-repressed terror, but she was there.

If I hadn't already loved them both like blood sisters, that moment would have clinched it. But I did, and they were already my sisters in every way that mattered.

Leigh glared defiantly at his eyebrows, not daring to make eye contact despite her bold statement.

He dropped his nose into my hair and drew in a deep

lungful of my scent before asking softly, "Do you want them here?"

I nodded, just once, still unable to speak over the intense pain in my middle. He stepped into the room, leaving the door open for them to follow.

But it wasn't just them, because Gael and Reed were right on their heels, and didn't bother to ask before following us inside and locking the door.

"What the hell just happened?" Gael demanded, looking rapidly back and forth between me and Kane, though Kane was ignoring him, adjusting the pillows on my bed in silence, before settling himself against them, still holding me tightly.

Once the motion stopped, it started to sink in that I was clutched against his very hot, very *bare* chest, and my heart sped for an entirely different reason. It was absolutely the wrong time to be turned on, but tell that to my lady bits, which practically flooded at this proximity to all his hard muscles wrapped in seriously the best scent I'd ever smelled.

I wanted to lick him, trace every deliciously cut muscle with my tongue.

Holy hell, I needed to slow down. I didn't even *like* this guy, and I wasn't going to be licking anyone, whether or not that denial made my wolf whine sadly. *Suck it up, buttercup. We don't lick dickish alphas who think they're too good for us, no matter how good they smell.*

Or how achingly right it felt to be hugged against his chest, cradled as if I were precious to him.

She huffed and lay down, dropping her head to her paws. It was then I remembered that we were very much *not* alone, and Gael was waiting on an answer that I didn't have.

"He touched her. Not a handshake. He pulled her against his body, and I defended her, as is my right as her—" He stopped as if grinding his back teeth, and then continued. "As is my right as Alpha here."

"Yeah, I clocked that part," Gael said drily. "I'm asking how the hell a *psi* was able to halt two alphas in the middle of a fight where first blood had already been drawn. I saw the look in your eyes. You were going to the death."

Kane nodded once in acknowledgment, but didn't offer an answer.

I certainly didn't have one.

"I'll tell you how. She's not a psi."

TWELVE

Kane

Reed's voice held such awe and disbelief, it pulled me from my intense focus on Brielle. I looked up to find his eyes glowing blue, his wolf pushing to the forefront in a rare loss of control.

It seemed we were all lacking in control since Brielle walked into my life.

It took a moment for his words to sink in, and I stiffened. "What do you mean, she's not a psi? How can you deny what's sitting right in front of you?"

A low growl echoed through the room, and it took a moment to realize it was coming from my throat. I cut it off, but the damage was done. He knew I was riled, on edge.

"That's just it, I'm not denying it. Her. When has a psi been able to do what she's done?"

I gripped her tighter, not sure where he was going with this line of questioning, but not liking it one bit, regardless.

"Just spit it out, Reed. We're all tense." Gael's tone brooked no objections, and Reed sighed.

"The instant you saw her, she triggered your mate bond. You,

Kane. The most powerful alpha on the grounds, save your father, who's already mated. She then rebuffed you and still managed to call a halt to a blooded fight between two *very* dominant males."

I growled again at the reminder of that damn Russo male, who dared to touch what was mine.

But... mating bonds?

I racked my brain, trying to follow his line of thought and coming up empty.

"It's rare, Reed, but it's not without precedent that an alpha's mated a psi before, and perhaps their bond is solidifying more quickly than usual. So what? Doesn't mean she's not psi." Gael ran a hand through his hair, looking annoyed with the entire discussion.

Reed took a step forward, that fervent light still in his eyes. "Tell me, Brielle, how do you feel right now?"

"Tired, mostly. My stomach hurts." I gripped her tighter at that. What was wrong with her stomach? If that bastard had hurt her—

"She's fine, Alpha. Please," Reed tried to calm me, but he only had eyes for my mate. "Do you smell anything different? About Kane?"

Brielle blushed and ducked her head, but her whispered response sent my heart thundering, nonetheless.

"He smells good, like cinnamon and oranges."

"Okay, that sounds good. What about me? Can you take a whiff and tell me what you smell?"

I ground my teeth as he stepped forward, and Brielle leaned away from me to take a tentative sniff.

"Umm... cologne? I don't know. You smell nice, but—"

"But not as nice as him, am I right?"

"Right."

That had a rumble of pride rattling through my chest, and she startled on my lap. God, she felt good. Her warm thighs were pressed down tight against my lap, and I had to resist the urge to press up into her heat. So close, and yet so far.

I knew without a doubt she'd be paradise, but I hadn't earned her yet.

I would, though, if it killed me. Whatever it took to get her to accept my bond, my bite, my dick... I would do it. Just having her on my lap was enough to make me never want to let her go, never let her *look* at another male again. She was mine, and the sooner she realized it, the better.

"Mate scent. Gael and I have both known Kane since childhood, and I can tell you with absolute certainty that he doesn't smell like cinnamon or oranges. Unless I've missed something, you two haven't even kissed, have you?"

She shook her head, but I didn't miss the embarrassed look she shot her friends, hovering on the other side of the bed. My mate was shy, but I'd get her to open up.

"As I suspected. The mate bonds usually only progress with increased physical and sexual contact. That's why the very first sign is the physical pull toward your mate. You two are already several steps in, and you've barely begun to accept it, let alone progress physically. And today, what we all witnessed at the mixer? I believe that was a power pull."

Gael snarled and turned on Reed, closing the distance between them with a look that would put a lesser male on his ass. "Just what are you implying, Reed?"

"You know. You're only mad because you *know*, Gael. Think about it. What else is there? She pulled *Kane's* alpha, used his dominance to subdue him and the Russo alpha, without even realizing she was doing it. She's no psi."

Gael froze, his gaze hard as ice when it turned on me, enough to bore me into the wall as my breath froze in my lungs.

Not a psi.

Rapid mate bond.

Strongest alpha.

Power pull.

"Omega." The word slipped between my lips like gossamer silk, and she shivered, turning her wide brown eyes on me.

"What? No. *No.* That's not possible. Omegas are illegal, killed at birth. If she were, the Omega Defense League would have killed her before she was a week old. Guys, this is *crazy* talk," Leigh argued.

Brielle clung to my arms, but didn't say a word. Did she know? Was it true?

"Shit. The ODL is *here*." Reed's mind was moving faster than mine, and I didn't think anyone else except him would have put together the signs. Omegas had been gone so long from our world, surely she was safe from reprisal, wasn't she?

The implications of what he'd said propelled me into motion. Or would have if she hadn't started shaking again, her body trembling like a sapling in a hurricane against my chest, and I gripped her tighter, unable to stop touching her, even if the horrifying accusation was true.

I kept my place on her bed—I'd known it was hers because of her delicate jasmine-and-apple scent covering the pillows—and debated what to do next. If Reed's wild theory was correct—that was a big if, though my mind was already latching on to the idea. She was special, and my wolf had known it instantly. But the logistics of it were a big question. How could she be alive? Leigh wasn't wrong. Omegas were killed no later than three days after birth, no matter what.

And yet, she was showing signs I couldn't deny. Omega-alpha pairs were the only known pairings that had the ability to power pull, and it would explain how she'd cowed two alphas with a word. I couldn't dismiss the possibility, at the very least.

Gael was the first to regain his composure. "We have to turn her in."

THIRTEEN

Brielle

Good Goddess, these males were *insane*. First, they insisted I'm an omega—impossible, *hello*—and then they wanted to just hand me over to the ODL to be *killed*?!

I heard Shay gasp and Leigh shout, "No!" as Kane moved beneath me. One moment, I was perched on his lap, curled into his chest like he was my personal damn pillow, and the next, I was landing gracelessly on the bed, as he blurred across the room to tackle Gael into my roomie's bedframe. The furniture didn't stand a chance, splintered wood flying as they crashed into it, scuffling. Whether it was seconds or years, I couldn't tell you, but my heart lodged itself so firmly in my throat I was going to be tasting aorta for a month as they fought and thrashed, impervious to the rubble beneath them.

When they stilled, Kane was on top of Gael, who had blood trailing from his lips and a split eyebrow. Kane's left eye was beginning to swell, but it didn't stop me from seeing the feral light glowing from them as he pinned his second-in-command by the throat.

"She is mine." The words came out slightly mangled, and I realized his fangs had descended in a partial shift.

Dominance swelled through the room with suffocating force, and I found myself perched on the edge of the bed. I was teetering between running to Kane, flinging myself onto his back and begging him to stop or bolting for the door, though that hadn't worked so well last time.

"Fealty to me is fealty to her. If you move one finger against her, I'll kill you. If you cause harm to befall her in any way, I'll rip your throat out and bathe in your blood. Choose now. Honor your blood oath or drown in it." The words dissolved into a menacing growl, his human lips peeling back to reveal his wolf's canines.

Gael's resistance melted, the anger in his eyes turning to confusion. "I would never betray you, Alpha." He clenched his jaw and pointedly bared his neck, the act of submission costing him dearly. "I only want to see you safe. The threat of an omega is too great. You know the histories."

Kane didn't relent though, his claw-tipped fingers still holding Gael's throat in a punishing grip as he growled over his friend.

"Brielle," Leigh hissed. "You have to go to him. He's too far gone to come back himself."

I looked quickly back and forth between her and Kane, his back hunched as he held his friend on the brink of death. Was she right? Was this powerful alpha going to bow to me and come away, or was I going to get torn to shreds instead of Gael?

Deep down, I knew he wouldn't hurt me. No matter how far gone he was, I was safe with his wolf. I rose on shaky legs, crossed the few steps between us, and laid a hand gently on the broad expanse of his back.

"Kane, it's okay."

His muscles flexed under my palm, and I dug my fingers in slightly, gripping him as I dropped my other hand down to caress him as well. We were like magnets, and even in this awful situation, I couldn't hold back from touching him. His back was a work of art, finely honed through years of hard work and shifter metabolism, but I didn't want to appreciate it like this, with him threatening his friend.

His head rose and his eyes bored into mine, but he still didn't let go of his friend. What would make him come back to me?

"Please? There's no threat here, because I'm not omega. I'm psi, have been my whole life. My stomach stopped hurting while you were holding me, and I need—"

I was swept off my feet, clutched back to his chest, my head pressed against his bare shoulder, before I could blink.

A sense of calm broke over me, and I sighed, unable to hold it in. He felt right, though my mind was still grappling with the idea of me—a complete weakling who could barely shift—being mated to the second-most powerful shifter in the *world*. And power pulling? I couldn't go there, not yet. That was more than I was ready to handle without copious amounts of Oreos and both of my besties in our ugliest pajamas.

Kane didn't settle back onto my bed. He simply held me, breathing into the top of my hair, and slowly, so slowly, I felt him come back from the brink. When he lifted his head, I looked up, finding his eyes back to their normal human green with gold flecks, fringed by dark lashes any woman would be jealous of.

His mouth was pressed into a hard line as he looked back and forth between Gael—now on his feet next to the rubble, strips missing from his black T-shirt and revealing tanned skin underneath—and Reed, who still studied me with hope that made my heart hurt. Why did he want to believe I was omega? It was impossible, no matter what they thought.

"We need a plan."

I couldn't concentrate on Reed's words, only on the fire in Kane's eyes. It was all-consuming, and his hands felt like brands where they connected with my arms. All heat, all flames. Licking, stirring up something deep inside me. Something primal, some part of my wolf.

He sucked in a breath as I looked up at him, deep into his glowing green eyes. He took one hand off my forearm and brushed it across my cheekbone so gently, it felt like the shadow of a real touch.

"Your eyes. They're stunning," he said, his voice still gravelly with his wolf's influence.

His face was sharper, more vividly colored, and I realized my wolf must be shining through as well, pushing forward to match his, *her mate*.

Holy hell.

I had a mate. And not just any mate, but *Kane*, son of Kosta, heir to the high alpha-dom of the world.

"What is it? Is it your stomach again?" He shifted his grip to my upper arms, holding me up as my body tried to go limp and gently easing me to the edge of the bed. "Reed!" he snapped, not taking his eyes from mine.

"Yes, Alpha?"

"Is this normal for omegas? Why is she in pain?"

"I... I don't know, Kane. There are only legends, and none of them that I've read mentioned this. Omegas have extra gifts from the moon Goddess, but nothing mentioned—"

Kane snarled, and I lifted my hand to tangle in his close-cropped hair. "Shh, Kane. I'm sure I'll be okay. It was just a lot today."

His eyes fell closed, and he leaned into my palm as if he was a parched desert and I was summer rain for him to soak up. And I never, ever wanted him to stop.

Which was insane. But perfect too.

"The mate bond does seem to be progressing differently than typical. Perhaps it's a side effect? Usually, physical intimacy would precede this level of bond, but... no, I don't know. I don't want to make a guess and be wrong."

Kane growled, the sound a low rumble in his throat, but something had clicked into place for me. Our mate bond was progressing with unusual speed. Usually, it was a slow unfurling of weeks or months, sometimes *years* mates could know each other, before the bond progressed past a strong attraction and the physical pull.

My stomach pains... If I were sick like my mother, would my wolf somehow be able to accelerate the bond, tie me to Kane? She'd never been very strong, but she had been pushing constantly when he was around, in a way she never had before.

Oh, Goddess. No. I could hear Gael, Reed, and Leigh all talking, but their voices were a background hum to the sick realizations spinning through my mind.

Wolves rarely fell ill, our pack healers primarily setting bones, cleaning up fight injuries, and helping deliver pups when a mated pair was blessed with them. But my mother... my mother had been sickly my whole life.

It was strange, and we lived a life secluded from our pack due to her illness. My father did everything for her, tried everything to save her, even increasingly involved spells and potions from her best friend, a witch, Karissma. It was why I studied medicine, why I wanted to see what differences existed between humans and wolves, to finally figure out why my mother's wolf genes *hadn't* worked like everyone else's.

But now, I'd found my mate—that word still felt so foreign, but it was rapidly growing on me—and at the same time, developed awful, racking stomach pains.

Just like my mother.

I needed a lab. I needed to look at my blood, see if anything had changed from my last sample, what was causing this. See if I could spot any disease markers not present in the other samples from my friends and pack who'd been willing to trust me with them. I needed—

"Everyone out. Leave us." Kane's voice held an alpha

command, and four sets of feet began shuffling toward the door, none of them quickly.

"Brielle! Do you want to come with us? You don't have to stay with him. He can't force you. Brielle, look at me!" Leigh's tone snapped me from my panicked train of thought, and I spun around on the bed to where she was gripping the doorframe with white knuckles.

"It's okay, guys. I'm fine. I think I just need rest."

"Did you not hear anything we just discussed? You're not going to get *rest*. We think you need to deepen the physical connection to fix your mate bond, and if that doesn't work, they're going to— Ahh!" She lost her grip, and the last thing I saw was Gael's grim face as he settled a hand on the doorknob.

"I'll take one of the hallway positions, Alpha. If you need me, I won't be far." With a nod, he turned the lock and shut the door with a resolute click.

And just like that, I was alone with the wolf prince.

FOURTEEN

Kane

"No, we can't. I won't let you deepen the bond, Kane. It's not safe." She tried to scoot away from me, back herself across the bed out of reach, but I pinned her thighs to the bed with my forearm. What did she mean, it wasn't *safe*? Did she think I was going to hurt her because she might be omega?

My wolf growled angrily at the thought. I could never. To raise a hand to your mate was to hurt yourself, the other half of your soul. She was more precious to me than any other person on the planet, and I would lay down my life for hers. Hurt her? Never.

"Shh, Brielle. We don't have to do anything you don't want to do, but don't run away from me." She stilled under my touch like a rabbit in a wolf's sights. Her chest heaved, pressing her beautiful breasts tightly against the thin shirt she wore. Wholly inappropriate for Alaska weather, but so stunning. I couldn't let myself get distracted by her body right now, though, when something was wrong.

She had stopped trying to escape me, so I eased the pressure, sliding my hands to her thighs instead, rubbing gentle circles with my thumbs over the denim of her jeans. The heaving stopped as I traced the seam along her inner thigh.

"Breathe, my heart, and talk to me. Why do you think it's unsafe to follow this bond between us? Our wolves have chosen. Tell me you feel it."

Her eyes were glowing again, and I knew I was right. Her wolf wanted mine, even if the woman hadn't yet acknowledged it. She was intelligent; she just needed time to come to grips with what it meant, work through all the details.

Goddess, I hoped that was all. My cock was aching, being this close to her, but unable to ravage her like I wanted, no, *needed* to. To slide the white T-shirt up and over her flat stomach, kiss a trail up to those gorgeous breasts and free them from the confines of her bra, suck and kiss them until she was crying for me to take her, make love to her, claim her.

The wolf was riding me hard, but he'd never hurt her either. And so, we waited. With an ache in my balls and an iron fist on my control. For this was the truth of wolf mates: the female had the power. She could deny me, or she could make my dreams a reality. But either way, I was hers. Even were she to reject me, there would be no other for my wolf.

Which meant I had no choice but to win her over, because not having her was not an option.

"Tell me why you don't feel safe," I said, trying hard not to demand, to push, even though it was my nature.

She shook her head, biting that delectable lip between her teeth, and I reached up to free it with the pad of my thumb. I gently tugged it free. "These are mine to bite. Talk to me, Brielle. Whatever it is, I'll fix it. You have my word."

"You can't fix this, Kane. Nobody can."

"Is it the omega issue? I don't care if it's illegal. I don't care if I have to burn the Omega Defense League to the ground with my own two hands, I will do it for you. This is an obstacle we can overcome together."

Her eyelids sank down, hiding her gorgeous brown eyes from me. And to my horror, fat, slow tears began to leak from the corners of her eyes as she shook her head.

I wrapped myself around her waist from my kneeling position, holding her tightly and hearing the thump of her heart. This was more than just a reaction to the bond. But what was I missing?

"Tell me, Brielle. Please."

Words began to tumble from her lips, and I leaned back just enough so that I could see her face. She kept her eyes screwed shut, blocking me out at the same time as letting me peek into her past.

"My mother... She was sickly. My whole life, she was never well, always fighting, always struggling. My father did everything he could. Spoke to every healer we could find, but nothing worked. Her best friend was a powerful witch, and she made potions to help her, but the sickness always came back stronger, worse."

She swallowed, and a horrible feeling started sinking into my gut. A sickly wolf? That wasn't possible. It was unheard of, because it went against our very nature. The moon Goddess had truly blessed her children with good health, and rapid healing.

"What was wrong with her?"

"She had these awful stomach pains that mimicked stomach cancer in humans."

The feeling in my stomach turned to stone, and sour bile rose up the back of my throat. No, not my mate. I could deal with her weakness, I could deal with the fact that she would be hunted for her omega gifts, though that was a shock in and of itself. One that my wolf had already decided was true, despite her own denial. But to watch her suffer, day in and day out? It would crush me.

"What happened to her?" I asked the question I most

dreaded the answer to, because I couldn't not. Her voice was small, her eyes finally flickering open to meet mine, loaded with sorrow when she answered.

"She died when I was seventeen, taking my father with her."

I buried my face in her stomach to muffle my wolf's howl of pain. To know our mate had suffered so much, so young, gave me all the more respect for her. She was strong, if not in the sense that I knew. Physical strength, or might. She was strong in her soul, and my wolf had seen that from the start. Not her beauty, not her intelligence, though it sparked from her deep brown eyes undeniably. No, it was that inner strength, that fire, that had bonded my wolf to hers.

She had lost so much, and yet here she was, the she-wolf of my dreams.

And I would not lose her. Not if I had to turn over every stone on the planet to find a cure, an answer, I would, and I would do it with a smile. She was mine. My heart. My love.

"And that's why I can't bond with you, Kane. I'm so sorry. But it's a death sentence, and I can't—" She broke off on a sob and covered her face with her hands. "I don't know how, but I already feel too much for you. If I have to die, that's one thing. But I can't take you with me, Kane, and if we bond, the mate bond will drag you after me, just like it did my father. So we can't—we can't deepen the physical bond. We can't complete the mating. I'm sorry. I'm so, so sorry."

"No," I growled, unable to restrain my wolf. He wasn't going to accept a rejection from her, not now, not ever. The wolf didn't see shades of gray, only the truth: she was ours. It wasn't right to live without your mate. We were meant to be hers no matter what, and we had to make her see that.

I climbed onto the bed, urging her back to the comforter. Her face was no less beautiful for being tearstained, and I pried her hands up and over, pinning them to the bed, stretching her beneath me. But this wasn't about sex or dominance. I had to make her *see*.

See that we could tackle this problem, together. That the only way I would accept this was with her at my side.

"Kane, no. Let me up. We can't do this. We can't take things any further. You should distance yourself from me now, before it gets harder to—"

"Never, Brielle. *Never*. Don't you see? It's too late. My wolf has claimed yours. Your wolf has claimed mine. Maybe this is exactly what was meant to happen. You may be sick, and your wolf knows you need my strength. Has she ever pushed you like this before? Tried to mark anyone else?"

She shook her head, biting that lower lip again. The urge to free it with my own teeth was strong, but I held back. I wanted her, but she had to say yes. She had to accept me, accept the bond first. I could convince her if that was what she needed, but she *would* say yes. If it took me a hundred years of wooing, she would say yes.

I dropped my nose down to her neck, at the place it joined with her shoulder, and sucked in a deep drag of her scent. It bloomed beneath me, confirming what I thought. But how did I get her mind to catch up with her body? Get her to say that one little word that I needed to hear?

"Your scent is intoxicating, Brielle. Do you know that? I've never smelled anything like your perfume. Your body wants mine, and this is how it tells me." I dragged my nose slowly up the length of her neck to the delicate shell of her ear, whispering, letting my breath play over her skin. "Why are you saying no, when everything in you wants to say yes? Can you trust your wolf? Can you trust me?"

I let my tongue trace up from her earlobe, rimming the shell of her ear, and she bucked her hips underneath me, grinding against my erection with a little moan that lit my blood on fire.

Yes. Come to me, baby.

"There's my girl, my dirty little mate. You liked that, didn't you?" She whimpered, and I knew I was on the right track. "I want to give you more. *So* much more. But you have to want it too. You can't tell me no and get all this. My wolf needs your yes. Craves your yes, your submission. What does your wolf want? What does Brielle want? Don't think about me. Don't think about anything else. Tell me what you want, and it's yours."

FIFTEEN

Brielle

Oh Goddess, Kane was going to kill me. My body was burning up under his touch, and he had barely begun to tease me. It was pathetic how badly I wanted him, but I didn't care. Didn't think about how many women he'd used his wicked words and tongue on before me, or what the implications were of giving in, saying those words he wanted.

I shouldn't, oh, I knew I shouldn't. But he asked.

He *asked*.

What did I want? I wanted him. Every hot, hard plane of his perfect body, crushing into mine, claiming, taking, wild... I wanted it. More than I wanted my next breath, I wanted his lips on mine, his dick grinding into me like he owned me. Because if I were being honest, really honest, I knew I couldn't stop this thing growing between us.

I hated it, because I had already seen the future. I'd lived it. I'd lived the slow decline and descent into heartache. My parents had suffered, my mother with the illness, and my father being slowly hollowed out by watching her endure the pain and being unable to stop it.

But that was the past, and right now, all I could see was the heat, the force of nature that was Kane, growling so sweetly with need above me.

And I wanted him. Selfishly, I wanted him. And he was offering himself up, mine for the taking, this big, powerful alpha. This wolf who would one day rule the entire wolf world. He wanted *me.*

"Yes." The word slipped from my lips like a prayer over the altar that was our joined bodies, and he dove down, not giving me a second to hesitate, to change my mind. His lips crashed so sweetly with mine, I couldn't help but gasp.

He took advantage, pressing into my mouth, sweeping through me with his tongue, plundering, invading, *owning* me. And I pressed right back, wriggling one hand free from his hold overhead, grabbing the back of his neck and pulling him harder, tighter, stronger to me. I wanted it all. I wanted the wild. I wanted him unhinged.

Our lips tangled and teased, fought for control in the sweetest war of all time. My chest was heaving, and I could feel my wolf shining through when he finally pulled back, his own eyes aglow, and a sheen of sweat coating his rock-hard chest.

Goddess, I wanted him. Wanted to lick every inch of that tempting muscle. Slide my hands under his waistband, peel those pants off him, and keep on going—

He dropped his forehead to mine, lowered himself to the bed beside me, and wrapped me up like a human burrito against his warm, naked chest. Goddess, I would never get enough of his skin. I traced little patterns across one firm pectoral, scraping gently with my fingernail, and he shivered at the contact.

"Thank you, my heart. My Brielle, my mate. Thank you." He said it so softly, I almost didn't catch those last words. But I did, and I locked them away in my heart to keep forever. Because for all his power, for all his wolf's strength and dominance, this male wanted *me.* And I never wanted to forget this moment.

Heat blossomed in my chest, unfurling like the most delicate flower, as a new awareness flooded my body. He grunted, and I knew he was feeling it too.

The bond. We'd done it. I'd accepted his kiss, let him in, and now—the gentle heat coalesced, built in intensity until it reached its crescendo, centering over my hip bone.

The pain in my stomach was gone, lost to the passion between us, and the only thing I felt was liquid heat, like my limbs were made of molten Jell-O.

"Did you just feel..." He stopped, moved to rest a hand over his left pectoral muscle.

"I did." I dropped my hand down to my right hip bone, where I was sure I now had a brand-new mating mark, the irrevocable proof that I'd found my fated mate, the other half of my soul. The strength to my softness, my protector, my one true love.

He rumbled, the soft vibration soothing under my ear. "May I see it? See your marks?"

I sucked in a surprised breath. That had been a hot kiss, but the mark was in an intimate place. He was so perfect. Was I ready to let him see all my flaws?

Did I want to keep him out? No, I didn't. I wanted to see him look at me like that again. Worship me with his eyes. For the first time in my twenty-seven years of life, I didn't want to hide.

"Yes." The word was stronger this time, resolute. "But I want to see yours first."

He propped himself on one elbow, leaning himself up so I could see the hard planes of his chest. I let my fingers trail over his smooth, tanned skin. There was a sprinkling of hair there, and I skated over it to his pec, where a swirling blue design now bloomed on his chest.

Every mating mark was unique, and I traced the strong lines of his with awe. These were for me, proof of my claim on him, my bond with him, a sign to every other female that he was taken. Pride swelled in my chest at the sight, and when I'd looked my fill, I rolled onto my back so he could see mine.

He leaned down and kissed the hollow above my collar-bone. "Where is it?"

I tugged up the hem of my shirt in answer, exposing the top of the mark on my hip. He hissed through his teeth, that gleam already back in his eyes as he scooted down the bed, getting himself eye level with the mark. He traced it reverently with his fingertips, stopping at the waistband of my jeans.

"May I?" He was running his fingertips so tantalizingly over the tender skin there, softly enough that it *almost* tickled.

I opened my mouth to answer, but a frantic knock on the door froze us both in place.

Gael's voice was every bit as frantic when he spoke. "Alpha! It's Gracelyn. We need you."

SIXTEEN

Kane

"Coming."

I mentally cursed the interruption, apologizing to Brielle with my eyes, but her worried frown told me that she wasn't angry, and it proved once again that she was the perfect mate for me, despite my initial reservations. The Goddess had blessed me with a caring mate, one who wouldn't rant and rave that our alone time might be interrupted by the needs of a pack.

"I'm coming with you," she said as she gestured for me to pull her up from the bed. I clasped her hand between both of mine, but didn't pull yet.

"How do you feel? Any pain?"

She frowned again, and I smoothed my fingertips over the cute little line between her eyebrows she got when she concentrated.

"No, actually. I feel... really good. But I want to check on Gracelyn. She had a lot of swelling, and I recommended an herb, but Gael wouldn't sound like that for simple swelling. If something else has happened..."

I pulled her from the bed, happy to keep her by my side, where I could protect her.

"Let's go find out."

IN MINUTES, we were standing at the front steps up to Gracelyn and Adam's cabin, the sturdy logs some of the first we'd cut here after the main lodge was finished. The whole pack pitched in, as was our way. It was fine workmanship, but we weren't here to admire it.

Adam stood with his shoulders slumped, leaning against the front door, one hand resting on it, pleading with his heavily pregnant mate through the door. "Please, my love. Please. Let me in, and take some rest. The stress isn't good for you, or the little one."

His voice was that of a broken man, and I could feel his desperation through the pack bond. I sent a rush of soothing energy through it as we climbed the steps, and I dropped a hand on his shoulder.

"What's the problem, Adam? What's happened?"

"Alpha, she found out that the ODL is here, and flew off the handle. She's angry I didn't tell her, and I deserve that." He hung his head, and I squeezed his shoulder. "But I didn't want to stress her. She's had such a hard time, I wanted her to have as much peace as she could. But she got angry, and kicked me out. She's trying to hide it, but I think the stress has sent her into early labor. I'm getting glimpses of pain through our bond, when she stops concentrating on blocking me. Goddess, it's not supposed to be like this. I'm scared, Kane. What if I lose them both?"

His voice cracked, and my heart lurched at the pain I could feel radiating from him through the pack bond, and the naked fear in his voice. It was a very real possibility that the delivery could go badly, but I couldn't dwell on that. As Alpha, I had to be the rock he leaned on.

"Excuse me," Brielle interrupted, elbowing past us without hesitation. "Gracelyn. It's Brielle. Remember me from earlier?"

There was a muffled snuffling sound from inside, and then Gracelyn's soft voice on the other side of the door. "Yes, I remember."

"Great. I have some ginger and red raspberry leaf tea right here for you in my bag. Could I come in, please? I think you might need the healer."

"Just you." There was a deep groan from the other side that rocked me back on my heels, but Brielle didn't blink. "Nobody else is allowed in. *Nobody*."

"That's fine. We don't need these guys taking up all the space, anyway. I could check on you, if you're okay with that."

"Yes." The door lock clicked open, and Brielle leveled a stern look at me and Adam, who stood like he was about to shoulder that door open like a linebacker.

"You two are going to stay right here and respect her wishes. Are we clear?" She may have been a psi—or an omega—but in that moment, she was all alpha female, and she was glorious—protective authority practically rolling off her.

"Yes, mate. Go to her. If you need us, call." I gripped Adam's shoulder tighter as Brielle slipped through the door, turning sideways and shutting and locking it immediately, not even letting us have a glimpse inside.

How could I ever have thought her too weak to be mine? Brielle was fiercely protective, and I loved her even more for it.

SEVENTEEN

Brielle

"How are you doing, Gracelyn? Can you tell me what's going on?" I tried to keep my voice low and soothing, because from the looks of things, Gracelyn had been struggling for a while. The small front room of the cabin was a wreck, with just about everything out of place.

Not like a temper tantrum, but more like she kept knocking into things while she paced, which she was still doing, completely ignoring me as she grabbed at her heavily pregnant belly.

"Can you sit down for me so I can check your ankles?"

She grimaced and clutched her lower back, but didn't stop moving. *Hell, she really might be in preterm labor.*

"Okay, you shouldn't be having contractions yet. It's time to sit down and put your feet up."

When she didn't respond, I crossed the room, wrapped my arms around her shoulders, and pulled her to me in a hug. She shuddered and then clung to me, sobs racking her shoulders.

"They can't take my baby, Bri. I won't let them. I would die, just die. Do you know how long it took us to get pregnant? A hundred years. A hundred years of hopes and dreams, and they might take her. Please, please, promise you won't let them take her. *Please.*"

Wolf shifters were not a fecund species, despite our longevity. It was typical for children to be rare, and spaced far, far apart if a couple were blessed with a second pregnancy. But even knowing this clinically, seeing the toll it took on Gracelyn in the moment, it hit me harder than it ever had before. I had a fated mate now, and it was all so much more real. Visceral.

"Shhh, Gracelyn. It's going to be okay. Nobody is going to hurt you or your child. But if we can't get these contractions to stop, she might come too early, and we don't want that. Do you think you can lie down?"

She nodded, still gulping and gasping through her flood of tears. She let me steer her out of the front room and into a larger living area, with a big, fluffy chaise lounge next to a love seat. I guided her down onto it and grabbed a few throw pillows to arrange behind her back. Once she was comfortably reclined, I sank down onto my heels and checked her pulse at her wrist. It was a bit fast, but nothing dangerous.

She groaned again, and I placed a hand lightly on her belly. Rock hard. I acted on autopilot, relying on my studies but also instinct. Seeing a female in trouble drove my wolf, had her pushing me to act and act quickly. I found their bedroom and grabbed more pillows to stuff under her feet. I positioned her on her side and then went to the kitchen for an ice pack. I wrapped it in a towel to keep it tolerable on her flushed skin. I settled it against her neck, and she shivered.

I settled back down on my knees next to the chaise and ran my thumb over the back of her hand, back and forth, just trying to give her something to focus on. After several minutes of silence, she spoke.

"He didn't mean to upset me. He never does, really. He's just so scared, he didn't want me to, to—" She hiccupped, then groaned. "He didn't want me to do *this*," she gestured to herself, upset and contracting, "but I can't help it. It's every wolf's worst fear, come to hang over the end of my pregnancy like a guillotine. I just want them gone, Bri. When they're gone, I can pretend they don't exist. But having them here, waiting. Who would call them here? Who could be that cruel?" She started sobbing harder, her shoulders shaking, and I leaned forward to hug her again.

"I don't know, honey, but Kane's going to find out. Nobody wants them here, and nobody wants them putting pressure on you." I stroked her hair, shushing her softly until her sobs softened to gentle, even breaths. As gently as I could, I pulled back to grab the soft chenille throw from the back of the love seat and tucked it over her. Instead of covering her feet, though, I pulled the hem of her stretchy black leggings up a few inches so I could see her ankles.

Definitely swelling, maybe more than the alfalfa I'd grabbed on the way out of the room could help. We needed juniper, and she needed to be off her feet until it kicked in and knocked this swelling out. Tucking the blanket around her feet just so, I walked back to the front door and opened it a crack. Adam was slumped against one of the support posts, eyes sunken and grim, the very picture of a worried-sick male. He nearly leapt at me, but Gael's hand on his arm halted him in his tracks.

Kane closed the distance, but I held up a hand. "No one else is coming in until she's okay with it. I got her comfortable and lying down with her feet up, to see if we can stop the contractions for now, but she's got more swelling than I realized, and that's putting strain on her too. I need somebody to get some juniper berries so I can make a poultice for her."

Adam let out a tortured whine and pulled against Gael's hold. "Please, Alpha. She needs me, even if she's too stubborn to admit it. I won't do anything but hold her. Please." My heart clenched at his pleading, but this wasn't my call to make. It was Gracelyn's.

"I promise I'll call you the second she asks for you," I reassured him as softly as possible. My gaze swung to Kane, who had his hands clasped together behind his back. "Can you send someone for the berries?"

He nodded once, his eyes never releasing mine. "Anything you need, anything she needs."

"Thank you. Can you tell Leigh and Shay—I don't know. At least where we are? I don't want them to come looking for me and worry..." I couldn't say the words. *That something had gone wrong.*

"Of course. Do you want them here?"

"No, no. I don't want to stress her any more than she is already. They'll understand."

"Consider it done." He stepped forward, anchoring me with a hand around the back of my neck, giving me a gentle squeeze, before dropping his lips to mine, the chaste press of lips nothing like his earlier claiming, but still I swayed forward, inexplicably drawn to him, no matter the circumstances. "Thank you for helping my pack mate."

"Of course, Kane. I could never leave someone in pain."

His lips twisted into a smile as he stepped back, barking orders that sent Gael and another wolf I didn't know off at a jog in separate directions, and I softly closed the door again, returning to Gracelyn's side.

WHEN SHE WOKE AN HOUR LATER, it was with Adam's name on her lips. I stopped grinding the juniper berries to get him, and he bolted past me like his tail was on fire. I didn't mind, though. They were sweet together, tiff or no. As soon as the berries were smooshed to my satisfaction in a smooth paste,

I sprinkled over some dried alfalfa, stirred it in, and then walked back to the living room. She was clinging to him, nose buried in his neck as he stroked her hair, a look of peace finally on his face.

I set the bowl of poultice on the low coffee table. "I think her contractions have stopped for now, and she really needs to rest. If you two will be okay, we can smear this on the soles of her feet, slide some socks over it, and let her keep it on until morning. It might take a few days, but it should help her ditch the extra fluid and feel a lot better."

Adam nodded solemnly. "Thank you for your help today. If the contractions start again..."

"Just call me. I'm in the second dorm, so I'm not far."

"Thank you, Bri." Her voice was still drowsy, and I smiled at how content she was, tucked up with her mate. He would take good care of her.

"You're welcome, Grace. I'll let you two get some rest."

I let myself out of the cabin and into Kane's waiting arms. He lifted me off my feet like I weighed nothing, and it was so nice to let someone else take care of me, for once. I was suddenly exhausted, eyes blinking shut as soon as my head hit his shoulder. His warm, comforting scent and solid arms lulled me to sleep before we made it back to the dorms.

EIGHTEEN

Kane

Reed was waiting outside my office after I tucked Brielle into her bed, pacing a pattern in the rug. He didn't look up until I was a few feet away, clearly lost in thought. He froze and drew himself up to his full height as soon as he realized I was there, putting on his usual business mask.

We'd known each other since childhood, though, so I knew something was bothering him, and I had an inkling of what, though I'd let him bring it up. Half of being a good Alpha was learning when *not* to steer, to let people make their own decisions. Reed and Gael were my most trusted; I rarely steered them at all, unless it was for the good of the pack.

Or my mate.

As the personification of all my wolf's desires, wrapped up in one soft, beautiful, perfect package, she brought everything into sharp focus. She was my world, and I would do anything for her, even if it meant putting my most trusted into place, as I had earlier with Gael.

"Come in," I said as I entered the code on the keypad and pushed open the door. It was a formality for him to wait. He had the access codes.

Whatever he wanted to talk about, it was important.

I strode behind the desk and sank into my chair, steepling my fingers as I watched my lifelong friend perch on the edge of one of the wide, comfortable chairs across from my desk. He ran his hand through usually perfectly gelled hair, knocking a hank askew as he met my eyes.

"She might be able to save Dirge," Reed said. Real hope tinged his voice for the first time in years, and I struggled not to react so he could say what he needed to without my influence.

Dirge was his twin. He'd gone feral three years ago, and despite Reed's endless efforts that first year to bring him back to the pack, he'd strayed farther and farther afield, and had not responded to any of Reed's attempts to communicate, whether in human or wolf form. I leaned forward heavily on my elbows, listening. I didn't know much about omegas, but if Reed thought an omega could pull a feral alpha back from the void, a lot more about his unexpected knowledge from earlier made sense.

"It's a long shot. I mean, it's speculation. I know I'm the one who said it was likely, but how could she slip through the cracks? The more time goes by, the more I question—"

"I don't."

He froze, eyes lighting with fervor.

"I think you're right. After having some time to think about it, my wolf agrees. He's wanted her from the beginning, and it never made sense before—"

He cut me off in his excitement, a rare slip from my ever-poised third. "I agree. A psi is a poor match for an alpha, but an omega... They're special."

"Brielle is special. Did you see how she was with Gracelyn earlier? She's a wolf the females can rally behind, even if she's not the conventional alpha female. She has that something about her, a healer's touch."

"Healers have always been respected in packs, Alpha," Reed

agreed, though his mind wasn't on Brielle. Not that I could blame him. His brother had been spotted only once in eighteen months, fur shaggy and eyes unrecognizable, hard, red pits.

It wasn't known how long a wolf could stay feral and still come back, but somewhere deep down, I knew Reed feared he was precariously close to being lost to us forever.

"How is an omega supposed to bring him back?" I asked, cutting to the point. If she could do something the rest of us had never managed, it would be another tick mark in the box of proof for her omega status.

I wasn't about to call the Defense League and ask them to test her, so we'd have to figure it out on our own.

Along with why they couldn't sense her, how it was possible, and... My fists tightened in fear and anger as I thought of her gut-wrenching pain. To find my mate and then lose her? No. I wouldn't let it happen. I didn't care what it took, I would figure out the problem, and fix it.

"—it's just a theory, but not much is known about omegas anymore. I think if we get the two of them in the same room, instinct should kick in. I hope."

I hummed noncommittally. I wasn't signing up to put Brielle in the path of a feral alpha until we had a lot more than a theory. But knowing what little I did of her so far, I had no doubt she'd jump into the fray if she thought there was any chance she could help. Keeping her safe at my side was going to be a lifelong challenge, and frankly, I couldn't wait.

"We can arrange a search party, try to find Dirge as soon as this gathering ends. But we've got some issues to deal with first." I dropped my fists to the table, leaning back against my office chair.

"Anything, Alpha. What can I do?" Reed's enthusiasm was interrupted by a double rap at the door, Gael's signature.

"Enter," I ordered, and he slipped inside, locking the door behind him. I watched closely as he crossed to the chair next to

Reed, checking his posture for any signs of defiance or unease, but found none as he dropped easily into it, lounging back and sprawling to cover the entire surface. He was my second, and I'd expected him to accept the correction, but I didn't want any anger left to fester and corrupt our relationship.

His easy stance told me everything I needed to know. This was one of the few places he relaxed, as he was always on guard when he was on duty. We were good.

"What're we talking about?"

"Kane was about to tell us," Reed said, glossing over his hopes about his brother.

Gael nodded, and then two pairs of intent, wolfish eyes studied me. I poured it all out for them, holding nothing back: the intense and unexplained pain, her mother's unusual and early death, and my determination to change what she saw as her future. The color drained from Gael's face as I spoke.

"Alpha, I'm so sorry. Had I known, I never would have said—"

"You're a Boy Scout, Gael. You'd still have said it because that's your knee-jerk reaction every time. But this is a law that's been repressing wolves for centuries. It's high time things changed." Reed's irritation shone through the words, though he tried to hide it.

Gael glared and shoved Reed's shoulder. "I wouldn't have said it *in front of her* and added stress if I'd known she was sick!" Amazing how two grown men devolved into teen antics when you took the stress off their shoulders for a few seconds.

I raised a hand, not even having to speak, and they fell silent. "All is forgiven, Gael. My mate is strong, despite this illness."

Even as I said the words, they didn't feel right. My wolf was pacing, something niggling at the back of my mind, but I couldn't put my finger on it.

"So, what are we going to do to help her? I'm assuming the

first stop is our healer, no?" Gael asked, more than happy to have a problem to solve.

"She *is* a trained doctor. Didn't you read the files the Alphas submitted? If there was a simple medical solution, I'm sure she'd already have found it."

"Of course I read the files. I checked every single person for security risks, interpack feuds, and anything else before signing off on rooming assignments. In fact, I remember thinking she could be trouble because she's been studying wolf physiology and how we differ from standard-variety humans. There's no way that would fly in a bigger pack. Heck, half the packs here would be none too pleased to find out her field of study."

Was this mystery illness why she studied medicine? It was unusual for a wolf to take ill, and even rarer to actually die from it, so I could understand the impulse. But Gael was right. If she continued her career, that could cause major problems for interpack relations once we were mated. Shifters didn't take kindly to anything that brought to mind being tested like lab rats.

That was a bridge to cross when we got to it. For now, I wanted to make sure she stayed alive and well to argue with me about her chosen profession for many centuries to come. Besides, my father still had a good hundred years of ruling as high alpha ahead of him, which was why I'd started my own pack, on a whole separate continent. He was only five hundred seventy. Knowing him, he'd live to be a thousand just to prove he was the stubbornest bastard on the planet.

"We can ask John Henry to take a look at her, assuming she's okay with it, but I doubt he'll find anything she didn't, given she's been working on it for so long. I was thinking more outside the box. Do you think Inuksuk would be willing to meet with us?"

"That's definitely outside the box. He didn't come for the Athabascan pack—they only had two single males, and they sent them alone since they're so close. He's ancient, so we'd have to go to him."

"I'm willing to do that." *I'm willing to find the moon Goddess herself, if that's what it takes.*

"I'll reach out to their pack line, see when we can visit," Reed said.

"Thank you. The sooner, the better. Though I'll have to tell my father something. He should be happy I've found a mate so quickly, at least. That's the whole reason for this shindig."

"Your old man is wily. Or maybe he's got himself a seer we don't know about," Gael joked.

I couldn't stop a snort. Seers were almost as mythical as omegas. Though I wouldn't put anything past Kosta, son of Konstantin. He'd delivered my fated mate to me practically on a silver platter.

"Are you going to tell him what we suspect?" Reed's eyes were sharp, and I knew he had my back, whatever I decided.

"We'll see how he reacts to the news I've found my fated mate first."

NINETEEN

Brielle

I'd slept better on a random bed in a dormitory after my time spent with Kane than I had in my own bed back in Texas in months. The man was some kind of miracle worker, that was for sure. Although, it was barely nine a.m., and already I was replaying our brief interlude the day before. It had been divine, and at first, that was all I remembered. But the more times I turned it over in my head, the more worried I'd gotten.

We had mate marks, the kiss had been hotter than a Fourth of July Texas parade, and I was raring to go again... but he'd stopped. When I thought back, it was really just one hell of a kiss. Why had he stopped? We'd gotten interrupted, sure, but by that point, he was already wrapped around me like my own personal big spoon.

Was he not that into me? I found it hard to believe since an impressive erection had been grinding into my hip.

And yet, the evidence didn't lie. He'd had me stretched out on a bed underneath him, and there had been no wandering hands and no clothing removal.

I bit the skin on the side of my thumbnail absently as I

opened the door to see if Leigh and Shay were ready to head down for the day's activity.

Okay, let's be honest. I just wanted to give them the recap and have them reassure me I wasn't an unattractive troll incapable of keeping my hot alpha happy. I was a little fluffy, and most of the time I owned that shit, but every now and then... I let being surrounded by perfectly toned she-wolves get to me.

When my door swung open, however, it wasn't to an empty hallway. A fiery redhead in a miniskirt and white crop top nearly stumbled straight into me.

"Whoa, wasn't expecting that to open. You my roomie?" She swayed on her feet, the faint scent of wine and a male wolf rolling off her like stale perfume.

"Umm, maybe? Are you Cherry?"

"The one and only." She waggled her eyebrows at me. "I've gotta hit the showers before this thing gets started. I'm already in deep crap with my Alpha for missing the opening meeting yesterday, so I've got to be on time today. See you later!" She pushed past me, and I was still shaking my head at our interesting introduction when Shay opened the door and gestured me inside.

She wrinkled her nose and leaned in to take a bigger sniff. "You smell like a stranger, and is that... sour fruit?"

"I met my roomie in the hallway."

"Ahh. Leigh's still in the bathroom. You know how she always takes forever," She raised her voice on that last bit, and I heard an answering grumble from Leigh.

Shay dropped onto the foot of her bed and shoved her feet into her favorite black sneakers. They were adorned with three different silver buckles instead of laces, and they jangled just a bit when she walked. My quiet bestie loved music, and even her footwear reflected it.

"So, how was the rest of your evening?" Shay asked without looking up while she finished buckling her sneakers. There was no judgment or cattiness there, and I loved her immensely for it.

My face went hot, and I knew I was blushing as my brain gave me the ninety-seventh replay of the hottest kiss of my life, and my panties grew damp at the memory. Just like the last ninety-six times.

I was a hopeless goner. I'd even put on my sexiest pair of cheeky panties today, *just in case* he could be tempted to continue where we'd left off. No granny panties for Kane, not today.

Though, I did love granny panties, and if we were going to be mated for the next five hundred plus years, he'd see them eventually. But not until *after* he was good and in love with me. Seemed safest.

"That good, huh?" She arched an eyebrow up at my silent blush.

"Umm, yeah. I mean, we weren't actually together that long after you guys left, since Gracelyn was having contractions, and we—well, he, but I wasn't about to not go check on her—got called over there." I stopped myself, feeling the urge to ramble building in my chest. If I didn't stop now, the word vomit would get a lot more personal real quick.

"Was your time together... good?" She kept it polite, but I knew exactly what she meant. *Mate signs.*

"We kissed, and it was the best kiss of my life," I gushed, unable to stop the flood of words after all. Leigh's head popped out of the bathroom, flat iron in one hand, toothbrush in the other.

"Did I hear someone say there was a life-changing kiss? Please, do go on. Don't skip a single detail." She waggled her eyebrows salaciously, and I ducked my head into my hands. These two were yin and yang, but I wouldn't trade them for all the other besties in the world.

Dropping my hands and shoving them into my back

pockets where they couldn't betray my embarrassment any further, I nodded. Leigh's excited squeal was so loud, I'm pretty sure a mirror somewhere shattered. She abandoned the flat iron and frantically scrubbed at her teeth while she sank onto the foot of Shay's bed next to her, gesturing for me to hurry up and spill.

"Okay, okay. So, you guys left, and we talked a little. I really didn't intend for anything else to happen, you know? I mean, you guys know about my parents. I never really expected to find a mate, but even if I did, it's too risky." I sucked in a deep breath, not needing to tell them what was at stake. "But he didn't care. In fact, he pushed even harder after I told him. I never expected that, and when he started kissing me, well, I just couldn't say no. It was like he lit my whole body up from the inside, and I've never felt anything like it. The pull toward him is unreal."

Leigh grinned around her toothbrush, and Shay's warm expression told me they were both happy for me. I was too, except...

"What is it? Where'd that happy glow just skip off to?" Leigh's words were mostly intelligible around her toothpaste.

"I— He—he stopped. Stopped kissing me. I was a hundred-percent onboard, right there with him, and then he just stopped and curled up behind me like that was that."

"And that's a bad thing?" Shay asked, her voice gentle.

Leigh waved frantically toward her face and the bathroom, ducked inside, and back out a moment later. "Okay, listen. I can practically see the freak out exploding out of your chest, but it doesn't have to be. There are about eight million reasons why a guy might not go *straight* for the gold, so to speak. None of them being that he's not into you. He was raised by Kosta, who, by all accounts, is a traditionalist. You guys just met a few days ago. Even for fated mates, there's no expectation that you jump straight into bed, okay? He probably wants to take it a little, tiny bit slower, so he can get to know you first. And finally—and I cannot stress this enough as the one with the most relationship experience—guys are *not* mind readers. If you want more, it's okay to *tell him*. You're shy and studious and hot as hell, lest we forget that very important puzzle piece. But you're also allowed to let go, get wild, and ride that stud pony whenever you're both ready, mm'kay?"

I about choked on my tongue at *ride that stud pony*, but her point was spot-on. I was shy and not the type to ask for what I wanted, especially not with someone as intimidatingly gorgeous as Kane. But, could I?

I thought back over the kiss and how patient he'd been, how determined to get my consent every single step of the way. Did he stop because he thought I wanted him to?

Au contraire. My dry spell had been running a long damn time, and I had never felt anything for a man with one-tenth the intensity the new mate bond had coursing through my veins. Did I know him like my longtime besties? Well, no. Did I know enough to take it to the next step?

My perpetually needy lady bits said *hell yes*.

"There she is! Look at that face! She's going to get some tonight." Leigh elbowed Shay, who just rolled her eyes and gave me a knowing look.

Leigh was a little loco, but she was ours. And we loved her for it.

Besides, she wasn't wrong. If I had any say in the matter, I would be getting some. Because I wanted him, and unless I was *way* off base, he wanted me too.

It was time to go out and get it.

TWENTY

Kane

I stalked up the hallway to my father's temporary corner office to tell him about my newly minted mate bond. It used to be a large storage room, but we'd cleared it out and furnished it for the great pack gathering. Otherwise, he'd have taken over *my* office, and that wouldn't have worked for me. He was high alpha, but I was dominant, and even for my father, I couldn't concede my territory anymore. My wolf wouldn't have it.

I didn't even make it to the office, though, because his third and fourth were standing watch just outside the door, arms crossed over their chests, eyes assessing as I approached.

"I need to speak with Alpha Kosta."

"He's unavailable. He's meeting at present with Alphas Jose, Dominic, and Stephan," Andrei said, bored.

I let out a low growl, but wasn't truly surprised. My father was a prominent male who didn't bother coming to this side of the world often. I'm sure many of the alphas here for the gathering intended to make use of his proximity to try to garner some favor or another.

Hopefully, they weren't all trying to pitch their daughters as a match for me. My wolf snarled at the thought of any mate but our Brielle. Her creamy, smooth skin and that way she gasped with a hitch in her breath when I'd run my tongue— I cut off the thought, not wanting to get an erection standing three feet from my father's men.

"Let him know I need to speak with him at the earliest break in his schedule."

Andrei nodded, and I turned on my heel to go find Gracelyn. Reed had already touched base this morning, and she was stubbornly refusing to let one of her assistants take over today, so Adam was once again parked at her side in the oversized recliner. I wanted to make sure that my men and I were in every single group with Brielle today, and I had the mate marks to prove my claim. Not that she'd argue. Gracelyn might get a little dictatorial with an event to run, but she was a sweet she-wolf and a solid member of my pack.

Maybe soon, it would be Brielle with her belly rounded with our pup, bossing me around. My wolf rumbled low in his chest at the thought, a contented feeling washing through me. He wanted our mate pregnant as quickly as possible, and the realization that I agreed with him nearly knocked me on my ass. I stopped midstep, letting myself delve into the fantasy.

Her in my cabin, tucked into the corner reading nook I was mentally designing just for her, a book propped up on her big, rounded belly, and her glasses sliding down her nose as she smiled over at me. She wiggled her finger at me to come over, and I sank to my knees, spreading her thighs. As I delved into her sweetness, the book fell to the rug with a thud as she moaned my name...

I'd never considered myself much of a family man—running a whole damn pack was plenty, thank you. I didn't need rug rats underfoot any time soon—but Brielle... One whiff of her scent, and I'd give her anything she wanted. That had to be pups, right?

I started walking again, shaking the tantalizing fantasy from my thoughts. I couldn't afford to be distracted yet. I had too much to do.

"I AM NOT SHUFFLING the entire day's roster for you, Kane."

Adam grunted uneasily at her side, and she rolled her eyes at him.

"Excuse me, *Alpha Kane*. You may be Alpha, but you entrusted *me* with these activities, and I'm not going to juggle —" The words died in her throat as I tugged down the collar of my shirt, exposing the deep-blue ink sprawling there.

Tattoos weren't at all uncommon among wolves—some were pain junkies, and we healed quickly—but there was no mistaking a fated mate mark.

"That's... oh. My. Goddess. You found a mate!" She squealed so loudly, Adam and two of her assistants jumped practically out of their skin.

"Shhh, yes. Yes, I did, but I want to keep that between us until I've got time to pull my father aside and tell him. But... I also don't want her out of my sight."

"That's a dangerous game, Kane. How are you going to handle it if one of the other wolves gets too close?" Adam's question set my teeth on edge, because I knew I wasn't going to handle it well. But what choice did I have?

"I'll stay close enough that nobody else dares. Today's a run. Should be simple enough."

Gracelyn shook her head slowly, clearly disagreeing. "You're an idiot, Kane." Adam cleared his throat, and she sighed. "He knows he's the Alpha, Adam. Shush. Now listen, if you have a mate, a *fated* mate, and haven't completed the bond, that's a volatile time. You have too much power to take any risks of her coming into physical contact with anyone else. Your wolf won't handle that well *at all*. When we were still unbonded, Adam nearly ripped Lucky's head off because he touched my shoulder handing me my bag. You don't want a reputation as a hothead, do you?"

"I'm *not* a hothead, and we'll be completing the bond as soon as physically possible, Gracelyn. I know it's best to get it over with quickly, so things settle back down. Now—"

"*What*?" The single, spluttered word from behind me froze me in place, and I knew down to the tips of my wolf's tail fur that I'd stepped in it. Because when I turned around, there were *three* pissed-off she-wolves standing with their best impressions of a death glare, all aimed right at me.

Balls.

"Get it over with? Really, Mr. High-and-Mighty, really? You get blessed with perfection in one ultrahot feminine package, and you want to take the most intimate, important communion possible between two shifters and *get it over with*?" Leigh was the first to flay me with her words, but no matter how true they were, it wasn't her words that cut me. No, it was the look of real hurt on Brielle's face after she overheard my casual dismissal that I would remember to the day I died.

Damn. Hell. Shit. *Fuck*.

"That's not at all what I meant. I promise you, if you'll let me explain, you'll understand."

Brielle held up one palm and shook her head. "No, Kane. *No*. I don't want to hear it. Not right now."

"Come on, besties. Let's find some less *assholish* air. I think I spotted some hot wolves over there. Outside. Away from Alpha Asshat," her tall blonde friend spat, glaring daggers through my forehead. Even in her anger, she was careful not to make eye contact.

"Brielle, please—"

Leigh was all hot temper when she spun on her heel, taking Brielle with her, but it was the last, sad look Brielle cast me over her shoulder that had my wolf howling with irrepressible rage.

Her quieter friend didn't follow them immediately. She looked as if it cost her, but she whispered a lifeline to me before she ran after them, and I grasped the words like the last, fragile tether I had to my mate.

"She's afraid you don't want her, Alpha. If you do, you need to show it. She doesn't give second chances."

I would make damn sure she knew that she was more important than my next breath, no matter what it took.

TWENTY-ONE

Brielle

I was going to be sick. The awful pain in my stomach was back. Kane's cold dismissal of the most important bonding rites mates could share was rattling around my head like a sick and twisted echo, and if I didn't lose my coffee and half a piece of wheat toast before this next activity, it would be a miracle the size of my home state. Leigh was talking a mile a minute as she dragged me across the clearing toward a tree line of towering spruce trees, but the words were washing over me like a swift current at the moment.

The impressive scenery in front of me couldn't dent the blurred, achy vision of Kane's taut back as he brushed off our mating, followed swiftly by the look of gut-wrenching horror splashed over his handsome features. It was burned into my retinas, and even the tears accumulating at the corners of my eyes couldn't blur it out of focus completely.

"What if he rejects me, Leigh?" The words tripped off my tongue, as I was unable to hold the fears back another second.

I'd never wanted a mate. And never finding your fated mate? It wasn't ideal, but not uncommon either. There were only so many wolves, and some settled down with humans when they got tired of waiting. You could still find happiness, if not a soul-deep bond. I'd been okay with that.

But never, not in my wildest imaginings, had I envisioned him rejecting me.

"He's not that stupid. Hey, look at me." I nearly ran into her boobs when she stopped. They were right at eye level since she was a good head taller than I was. "He might not realize what a dickish thing he just said, and how callous it is to brush off the importance of the bonding ceremony. But there is no way in hell, Hades, or purgatory that his wolf is going to let him walk away from you. Don't shake your head. I know you want to live in the worst-case scenario, but I'm right. And we're going to show him what a dick he was by using the oldest trick in the book."

I frowned up at the devilish glint in her eyes. "And what is that, exactly?"

"We're going to make him so jealous he swallows his tongue."

I groaned. "Leigh, this is a bad idea. He's dominant. He already fought Shane over a hug—"

"Exactly. You're irresistible, baby. You're sending off all those good mate-me-and-impregnate-me pheromones right now, which means the dudes are gonna flock to you like turkeys to a pile of corn. All you have to do is be yourself and not hide. That's it. Nothing wrong or sleezy. Show him what he's risking by being an idiot, and he'll come around quicker than you can sneeze."

I bit my bottom lip, entirely unconvinced that what she had in mind was wise.

"Give him a chance to make it up to you, Bri." Shay's calm reassurance was accompanied by a hand on my shoulder, and I realized I'd been holding them tightly enough to crack a pecan between my shoulder blades. I let out a long, shaky breath and nodded.

"I'm not doing anything intentionally to rub it in his face." The words felt right, like a good decision. Even if I were tempted. I wasn't a tree he could just pee on and then ignore.

"Fine, fine. Dr. Responsible, as usual. But don't let him back in *too* easily. It's good for a man to see you're desirable, and not just to him. You've got options, baby. Now, let's go strip for this run and show him the wonderland he's not getting near tonight."

I groaned at the idea of a run as she pulled me along by the hand, Shay keeping pace at our side. Could this day get any worse?

I HAD my answer as I looked around the group gathered around one of Gracelyn's assistants. Shane Russo was in it, and he had three men clustered around him, who had to be pack. The whiff of their scents that reached me from our position at the edge of the crowd smelled like Russo. The rest were a wash of different packs, several of them nice males I'd shaken hands with during the activity yesterday. A few even nodded and smiled at me, which I returned politely, though my eyes were restlessly looking for one particularly stubborn he-wolf.

Mate. My wolf paced back and forth doggedly in my mind, and for once, I was hopeful that my shift would go well.

We'd found our mate. She'd been more present with me since we'd arrived in Alaska than ever before. Maybe I'd be able to shift here? Everything was bigger. The mountains, the weather, the sky—hoo boy, *the men*—maybe my wolf's abilities would be amplified?

Couldn't hurt to hope... unless I ended up face down in the dirt, passed out and mocked by all my proposed suitors, and that very same mate realized I really *was* unsuitable for him. We were fated, though, so he'd just have to deal.

Unless he really does reject you.

Dread pooled in my stomach, and I sucked in a fortifying breath through my nose. He hadn't said he didn't want to mate me, just that he wanted to get it over with. Insulting as hell? Check. Wholly unenthusiastic? Also check. But flat rejection? Not quite.

Not yet, my inner voice whispered, but I shut that bitch down. Kane might have made my knees go gooey—and all parts below the belt, who was I kidding. He *owned* my lady garden, and he hadn't come within a mile of it yet. But I'd gotten along before him, and if he really did decide he didn't want to mate with me, I'd make it again without him.

My wolf howled, and I fought to ignore her anguished denial. She wanted him with a passion that eclipsed even my inner horny goddess.

"So serious. Not a fan of running?" Kane's whispered words brushed my ear and sent an electric jolt straight through me, as if his tongue was already connected to my clit, even though he didn't touch me.

Jerk.

Irritation at my body's reaction to him even when I was angry rose, staving off the lust. I spun to answer, realizing my mistake a split second before I crashed straight into his chest. He steadied me with surprisingly gentle hands, one at my shoulder and one at my hip. I felt his heat like a brand, marking me irrevocably.

Had anyone touched that hip before? I couldn't remember. All I could feel was him, hot and enveloping and—

"Get your grubby mitts off her, you jackass!" Leigh snarled, fangs lengthening as she stepped up to the *literal prince of all the wolves* like she was about to throw down.

Before I could talk her off the ledge, I was shocked by a harsh alpha bark.

"Leigh!" Gael appeared like an avenging angel over her left

shoulder. His face was all thunderclouds, and I couldn't help myself from shrinking back from his thick, rolling alpha energy. Kane was stronger—my wolf preened at the thought—but his alpha energy felt like electricity. Gael's felt like somebody rubbed my fur the wrong way, plucking at my nerves and sending unpleasant jitters through me.

Kane growled low in his throat and tucked me against his chest. The hand on my shoulder floated up to cradle the back of my head, tucking my nose against his neck, where all I could feel, smell was him. I calmed instantly even as Leigh and Gael squared off three feet away.

"He doesn't get to just lay hands on her! I don't care who he is! She's mad at him, and he needs to respect her space!"

"If she wants space, all she has to do is say so and his wolf will comply. Immediately. You know it as well as I do."

"You're *infuriating*! Why are you even here? Nobody asked you to be here, and this has nothing to do with you."

"Right, because as the alpha's second, I should stand by and let you deck him?" I could *hear* the eye roll, even though I couldn't see anything but the tanned expanse of Kane's neck. I sucked in another lungful of his glorious cinnamon-orange scent, and to my surprise, my mouth started watering as, for the first time in my life, my fangs dropped.

Holy hell on a double helix.

Fangs.

Neck.

Mate.

My wolf snarled again, and I jerked back out of Kane's arms. He let me go, and I caught the briefest glimpse of sorrow on his face before he pulled his alpha mask back into place.

I couldn't speak, my wolf's fangs still low and awkward in my mouth, the desire to leap into his arms and sink them into his perfectly golden neck still pulsing in my veins. It took everything in me to resist, as the polite aide interrupted our little spat.

"Everything okay over here, Alpha? Some of the other males are getting antsy." She cast a nervous glance at the ruffled group of shifters, more than half with their wolves shining through their eyes as they watched our ridiculously public show.

So humiliating. I'm a doctor, for Goddess's sake, not a teenager!

I was as horny as one, but that was neither here nor there.

"Everything's fine, thank you, Emory. Please, go ahead and get things started. We won't be any more trouble, right, everyone?" His eyes hardened as he skated past me and into Leigh and Gael.

"Yes, Alpha," Gael said, dropping into a fighter's rest stance, hands behind the small of his back and shoulders straight.

Leigh's jaw was set in that way that said *this isn't over*, but she also nodded tightly in response.

"Greeeeeeat," Emory drawled, but she hurried back to the center of the group to get things rolling as she was told.

"Okay, everybody! Show's over. This is a group run, but there are still rules. Keep it friendly. No hunting inside the camp perimeter. Mix and mingle, but keep physical contact friendly and minimal. If you wouldn't want your mother to see you do it"—she shot a pointed glance at the five of us, and I resisted the urge to hang my head—"don't do it. You're all adults. Don't make your Alphas whoop your asses. Now, run along and have fun."

She waved her clipboard vaguely toward the woods with far less chipper enthusiasm than Gracelyn, and then stepped back quickly as people started shucking clothes to the ground, modesty forgotten in typical shifter fashion. Nudity was a fact of life.

Leigh cleared her throat loudly, and when I looked over, she shot a pointed glance at me, then over to Kane.

Ahh, Operation Forbidden Wonderland. I rolled my eyes at her, but stepped away from Kane and to her side, Shay following suit and flanking me as well.

I locked eyes with Kane as I tucked my thumbs into the waist of my favorite black yoga pants, and his Adam's apple bobbed as he swallowed, not breaking my gaze.

I slowly lowered the pants, exposing my lacy plum, cheeky panties inch by inch as a low, rumbling growl reverberated from his chest. When they reached my knees I let them fall to the ground, stepping each leg out much more slowly than necessary.

I froze as he started with his shirt, doing that guy thing where he reached over the back of his head and pulled the whole thing off by the back of the neck. It was a lovely green Henley that brought out the gold flecks in his eyes, but my mouth started watering again as it hit the soft grass underfoot, leaving *so much muscle* on display.

Damn, I wanted to jump him again. Why did I want to jump him every time we were within three feet of each other? I wasn't normally a sexually aggressive girl. Sure, I enjoyed an energetic romp as much as anyone, but I liked to let the man come to me and do the pursuing.

With Kane? I wanted to jump into his arms, take that blisteringly hot chest to the ground, and ride him until I collapsed. Goddess, I was as bad as Leigh with her *stud pony* jokes.

Yeah, I had problems. Not the least of which were Leigh's throat clearing and the snap of bones around us signaling that we were taking way too long caught up in our own stripteases, as other wolves were already in fur, leaping around and nipping each other's flanks and tails playfully. Kane stepped out of his black pants, leaving nothing but tight, black boxer briefs underneath.

I swallowed hard and grabbed the hem of my long T-shirt, but it was barely above my navel when Shay gasped.

"Oh my Goddess. Are those *mate marks*?" Leigh's words weren't quiet, and they carried through the clearing. Wolves stilled almost as one, and I could practically feel the dozens of eyes burrowing into the tiny strip of exposed markings on my hip.

A blush burned up my cheeks—I couldn't believe I'd forgotten in the heat of the moment. They were nothing to be embarrassed of; in fact, they were often prized and cherished, much like human women's wedding rings. But, Kane hadn't even seen them yet, and here I was about to flash them to the whole pack.

It was skipping a *lot* of steps.

I didn't even have time to process all that before Kane's arms were around me, spinning me so that his back—his naked, naked back—was between me and the crowd of nosy wolves.

I buried my face in my hands, perhaps in the childish hope that if I couldn't see them, they couldn't see me, and this would all just vanish when I next looked up. But Kane's fingers were persistent, and they ever-so-gently pried my hands away from my face and tilted my chin up. A little thrill shot through me when his eyes met mine. So few people ever had the privilege, and before him, I certainly never had as the lowest she-wolf on the pack totem pole.

But his eyes were warm and vibrant green, gold flecks sparkling in their depths and sucking me into his gaze. They were utterly gorgeous, and staring into them had a piece of my heart chipping and falling off, right into his waiting palms. Hopefully he didn't crush it to dust, because I was helpless to take it back.

I didn't want to take it back. I wanted *him*.

"These are mine," he whispered, grazing his calloused fingertips lightly over the skin of my hip, sending a forest fire's worth of heat sparking through my veins in their wake. "And I admit to feeling jealous at the idea of my pack mates and a bunch of other wolves seeing them with me for the first time." His fingers skimmed up, up, up, under the hem of my shirt, stoking that fire to molten, liquid heat.

"Mmm, your wolf likes it when I'm a caveman, huh? I can't wait to see her. I bet she's as beautiful as you are, with those deep brown eyes and all this irresistible skin." He dropped his mouth next to my ear, and I couldn't help arching my neck toward him, bared for his fangs like a good little mate. Goddess, who was I? It was a brazen invitation, the crowd of wolves utterly forgotten as my world shrank to just us. Brielle and Kane. *Fated mates.*

Kane ran his nose up my neck, the tiny touch electrifying. When he reached my ear, he whispered low so the onlookers couldn't hear, his lips brushing against the tender shell of my ear. "I can smell your arousal. Are you wet for me, Brielle?"

My knees shook as my wolf whined, and he chuckled, low and dark. "I can't wait to feel you, baby, but now is not the time. The first time I take you, it will be just us. I'll make sure you forget every other wolf but me. But now... will you let me see these marks? My wolf is dying to get out and howl about how lucky he is to have the most beautiful she-wolf there is as a mate."

I nodded and almost self-combusted when he pressed a hot, open-mouthed kiss on my neck just below my ear.

His other hand slipped under the hem of my shirt as well, one anchoring me at the hips as the other lifted the T-shirt. All thoughts of embarrassment fled as his hot eyes met my flesh, inch by painstaking inch. He growled low in his throat when the full mark was exposed, bisected by the thin strap of my panties.

His touch over the beautiful blue swirls was reverent, tender. His wolf's green eyes shone through, proving he was as on edge as I was.

How could I have thought he didn't want me? The look in his eyes right now would swallow me up, drown me in his passion, if I let it.

Gentle strokes vanished, he stopped toying with my shirt. He pulled it quickly off over my head, and his eyes darkened another shade when he saw my bra, lacy and sheer, with my pebbled nipples poking against the thin fabric.

"Goddess, Brielle. You are utter perfection. How did I get so damn lucky?" His hands skimmed up my sides, leaving goose bumps in their wake, every inch of me aware of his heat, his closeness, and how little clothing was still between us. The wicked thought that maybe he'd follow me to the ground right here and take me *right now*, seal this bond between us, if I reached for his boxers and slid them down, nearly overwhelmed me.

When his hands brushed the underside of my breasts, I nearly came unglued. They'd never been terribly sensitive with any past lovers, but Kane didn't even have my bra off, and I was ready to beg him to touch, hold, *taste*. He traced the bra around to the back, deftly flicking the hooks apart. When it fell away from my chest, I closed my eyes and hissed out a breath, unable to take any other sensation as my bare breasts pressed up against his chest, skin on skin for the first time.

I clawed him against me tighter, and his hot erection pressed against my belly, his boxers doing nothing to disguise his arousal. *Goddess, he's huge.*

He rumbled contentedly and stroked from the nape of my neck down to the band of my panties, long and soothing strokes.

"Are you ready to run? Most of the pack left without us."

"They did?" I leaned back just far enough to peek around his large biceps, and sure enough, the clearing had emptied while we were lost in our own world. Leigh and Shay waited in wolf form just inside the tree line with Gael and Reed, all of them studiously looking elsewhere to let us have a private moment, and a bit beyond them were a few curious stragglers who weren't the least bit shy about staring. Dread pooled in my stomach, dampening some of the liquid heat Kane roused there when I recognized Shane as one of the waiting wolves.

Ugh. It was bad enough to have to tell Kane that I was a weak wolf, but to have the other arrogant alpha watch would make it all a thousand times worse.

That was the rub, wasn't it? Why Kane thought we weren't compatible.

My weakness would paint a big, fat target on his back.

I swallowed hard, trying to clear the sudden lump blocking my throat, blocking the words I needed to tell Kane.

"Baby, what's wrong? Did I push you too far? I'm sorry, I just wanted to make sure you knew where I stood, and that's the best way I know to—"

I pressed up on my toes and kissed him, my nipples dragging tantalizingly across his chest, racking me with a shudder.

"Not too far," I answered, hoping he could see the heat in my eyes like I had in his. "There's something else I need to tell you."

TWENTY-TWO

Kane

I didn't like that tone in her voice, the one that said she was about to tell me something awful. Like she was a *cat* person.

"What is it, baby?" She worried her bottom lip between her teeth, clearly not excited to spill it. "You can tell me anything, my beautiful mate."

She drew in a deep breath, pressing the perfect mounds of her breasts tighter against me, and then finally blurted it out.

"I can't really shift. Well, I *can*. A little. A few times a year, for a few minutes. I don't know why, but if I try to stay in fur for long, I pass out. Most full moons, I can't run with the pack at all, so I just stay in my lab and work." She stopped herself, and I could practically see the wheels turning as she forced herself to stop, grinding her teeth together to wait for my reaction.

And I was shocked. My mate couldn't shift? I'd never heard of such a thing. The wolf was as much a part of who we were as the man. To have one but not be able to access the other? My skin crawled at the idea.

It was a miracle she wasn't mad. Feral wolves couldn't come back to skin, but I didn't know of anything that could cause a shifter not to be able to go to fur, save an injury too grave to survive.

Yet here she stood, whole and flawless, and telling me she couldn't shift.

"Has your Alpha tried to help you with it?"

She shrugged one shoulder, looking away and down as if embarrassed. "Once or twice, but it's easier to just not. I don't know, he wasn't able to figure anything out the few times he tried to force my shift, and I never followed up with any neighboring Alphas. It's... not common. Nobody knew what to do."

Her cheeks bloomed red, her sweet, mouthwatering scent took on a sour note of shame, and my heart nearly broke for her.

"Well, luckily for you, I'm the second-most powerful alpha in the world, and my father is *the* most powerful. If I can't help you, he can for sure. But first, I think I need to see you shift. Are you ready? I promise not to let anything happen to you, even if you do faint." I kept my voice even, though the idea of her unconscious made my wolf pace anxiously.

She nodded once, still not meeting my eyes as she stepped out of the panties I'd be dreaming of for the next decade. They cupped her round ass cheeks in see-through purple lace, and I wanted to tear them off her with my teeth. Or steal them and keep them in my pocket.

Brielle drew in one last, deep breath and then took two big steps back from me, squaring her shoulders—Goddess, her decadent breasts were going to give me a permanent boner—and then closing her eyes.

Between one breath and the next, soft, smooth skin gave way to a delicate white undercoat. She sank gracefully onto all fours, shaking out dark-tipped fur and looking up at me with her glowing brown eyes. She was decidedly small for a wolf, but absolutely perfect in every way. My own shift was reflexive, as if my wolf was so overcome by the sight of his fated mate, that he couldn't help but spring forth from my skin, tearing right through the boxers I was still wearing.

The shift didn't even register. In one moment, I was an awed man. The next, a gloriously happy wolf, running in giddy circles around his mate and letting out happy barks.

She dropped to her forelegs, tail up and wagging high in the universal sign for *play*, and I raced around her, my claws cutting a circle in the earth with my speed. Turf flew up behind me as I showed off, letting the wolf do anything that felt natural. She began to trot after me, dodging and diving as I picked up the pace, keeping her guessing. When she began to slow, I skidded to a stop, ending nose to nose with the most beautiful, delicate she-wolf I'd ever seen.

We stared, frozen, with our wolves finally able to connect one to one. I was so blissfully happy, giddy sensations from my usually stoic wolf making me forget everything else.

That's when I felt it.

The *wrongness* about her. I sat back on my wolf's haunches, shocked by the deep, sickly *drain* I felt pouring out of her, that I'd never sensed before.

My wolf shook his head, as if clearing his vision might make it go away, but there it was, a fetid green ooze trailing from both her sides, seeping down into the ground beneath her.

Goddess, her stomach pain. This was like something foul flowing out of her. I paced forward, sniffing the air to see if I could discern anything about the taint.

She began to whine, sensing the sudden change in my mood. But I couldn't help it. All thoughts of play had flown out the window when I'd sensed it. Now that I was at her side, I tentatively sniffed the oozing magic.

Witch. My wolf sneezed, disliking the charred-bone smell that always accompanied a witch's magic. On closer inspection, I saw little sparks of silver mixed into the magic flowing from her sides. If this was some kind of curse, did that mean she didn't have a mystery illness? Had her *mother* died of foul play?

I didn't have time to process the implications further because, to my horror, her wolf began to sway drunkenly. She was fine and happy one minute, and the next, she struggled to stay on her feet. I wanted to shout, to warn her, to do *something*, but I didn't have the chance.

Because my beautiful, precious mate collapsed before my eyes, her shift reversing, leaving her naked and convulsing on the ground.

I WAS BACK in skin in an instant, cradling her head and yelling for my pack.

Gael and Reed skidded to a stop, anxious grimaces on both their faces.

"What happened, Alpha?" Gael barked, his wolf still close to the surface after such a short shift.

"I don't know, but something's wrong. Go get the healer. Reed, keep everyone back until he gets here."

Leigh and Shay were there, hovering in wolf form as soon as my men departed to do as I'd ordered.

Leigh shifted back, blurring from reddish-taupe fur to long, tanned legs in a second flat. I didn't care that a naked supermodel was standing in front of me; all I could see was my mate, arms thrashing and head tossing despite my best efforts to keep her still, safe.

"Roll her on her side! We don't know why, but this happens every time she shifts. She'll come out of it soon and be embarrassed as hell. I swear on the Goddess's tits that if you're rude to her about this, I'll tear your balls off and feed them to your asshole of a second."

I snarled at her implication that I would ever knowingly embarrass my mate, not in the least worried about her threats, serious though she was. In fact, I appreciated her undying loyalty to my female. She needed us, needed our strength, if we were going to figure this out. Leigh's hands were surprisingly gentle for such a brash she-wolf as she steadied Brielle's legs, supporting her knees and shins so she didn't bash them on the ground.

Shay didn't shift back, instead curling up at Brielle's side, inserting herself between me and Leigh to get to her friend. Brielle's tremors were beginning to slow, and she curled one of her hands into Shay's fur, gripping it tightly enough that it had to pull, but Shay never made a sound, only rested her canine head in the crook of Brielle's elbow. Worried wolf eyes met mine briefly before flicking away.

If I hadn't already known that Brielle was a woman of worth, the deep loyalty she inspired in her friends would have proven it, no question.

In wolf society, strength was respected. The strongest line ruled, the strongest wolf was Alpha, and only the strongest survived. But here was my mate in a moment of extreme vulnerability, and they hadn't attacked. They'd protected.

But how strong would she be once we removed that drain on her power? The longer I spent with her, the more convinced I was that she was no psi, and this drain only underscored that in my mind.

My heart clenched in my chest as I ran my hand over her sweaty temple, smoothing the hair back from her face again and again. I hoped she found it soothing, but it was as much for me as it was for her. I could no more stop touching her than I could lop off my own arm and walk away.

I sensed another male approaching me from behind and snarled back over my shoulder, only to find Gael, gray sweatpants clenched in one fist and a blanket tucked under his arm.

He stopped at my shoulder, dropping the sweats for me to put on, and offered me the blanket.

Careful not to move her, I quickly fanned the thin, soft material over her—and Shay, who refused to move. Leigh helped me tuck it around, and then I heard the familiar clank of John Henry's medical kit as he ran to where we all knelt, just inside the tree line.

"So, she fainted the first time she saw you naked, huh, boss?"

"Now isn't the time for jokes, John. Something is very wrong. She told me she's always struggled to call her wolf and stay shifted, but when she did, I saw—" I stopped short, the words refusing to come out. Now that she was motionless in my arms, a wider awareness returned, and that included the dozens of wolves crowding less than ten feet away, trying to see whatever they could around Reed's dress-pants-clad form.

No, better not to share every detail. Not here, when we didn't know who had called the ODL or what they were after. Besides, I wanted to know what her *friends* knew, as well. Surely they'd already tried to figure out what witch's magic was plaguing her?

"Lay her down flat for me, and let me check her pulse." John was all business, and I appreciated that he'd dropped the jokes. This was serious, and whatever was hurting my mate, it wasn't natural.

TWENTY-THREE

Brielle

I woke slowly, as if rising up through something sticky and dark, like muddy Jell-O. My tongue felt thick and dry in my mouth, and at first, I had no idea where I was or what had happened.

Then it clicked. Shame and humiliation flooded me, and I heard a groan from somewhere.

Gentle fingers soothed over the side of my neck, and a soft shushing sound broke past the pounding of my heart in my ears. Next came sensation, and I felt the soft plushness of wolf fur—Shay's, no doubt—against my naked front, Leigh's strong grip on my ankle and— I sucked in a breath, his cinnamon-orange scent comforting me while oddly making me want to cry at the same time.

Kane. My strong, dominant alpha mate, witnessing the lowest of the low of my weakness.

Something inside me cracked, and tears began to well over my cheeks.

There was no way he'd want me now. I'd tried to warn him, but there was just something different about seeing a majestic wolf collapse into a naked, vulnerable woman.

The truth was out there, and there was no sense crying about it. So why couldn't I stop the ever-growing river of tears tracing down my cheeks? I hiccupped a sob, and words also became part of my world again.

"Brielle, talk to me, my heart. What hurts? Please, baby, tell me what I can do for you. Tell me how to help you. It's okay, I'm here. I'm not going anywhere, Brielle, and we've got the pack healer to help you. Come on, baby. Talk to me, please. Tell us what hurts." Kane's soft crooning words were like a balm and a torment all at once.

I couldn't saddle this man with my weakness. It wouldn't be right, or fair. He was too good, and I was too broken.

He wouldn't turn me away, though. I saw that now, with my eyes still screwed shut, fist clenching Shay's fur.

Oh, too hard. I should probably let that go. I loosened my grip, tangling my fingers in it again without pulling. I wasn't ready to let go of that bond yet, not when the truth was staring me right in the face.

Kane was my fated mate. He had seen me fall out of my shift, seen what happened, and he still hadn't run. He was already loyal, already *good*.

Which meant *I* had to be the one. The one to stay strong, to do what was best for *him*.

"Her pulse is steadying, Alpha, and her temperature is a bit high, but nothing terribly unusual for immediately postshift." The healer rattled off details in a way that was pleasantly familiar. But I ignored him, because I already knew what he'd find. I was too focused on the realization in my heart to care what he told any of the other wolves here.

I had to be the one to say no to Kane, the one to break his heart.

"I'd recommend fluids and rest for now, and maybe when she's more aware—"

The one to tell him it couldn't work.

"—we can find out how long this has been going on, or if something specific triggers it."

The one to reject my mate.

My other half.

The one I somehow, impossibly, already loved. Because if I didn't? I'd take him down with me. And I didn't care what anyone said, Romeo and Juliet? Dying in each other's arms?

That wasn't romance. That was a tragedy.

"Yes, we'll get her back to a room. Mine is bigger, so I'll take her there. You can follow us and monitor her vitals for a while until she's feeling well enough to talk to us," Kane said, that familiar alpha command in his voice snapping me out of it.

No. I couldn't let him take me to his room, his space. I needed to hole up, get away. The more time I spent with this man, the more impossible it would be to break this off. And I had to. This wasn't some fairy tale where the power of love was magically going to fix me. My parents had been in love, been fated mates. And they'd *died*, leaving me alone and devastated.

I wasn't about to do that to Kane. Not ever.

"Leigh!" I gasped, my lungs and vocal cords not quite ready for speech yet.

"I'm here, Bri. What do you need?"

"My room. Alone. Us three."

Kane stiffened underneath me, and I realized I was half in his lap.

Leigh didn't wait around, didn't pause for the alpha's approval. She jumped to her feet, nudged Shay out of the way, and scooped me up under my armpits, pulling me right out of Kane's arms. He snarled, leaping to his feet as well.

I gripped around Leigh's neck, and she whispered, "You sure about this? No Alpha?"

"I'm sure," I croaked.

She arranged me to the side with my blanket, and my legs shook so bad, I was sure they weren't going to hold me.

Leigh didn't drop me, though. She held me with the steadiness of an iron grip, and her eyes were no less steely as she squared off against Kane, flanked on either side by Gael and Reed.

"What do you think you're doing? She is my *mate*, and you will let me take her to my quarters."

"She does not bear your bite, and even if she did, she doesn't have to stay with you. She wants to go to our rooms, she's going to our rooms."

Kane growled, and his hands started shaking. Human fingernails gave way to claws, and the tremors radiated up his arms and into his chest. When he next spoke, his voice was gravelly, his wolf pushing for control.

"You will not take my mate. She's hurt."

I couldn't look at him anymore. I couldn't, or I wouldn't do what I had to do.

"Please, Leigh. Let's go," I whispered, but she heard. We took a few steps forward, struggling to get coordinated, and Reed stepped into our way, hands held high in a placating gesture.

"I don't know what's happening here, but I know we all need to calm down." His words matched his body language, but when Leigh tried to steer us around him, he blocked us again.

Shay lunged forward, ears back and shoulders low, snapping at his chiseled abs with clear intent and sending him back several steps. She snarled, meeting his eyes with a pointed challenge.

His wolf's eyes began to glow, not liking the challenge, even from a she-wolf. He didn't flinch or look away, though, as Leigh edged us around the two of them. Shay skirted him without turning her back, keeping herself between us and the three males.

When we finally had a clear path to the dorms, Leigh took most of my weight and urged me into a jog, eager to put distance between us. The last thing I saw before the dormitory door swung shut was Kane's wolf exploding out of him, and his mournful howls followed my every painstaking step up the stairwell and down the hall.

He sensed the rejection, even though I hadn't said the words.

Couldn't say the words.

TWENTY-FOUR

Kane

She left. We had shared a moment. Of connection, of joy, of being *mates*, our wolves bonding. And then, between one heartbeat and the next, she left.

I could see that it cost her, smell her sorrow like sour roses. What I didn't know was *why*. But I wasn't going to give up. I would have her, and I would find all her objections and obliterate them, no matter what she asked of me.

I would do it for her.

I would solve the mystery of her pains. I would mate with her, protect her from the Omega Defense League. I would climb any mountain, protect her from any threat with my life. And pups. Though the idea terrified me, I would give her pups.

But first, I needed to know why she was distancing herself, pulling away from me. Second, actually. Because first I had to calm down. My wolf was raging, my heart was pounding, and I was staring through my two most trusted wolves like they didn't exist, as they stood shoulder to shoulder between me and the path to the dormitories. Where my mate had disappeared inside, taking my heart with her.

I shook my head, sucked in a lungful of air. Her scent still clung to me. It was a temporary mark until our permanent one could be forged.

"Alpha, we should go somewhere private and talk about this," Gael's voice was respectful and calm, the complete opposite of everything inside me.

"Yes, I'm sure there's an explanation. Maybe she was embarrassed, or got cold feet," Reed agreed. "That was a lot for a new couple. She's probably not proud of any show of weakness, and that one was particularly public." He shot a pointed glance behind me, reminding me that my simmering rage was *also* public, even though I'd shifted back out of wolf form.

I clenched and unclenched my fists a few times, trying to rein it in so I could listen to calmer heads. My men had my back, and they always would. This wasn't a problem we couldn't overcome.

I took one step forward, then another, when I heard it.

A snigger, a few feet back.

Someone was *laughing*. Then, the whispers started. I probably wasn't supposed to hear, but they were imbeciles to whisper in my presence. Wolf hearing was exceptional. Mine was better still than most.

"Did you see that? I'd heard the rumors that the Johnson City pack had a real dud, but she couldn't even hold a shift for five minutes!"

"You think that's bad? That dud just rejected the high alpha's son. *Publicly*."

"With mate marks," a third wolf added.

"No way she has mate marks already." I knew that voice. *Shane Fucking Russo.*

"And until the bond is complete, it can be challenged. She didn't seem too keen on him, so she's still fair game."

My spine stiffened, and I turned slowly to face the lingering crowd.

"She's got a hot ass, for sure, but I can't overlook being

unable to shift. Is she even a full-blooded wolf? Maybe she's a mutt." The smart-mouthed male was elbowed by his more attentive friend, and they both snapped to attention at the back of the crowd when the wolves in front of them began shifting uneasily on their feet. But I wasn't worried about them and their crude comments.

Let them out their bias and idiocy to every female here so they could spread the word about Tweedledee and Tweedle-dum. No, I was looking for a far greater threat.

She's still fair game. Like hell, she was.

I stalked forward, wolves scattering like chaff before a stiff wind as I closed the distance between myself and Russo.

He didn't budge, standing with his arms across his chest, staring me down as if he had the right. My wolf was already boiling for a fight, and for once, the man was more than happy to acquiesce.

"Stay away from Brielle." My voice was all grit and threat, the wolf's fangs descending into my mouth as I finished on a snarl. *Make the first move*, I dared him mentally.

He had the audacity to lean forward as he spoke again. "You heard me. She's available. That was a rejection. Everyone here is witness. Your marked, fated mate *left you.* I'm going by there tonight to see if she wants a better option."

"Somebody notify Webster, 'better' now means *inferior in every possible way*," Reed sniped from my right shoulder.

"You will not approach my mate, not unless you're willing to challenge me for her hand. You know the rules, Russo. There can only be *one*. It's me."

Shane waited, eyes narrowing, but didn't react like I'd hoped. Was it juvenile? Yes. But I needed to tear into someone, and he was a prime option. Better him than Gael, though he'd be more than happy to slake my need to fight off the rage building inside me. Goddess knew we'd done it for each other a hundred times before.

Dogging my father's leadership, calling the ODL—unconfirmed, but my wolf knew—being a grade-A asshole and putting his hands on unwilling women. *My* woman. I wanted to dig in my claws, rip him apart for daring to threaten my connection with my mate. Brielle was part of my *soul*, and he wanted to act like it was nothing? He deserved for his blood to soak my soil.

I sneered at the coward once more, then turned on my heel. I'd just have to find my release elsewhere. "Let's go."

I hadn't taken two steps when I heard the familiar snapping of bones, indicating a shift. The coward thought to catch me unawares? Attack my exposed back?

He had another thing coming.

I twisted and leapt to the side, shifting in midair. His steel gray wolf landed where I used to be, and primal glee exploded in my chest.

I used his confusion to my advantage, continuing my spin around to sink my teeth into his exposed flank. He howled with pain and rage, as his hot blood coated my tongue.

The taste of *victory*. But he dove away, rending his flesh to free himself from my first bite. When he faced me again, there was undisguised hatred in his eyes, canine or no. We circled for a moment, a pause to see who would attack again now that we were on equal footing.

The fat splatter of his blood hitting the ground had my wolf preening, but he didn't lose focus. I had a gut feeling that Russo would eventually snap, and I wanted to take advantage.

We circled three times before Shane lost patience and dove straight for my neck. The full-on frontal assault was dumb, and I deflected easily by ducking low and charging toward his inside shoulder, knocking him off-balance. He recovered quickly, but didn't waste time with more pacing. His claws slashed at my back leg, ruffling my fur, but not quite making contact.

I spun again, using my speed to give me the upper hand. He was a half-second slow, and I bit down on his tail, feeling the bones shatter underneath my teeth.

It wasn't a mortal wound, but it was an insulting one. He yelped in pain, but couldn't tear himself away lest he lose half his tail.

Even for a shifter, he'd be maimed permanently. I gave it a sharp tug, then dove up and over before he had time to move, nailing the top of his shoulders with both front paws, and rolling him to the ground. We rolled one over the other, tussling for control, back claws digging at each other's bellies and fangs snapping at throats.

I couldn't tell in the moment if he landed a blow, so single-minded was my focus on his throat. When my wolf tired of the tussle, ready to end it, we connected.

My jaws bracketed his neck, squeezing hard enough to restrict his breath and break the skin, but not hard enough to kill.

I growled, and he stilled beneath me. At that moment, I held his life between my teeth, and my wolf reveled in the power.

"Kane, son of mine! Stop! All of you, leave at once!"

My father's voice was all steel and dominance, and I froze, unable to finish the killing blow as I heard footsteps scatter like mice. My hackles rose along my back, my wolf unwilling to bow even to my father, with all the power of all the packs behind him.

"I don't know what's going on here, but we do not attack our invited guests. Kane, whatever insult he's paid you cannot be so great that you want to ruin our alliances with all the packs gathered here. Exercise some self-control and release him."

This wolf threatens our mate bond. He must die, my wolf insisted, managing to break through the alpha command enough to squeeze another fraction of an inch. The trickle of blood on my tongue sped faster, and my father's boots came into view a foot from our positions.

My father's mental words were no more gentle than those spoken, and his anger that I hadn't immediately complied almost bowled me over.

Kane, what's the meaning of this? You've made a sham of my peace treaty.

This wolf threatens my mate bond. He cannot be allowed to live.

Mate bond? My father hesitated, something I'd rarely seen in my thirty-three years of life. *You've found a mate, truly?*

Truly, Father. He's put his hands on her and threatened to try to take her from me.

Bah! Foolish words from one barely older than a pup. Release him, and we'll discuss this.

My wolf protested, and as soon as my father released the alpha command from me, I couldn't resist giving Russo one last shake before I pried my jaws off him.

Father stood relaxed, watching as we separated, Russo's glare poisonous as he stared me down.

"Shane Russo, my son tells me you've threatened his fated mate and my men tell me that you've also made unwanted advances toward the women under my protection at this gathering. As such, you and your pack are banished. If any of you are still on the grounds within one hour, I won't stop him from ripping your throat out. I'll help him, and leave your entrails for the bears." He made an expansive gesture toward the open wilderness, and the Russo Alpha began backing away. Slowly at first, before turning tail and running.

As soon as he was out of sight, my father turned to me, crossing his arms. "I presume you've got security on your mate until we confirm he's out of the state?"

Still in wolf form, I turned and spotted Gael, who gave me a serious nod and jogged off to oversee the Russo pack's exit.

"Come, then, shift back. I want to have a conversation with

you. It's not every day your son and heir finds his fated mate, after all."

I did as he was told, then slipped my pants back on, leaving my chest bare. I was still hot and thrumming with too much energy for more than that.

I would be until things were fixed with Brielle, but I owed my father a conversation before I could go and beat her door down.

I DISMISSED Reed and followed my father to his temporary office, which some of the pack's females had decorated and set up for him. They'd done an excellent job on such short notice. The room was the perfect blend of comfort and intimidation one would expect for an alpha of his stature. Dark mahogany furniture took up a good portion of the room, chairs grouped loosely in front of the desk, with extras against the wall next to a beautiful black chest, which I had no idea where they'd found it. It had shiny, gleaming hinges and a latch which seemed to radiate magic. His men, Sergei and Dimitri, posted themselves right outside the door as I shut the door behind me and took the chair directly across from him.

He sank into the oversized leather chair with grace fitting for a wolf of his age, letting his hands rest easily on the arms as he appraised me.

We were opposites in the moment. Him the picture of a still well of untapped power, me an agitated stream running over rapids and spitting angrily into the air.

"Well, tell me about her."

Such a simple request that held so much weight. Where did I even start?

"She's beautiful, intelligent—a trained doctor, actually, and her pack's healer according to her file—and she's compassionate, more than any other she-wolf I've ever met."

He drummed lightly on the arm of his chair, considering. His eyes fixed on the mate marks on my chest when he spoke next.

"And will she make a good leader?"

Would she? That was the only thing I didn't know. She was kindhearted, and many good wolves would be glad to follow a female like that. *I* would follow her to the ends of the earth. But not all wolves were good, and even some that were canted back to the old law, that only the strong were fit to lead. That didn't even bring in our suspicions that she was more than psi, but *omega*. That great danger that hung over our heads like Damocles's sword.

The idea of her being challenged by wolves like that nearly stopped the blood in my veins. But my father needed an answer, and I couldn't lie to him.

"She will have to be. She's my mate, and my wolf will accept no other."

He nodded, seeming satisfied enough with the answer. "And why were you fighting that Russo twerp when you could have been at her side?"

I sighed, dropping my head into my hands. The reminder of those circumstances was painful, like a finger jab to a fresh claw wound.

"She doesn't want to see me right now."

"I see. And what do you plan to do about that?"

Relief that he wasn't going to ask *why* was short-lived. What was I going to do about it? I didn't even know why she was rejecting me, so how was I supposed to fix it?

"I don't know, Alpha. What do you suggest?"

One side of his mouth quirked up as he appraised my stiff posture. "Go to her, son. Don't stand on pride with your mate, and don't let her either. The bond you two share will grow into the most important part of your life, but it's not indestructible. Focus on her and what she needs, not some petty tiff with a weak-spined alpha. You must *choose* to become one, to delve deeper, to hold tighter, to love stronger. The Goddess gave us this gift, but some have thrown it away over the centuries, nonetheless. You want my advice? Put aside your pride and go to her. Don't leave until you've solved the problem, whatever it is. You're both dismissed from scheduled activities going forward. Use the time wisely, son. There are no second chances in finding your fated mate."

A pounding on the door interrupted our father-son moment.

"High Alpha," Andrei called from the hallway. "The ODL is back."

He made to rise from his chair, but I growled. "Let me."

He nodded and sank back, steepling his fingers as he watched me. "Go. But don't forget what I've told you."

"I won't," I said, the words half growl as my wolf fought to come back out and deal with the ODL.

TWENTY-FIVE

Kane

I ran in human form, not bothering to shift to the wolf for such a short distance. Andrei had started off running in the lead, but I could smell the cat-piss stench of the lynx shifter at this distance, so I followed my nose and passed him.

I sent out a mental call to my top two, letting them know what was going on. Gael responded in the affirmative, and Reed was already running to stand guard outside Brielle's door.

I slowed just before the ODL reps were in sight, raking a hand through my hair and sucking in a deep breath for composure before striding into the middle of the clearing. Andrei paused at my shoulder, following my lead.

When we stepped into sight, the Omega Defense League representatives were spread through the same clearing where the group shift had gone so disastrously earlier in the day. The vampire clung to the edges of the trees, staring disdainfully up at the sun, but the lynx was in feline form, sniffing a pattern back and forth across the forest floor.

The lesser fae was harder to find, but he solidified into human form once my wolf spotted his misty, leaf-and-vine form. He scowled, sour that I'd seen through his mediocre talent.

"What are you doing back on Pack Blackwater lands?" I asked the question calmly, but I knew they saw my wolf pressing against my restraint. I never slipped and lost control, but they didn't know that.

"Investigating. We detected omega magic today, confirming the report we were already investigating. Something isn't as it seems, Alpha. And if you're hiding it..." The vampire let the threat trail off, but the glee in his ancient eyes at the idea of my punishment was chilling.

"We have nothing to hide. Frankly, I'm surprised you're all so chipper about the idea of finding an adult omega. Doesn't that mean that one of you failed spectacularly at your job?" I paced along the edge of the clearing, hands clasped behind my back and shoulders loose, as if I were out for a leisurely stroll and not to petrify the ODL into leaving us the fuck alone. "I wonder what would happen if it was found out that there was an adult omega?"

I let the question hang heavily in the air, ripe with unpleasant possibility. I might receive some small punishment for not immediately reporting an omega. But I had the benefit of the doubt; no wolf today would expect an adult omega to walk among us.

The punishment for a member of the ODL, who had enchantments specifically to identify omega females at birth?

Their fate wouldn't be so lenient.

The lynx hissed and spat, scratching at a patch of dirt. I glanced that way and schooled my features when I realized it was the exact spot where Brielle had collapsed.

The lynx transformed back into the man, fully clothed in his odious uniform.

Interesting. They've got witches providing spells to help them now, since they're keeping their clothes with their shift.

"This is the spot. There are traces of nonshifter magic here."

I snorted then, when it clicked into place.

"You've got no proof." They sensed Brielle's curse. The witchy-smelling, vile drain on her natural magic. Deep down, I was both relieved and concerned. Was this proof that Reed was right and she was omega, or were these assholes just getting off on bothering us?

There was no way to know, and my wolf was irate that we couldn't pinpoint the threat.

"Of course we have."

"*Nonshifter magic* isn't omega magic. Omegas are shifters. Vampires and fae, however..." I spun to face them, dropping all pretense that I wasn't intensely interested in what they were doing. "I would hate to think that your little squad is *harassing* this event, or Pack Blackwater."

Gael ran into the clearing, not stopping until he was just behind my right shoulder. The bastard wasn't even breathing hard, and he'd run full speed across half the pack lands.

"Do you need me to remove them, Alpha? It would be my pleasure." He growled the words, baring his teeth at the lynx male.

"We are not harassing anyone. We are serving our stated purpose, which is ratified by the Magical Race Accords. Werewolves are bound by its law, just as any other magical race."

"There are protections in place, Alpha, to prevent this sort of overstep." Andrei's low rumble held no hint of threat, only boredom. "Perhaps your father should call the chancellor, let him know that these three are breaking subsection twelve of the accords and are in need of advisory review."

"That won't be necessary," the fae said smoothly. His voice bubbled like a peaceful stream, infused with persuasive magic.

Fae were tricky, even lesser fae like this one. I let one claw shift and dug the tip into the meat of my palm to keep myself sharp.

"We'll be taking our leave now. I can confirm that this is indeed nonshifter magic. Alpha Kane is correct in that it cannot be omega. We'll consider this investigation closed and return once your pack mate has delivered her little bundle of joy."

The fae gestured for his squad mates, and they quickly joined him. With a wave and a whisper, the three of them shimmered and disappeared.

"Well, that was, as you pups say, sketchy as feck," Andrei said, his Romanian accent tripping him up.

"It's fuck, man. Sketchy as fuck." Gael clapped him on the shoulder, and they began bantering happily. But my eyes were trained on the spot where the ODL had stood, my wolf still unable to accept that the threat was gone.

"Alpha? You okay?"

"Fine, Gael. Thank you."

"Thinking about your girl? Reed says they're quiet in their room."

Brielle, my heart. A fresh stab of pain at our separation cut into me, and my father's words echoed in my head, pounding impossibly like a tattoo against the back of my eyes.

Go to her, son. Don't leave until you've solved the problem.

I left the clearing at a run, not able to wait another moment to see my mate.

So I didn't.

TWENTY-SIX

Brielle

Exhaustion, weighing my limbs down and making me feel like a lump of wet clay instead of a person, was all I felt that first afternoon. That, and searing pain in my heart. Shay curled up behind my back on the bed, back in human form now, and we lay back to back under the covers while Leigh hovered around, doing Goddess knew what.

Cups of hot tea and chicken noodle soup showed up at regular intervals, but I was so exhausted, I never took more than a sip or two.

The second day, I was able to sit up, and hunger stirred my belly as if I hadn't eaten in months instead of a day. My wolf was mournful, curled into a ball and ignoring me, but still closer than usual. Especially postshift when we'd been snatched apart so forcibly. Usually, I could barely feel her, but this time, I felt her disdain pouring through me like burning potpourri.

Unpleasant and rank.

I sipped a cup of herbal tea—my own blend, filched from my med kit, if I wasn't mistaken—and studiously ignored the plate of cold scrambled eggs sitting on the bedside table. Shay was showering, and Leigh was sitting at the foot of the bed, staring me down.

"Just spit it out," I murmured, taking another sip of the soothing brew.

"He won't leave. I've tried everything I can think of, but he won't leave."

"Who won't leave?" Surely she didn't mean Kane. He hadn't followed us into the dormitory, and even if he had, he had a pack and a gathering to run. He was too busy to wait around on me all day.

"Your alpha, who else? He's camped in the hallway like a damn hippie, has been since about an hour after we left the run. Stubborn, that one." She glared at the door, and I tried to filter through my shock to give her a helpful answer.

"I don't know anyone else who's stubborn like that," I blurted.

Her answering glare told me she didn't see the humor in their similarities at the moment.

But I was too floored to care. He'd been in the hall all night?

"Surely he went back to his room to sleep."

"No, he didn't. I was up last night and checked. He slept in the hallway, right on the floor," Shay said from the bathroom, where she was towel-drying her hair.

A liquid warmth pooled in my stomach at the thought of him, and try as I might, I couldn't push it away. With shaking limbs, I levered myself to standing. I was proud that I wobbled only briefly under Leigh's critical eye before steadying myself. *Who's a badass? I didn't even spill a drop of my tea!*

My third step toward the door, I tripped over a stray bag strap and nearly ate the carpet, were it not for the handy desk I caught myself on.

Okay, okay. Not a badass. Still impressive... sometimes.

Leigh made a distressed sound low in her throat as I reached the door to their dorm room, but she knew from past full-moon catastrophes that I was very stubborn postshift. And if Kane, son of Kosta, son of Konstantin, High Alpha Heir of the nine great packs was on his tail outside my doorway, I needed to see it with my own eyes.

My hand was rock steady when I reached for the doorknob and twisted to push it open. The soft scrape of the door hinges interrupted his pacing, his eyes jerking up to mine like we were two magnets, helpless to stop the relentless force pulling us together.

There were so many questions in his eyes, and I didn't have any good answers. I only knew I needed to see him, needed to make sure he was okay after my rejection, wordless though it had been.

"Brielle."

One word. Seven little letters. So why did they sound like a benediction on his lips?

He crossed the space between us in a heartbeat, but stopped centimeters shy of touching me, hands hovering.

I hated that space, but simultaneously needed to guard it. That space was to keep *him* safe. I owed him that, even if my weakness hadn't sent him running for the hills.

There was no choice but to stay strong, I told myself as I looked up into his bottomless green eyes. As my body swayed toward his without my permission.

"Kane," I whispered, unable to stay silent a second longer, or I was going to fling myself at him.

His eyes flickered shut, relief washing his features at the sound of my voice. My wolf hadn't woken yet, but I could still feel a primal *push* that was hard to deny.

"How are you feeling? Do you need something? Anything?"

Not *Why did you push me away? Why were you such a bitch? Who do you think you are?*

No, none of that.

How are you? Do you need anything?

Now it was my turn to let my eyelids droop, try to hold back the tears burning at the corners of my eyes. Goddess, why did he have to be so perfect? This would be so much easier if he stayed the alpha asshole I thought he was that first night.

I shook my head, unable to speak yet without giving away my emotions.

"Can we talk?" he tried again, and I looked back up. His sincerity made me want to weep, but I had to stay strong. Did that mean I couldn't talk to him, though? At least explain that we couldn't be together?

Goddess. It would shatter me to watch him move on, find a strong alpha she-wolf to make stunningly beautiful babies with. But he would, so long as I didn't tie him to myself, and my one-way-ticket-to-death faulty genetics.

"Please, Brielle. There's so much we need to say to each other. I'll wait as long as it takes. I already spoke to my father, told him about the mate bond. He's thrilled, and we're excused from all further activities. I just want a little bit of your time, and I'll make it worth your while. There are some beautiful hot springs not too far from here, and they're our pack's favorite place to go when we need a pick-me-up."

Sinking neck-deep into a hot spring sounded like utter bliss. But... it also meant swimwear. Could I keep my hands off him if I let him take me there? I could not let the bond go any further and risk him dying with me when it was my time to go.

I set my jaw. I could do it. What was one hour? I could do *anything* for an hour. I might not be physically strong, but I was mentally tough.

"Yes, we do need to talk. Hot springs sound great. I'll need another day or two, though. I'm not very steady yet—" As if to emphasize my point, I canted to the side. He caught me with a polite hand on my elbow, the virile heat of him singeing me even from such a simple touch.

"The hot springs have great healing properties. You'd probably feel better much quicker if we went right away. If you're willing, I'd gladly carry you the whole way. A mate's touch can also speed the healing process, which I'm sure you know."

I did know, and the offer made a lump rise in my throat. How could I say yes, but how could I say no?

"Come on, Brielle. I promise not to take advantage. I just want to talk about everything that's happened. Please. My wolf is demanding that I care for you, be with you. He wants nothing more than to see you well. Nothing... else."

I was barely upright and tired as hell, yet here came this sexy-as-sin alpha talking about *not taking advantage* and I wanted to jump his bones, right there in the hallway.

It was possible the mate bond was making me not right in the head. Yeah, let's blame it on the bond, and not the fact that I knew what tanned, broad expanse of muscle was hiding under his tight T-shirt.

"Okay, just let me get changed."

He grinned and nodded before stepping back just enough for the door to swing shut.

I CHANGED as quickly as I could into my favorite black bikini and a floaty, sheer cover-up. A hint of energy came back to me as I moved through the familiar motions of changing clothes, and anticipation built in my chest at the prospect of being near him again, despite my best efforts to squash it down like a cockroach.

That damn desire must be nuclear-bomb proof, because it wouldn't quit. Resisting him was going to drive me eleven kinds of crazy, but I *had to.* For him.

Resolve as strong as I could build it, I reopened the door. His eyes lit with heat as they skimmed from my hair twisted into a simple bun, down my neck, lingering on my bikini-clad cleavage, over my bare stomach, and down to the gold links on either hip which held my bottoms in place.

His wolf growled, the sound low and approving in his throat. He cleared it a second later as he skated his eyes back up to mine.

"It should be illegal to be this stunning. May I?" He gestured toward me, and it took my still-tired brain a moment to realize that he wanted to pick me up.

"Kane, it's not at all necessary to— Ahh!"

He swept me off my feet, leaving my strappy sandals dangling from my toes for dear life as he ignored my objections. My arms went around his neck reflexively, steadying myself against the sudden change in gravity.

His breath was hot against the shell of my ear when he spoke, the low tones of his voice making my nipples pebble tightly against my bikini top, "It's as necessary as my next breath, holding you. Feeling you against me. I'd like every inch of you spread out underneath me, but we need to take it slow, give you time to come to terms with this bond between us. I refuse to rush you, even though my wolf *very much so* wants to rush you."

He took the stairs easily, as if I weighed nothing, and I found myself relaxing into his strong arms, his solid chest. A feeling of rightness, of safety, washed over me as he jogged into the trees in a direction I'd never been in our short time so far on Pack Blackwater lands.

He ran in contented silence, and I rested my head against his shoulder after a few minutes. The scent of him was intoxicating, but also soothing. If I let myself, I could curl up with my nose to his neck and sleep. He would keep me safe, I knew it to my core.

But thoughts of sleep were fleeting when minutes later, he rounded a large boulder, wove through some tall piles of rocks, and stopped on the edge of a steaming hot spring. The still waters were clear enough that I could see down to a rocky shelf along the edge, and when he set me carefully on my feet, even the reddish-gray stone we stood on was comfortably warm.

"There are bigger hot springs about a hundred miles east of here, but those are public. These are private, known only to our pack. I put the word out that we needed some privacy this evening, so we won't be disturbed."

I swallowed hard, images of the two of us tangled together in the water coming to me unbidden, and a raging inferno of lust and need rising in my chest.

No. No, no, no. We can't. We can't take this bond any further, no matter how badly I want to feel him sink into me, claim me.

He stripped off his simple black tee, draping it over a stone bench carved right into one of the huge boulders protecting this oasis—someone in his pack was a very talented craftsman. I watched with hungry eyes as he also stripped off the sweatpants, leaving nothing behind but tight black boxer briefs, which showed off the largest erection I'd ever seen. I was swallowing hard again as he stepped to the edge of the hot spring and extended his hand, palm up, waiting for me.

Sucking in a shallow breath, I closed my eyes and stripped off my sheer cover-up, tossing it to float down next to his clothes on the bench. One step, then another, and our palms touched, the kiss of skin on skin more glorious every single time it happened.

My arousal burned even hotter with the small bit of contact, and he didn't release his grip on me as he stepped down into the steaming water. I dipped one toe in gingerly and moaned in bliss. It was hot, but not too hot, like the world's best Jacuzzi, only better.

I stepped down onto the shelf, coming chest to chest with him, waist-deep in the water. His straining erection couldn't be hidden, the rock-hard length pressing greedily against my hip, drawing all my attention.

He didn't push, though, or grind it into me the way I longed for. True to his word, he didn't act on his obvious desire, instead sinking down into the water and gesturing for me to do the same.

While the water lapped at his shoulders, it came nearly to my chin once I was seated. Another sigh escaped me as the warm water enveloped every tired, achy muscle, and I couldn't help but lean into his solid strength next to me.

His shoulder made a much better pillow than the stone, and our fingers twined beneath the water weren't enough contact.

Maybe I was the greedy one. But I couldn't be, couldn't be that selfish. I had to stay strong. That was why we were here, so I could explain. Make him see. Not to feed the burning desire inside me that demanded I climb into his lap, shove off his boxers, and sink down onto his rock-hard shaft.

No, that couldn't ever be between us.

The ache in my stomach came back with a vengeance, and I gasped, unable to keep it in.

Goddess, this was the worst kind of torture.

"What is it? What's wrong? Is the water too hot?" His fingers gripped mine tighter, and suddenly, he was hovering in front of me, leaning over me in the water with a worried line etching his forehead.

I didn't answer, instead reaching up and smoothing it out with my fingertips. The motion sent little trickles of water down his nose, and he wiggled it as if it tickled.

"I'm okay. Just a twinge, that's all. But we need to talk." I was proud of how firm I sounded, how in control. With me submerged under the water, even his wolf's nose shouldn't be able to pick up the smell of my arousal anymore.

I could do this.

I *had to* do this.

He sank forward, edging his torso between my knees,

bracing himself on the stone rim of the spring with one hand on either side of my head. It was a heady invasion of personal space, but I couldn't bring myself to push him away. Somehow, the contact gave me the strength to do what I had to do.

His eyes were serious on mine when he gave me a little nod to go ahead.

Here went nothing.

"We can't take the bond any further, Kane."

He growled, the sound low and anxious in his throat, but I didn't feel threatened. I pushed on, ignoring his objection.

"I'm going to die, Kane. Whatever this illness is, none of my years of study have found anything different in my genes. But, I know it in my *bones* that it's the same thing that killed my mother. And I've seen that future, Kane. I've seen what happens when, when one mate withers away, and—" A sob I wasn't expecting nearly choked me, and I buried my face in my hands.

"Shh, it's okay. Take your time. I'm not going anywhere." He slid one hand from the rock to my shoulder, tracing over the tender spot where my neck and shoulder joined, distracting me from my sorrow with little bolts of electricity jolting straight to my core.

I sucked in a few breaths and dropped my hands back to my lap, twisting my fingers together under the water to keep them still.

"Mating me is a death sentence. I won't do that to you, Kane."

"No." His face was dead serious, expression fierce as he kept tracing little patterns over my skin. *Distracting* patterns.

"You can't just... say no. This isn't a yes-or-no decision. I'm telling you, I won't subject you to sitting around and dying with me, and that's nonnegotiable. You can still move on, find another, stronger she-wolf to—"

"*No.*"

"Kane! Stop it." I glowered at him, annoyed by the little grin that twisted his lips as he watched me.

"I hear you. I understand that you think this is a death sentence. I understand that for some crazy reason you think I'm so disloyal that not only would I abandon my fated mate, but that I'd abandon her to die alone and rejected—we'll talk about *that* later, I can assure you—but Brielle, it's time for *you* to listen to *me*."

His finger trailed from my shoulder, up my neck, to press his fingertips up under my chin and gently force my tear-filled eyes up to his.

"I am never leaving you. I am never giving up on you, on our mate bond. If you won't have me, that's your choice, and I will honor it. But you'll be sentencing me to a life of loneliness and rejection right alongside you. I will not move on and mate with someone else like you don't exist. I could never, ever do that. My wolf has chosen, and so have I."

All the breath left my lungs in a painful rush. He wouldn't take another mate? Even if I rejected him?

"But, Kane, I'm going to *die*. At best I've got another fifteen years. *At best*. I've probably got more like eight to ten, based on how long it took my mother to succumb after the sickness started. That's it, that's all we'd ever have together, and then... then you'd die, Kane. Right alongside me."

"Brielle, my heart, my stubborn one, you're not hearing me. The Goddess intended for mates to be together, in life and in death. Do I wish for more than ten years with you? Of course. I'm greedy. I haven't even *begun* to explore you."

He leaned down and peppered hot, openmouthed kisses over my cheeks, down to my ear, my neck and collarbones as I absentmindedly rose from the water to meet his demanding lips. When he pulled back to speak again, I was dazed with unadulterated lust.

"But if eight, ten, or fifteen years is all the Goddess sees fit to give us? I'll enjoy every. Single. Minute." He punctuated each word with another kiss, driving me wild. "And even if you won't accept me, you're missing one very crucial point." He paused, waiting for my brain to clear enough to catch up with him.

"What's that?" I sounded breathless, even to my own ears.

"When you leave this world, I will leave with you. Whether or not you accept the bond. I won't live without you."

TWENTY-SEVEN

Kane

I saw her horror as the words sank in, but I refused to take them back. She needed to know that I was as deadly serious as she was. I would follow her to the ends of eternity, in life and in death.

Even if I didn't want to, the risk of an alpha of my power going feral? It wasn't safe. She was it for me, my own blessed gift from the moon Goddess, and I intended to take any scrap Brielle saw fit to give me. In time, hopefully she'd see my sincerity and agree to complete our bond, as the Goddess intended.

"Kane, *no*, you can't be serious." Her horrified words were half stutter, half shock.

"I am deadly serious, my heart. I won't live a single day without you, even if it would kill Gael to fulfill the task of sending me to the afterlife and back to your arms."

"But, Kane, you could have so much more. You could have a real life—"

I couldn't take it anymore, the way she kept writing off her own worth, her own *pain*. She was priceless to me, and she acted like I could just toss her aside like so much garbage.

"No, not another word of that. I heard you. You told me your why, but you need to hear me too. I am fully aware of the risks, and I accept them. I accept *you*, mate, exactly as you are."

Her face crumpled, and she buried it back into her hands, hiding herself from me once again. I was starting to see a pattern with her. Any hint of weakness, she hid. She only let the world see the strong, composed doctor version of herself. Everything else was tucked away, kept private.

My mate was stronger than she realized, but hiding from me was unacceptable.

"Mates are meant to face the hardships of life *together*. Let me prove myself to you, Brielle. Let me show you that our love was meant to be, written in the stars by the Goddess's own hand."

I sank down lower into the water, dropping my forehead to hers, and giving her a moment to compose herself. I wanted to wrap her up in my arms, but I needed her to come to me. I'd promised her that I wouldn't cross any lines, and I would always keep my promises to her.

Any scrap, any crumb she would give me, I would gladly accept it until she was ready for more.

"You don't have to prove anything, Kane. I believe you. I just hate this, hate that I'm forcing you—"

Her words warmed me, a flicker of hope blooming in my chest. Her trust was a gift I wouldn't squander.

"There's more, Brielle. I don't think your sickness is physical."

She froze, looking up at me with a confused furrow in her brow. "How on earth could a sickness be anything *besides* physical, Kane?"

"Think about it. You're a doctor, an incredible healer, and you've had years to study this and haven't found anything, right?"

"Right... but for a lot of that time, I didn't have any symptoms. Now that it's intensifying, I'll have a better chance of isolating the cause."

"Sure, but when you shifted, I saw something. Something was off with your magic, right before you collapsed and shifted back."

"*What*? What did you see?"

I explained the greenish magic and the witchy tint, as if something was oozing off her, draining into the earth. The shocked look on her face grew until, by the end, her mouth was hanging open, those perfect pink lips taunting me. So close, and yet, so far. My dick pulsed against the too-tight fabric of my boxers, demanding to be let loose to sink past those heavenly lips into the wet warmth of her mouth.

"How has no one ever seen that before? I've shifted in front of the pack multiple times over the years, but no one has ever suspected anything with my wolf. I've always assumed it was a weakness of the human side, something faulty in my genes."

"There's nothing faulty about you or your genes. You're perfect, and whatever this is, Reed's got a call out to a shaman who might be able to help."

Her mouth popped open again. I gently reached up, and ran a wet fingertip over her lips, unable to avoid the temptation another second. She had me keyed up like a live wire, my entire body one big, frayed, electrical pulse of *need*.

The shocked "Oh" melted into a blissful sigh, her eyes fluttering closed under my wandering finger. She was soft, plush, and a thousand times hotter than the focal point of any wet dream teenaged Kane had ever had.

"Do you trust me?" I asked, the question slipping past my determination to stay quiet.

"Yes." The word was so small, but meant so much.

"Do you still want to reject our mate bond?" That question burned like acid as it left my lips.

She hesitated for only a second and then shook her head.

Joy soared in my chest, right alongside a new determination to prove to her that it was the *right* choice.

"Will you let me love you, Brielle? Let me show you what we're capable of together?"

She bit her bottom lip between straight white teeth, and my fangs descended so fast at the sight that they nearly tore through my bottom lip.

Hot.

Damn.

Was that how it was with all fated mates? The smallest action, and I nearly came undone? My beast demanding I take her, mark her, mate her?

I'd never experienced anything close to this level of intensity, in all my thirty-three years.

"I won't take anything that you're not ready to give, I promise. I only want to make you feel good, take care of you. After watching you collapse... my wolf craves you. The taste of your sweet nectar on my tongue as I lap you up, make you come undone under my lips and tongue."

She shuddered, a hot flush rising to her cheeks at my suggestive words.

"Yes."

TWENTY-EIGHT

Brielle

One second, I was practically self-combusting just from his words, neck-deep in a hot spring. The next, he scooped me out of the water and planted my butt on the warm flagstone rim of the spring. My calves and feet were still dangling in the water, and then I couldn't focus on anything except the fact that his mouth was on me. My neck, my chest, covered by his lips. His tongue trailed down the strap of my bikini top, and my head fell back, arms barely holding me up at the onslaught of sensation.

Every single touch was a direct connection to my clit, and I knew my bikini bottoms were soaked with way more than just water from the springs.

I didn't have time to dwell on my reactions, though, because he was in constant motion. Teasing the edge of my breast peeking from the cup of my black bikini. Skimming his hands over my ribs, urging my hips closer, closer, just to the edge of the rock I was seated on.

His broad waist pushed between my knees, spreading me wide and leaving me feeling exposed, despite the tiny scrap of spandex between my pulsing core and his muscle-corded abdomen. When he pulled himself flush against my core, I almost climaxed just from the heat of him there, pressed tight. The damp bikini bottoms added a delicious friction, and I was on the razor's edge of pleasure in a flash.

His kisses trailed down between my breasts, over my navel, and, after a quick pause to press a reverent kiss against my blue mating marks, he laved the edge of my bikini bottoms with his tongue, and my elbows almost gave out. He somehow sensed it, because one second his hot hands were sending delicious spirals of heat over my skin, the next he was cradling my head and shoulders, lowering me down to the stones. He jumped out of the water with lithe grace, crossed the distance to the bench in two swift strides, and then tucked his T-shirt underneath my head before slipping back into the water, positioning his shoulders back between my knees, widening me even further.

Kane's mouth trailed up from my ankle, up the inside of my calf to the tender spot behind my knee, his hot tongue there making me arch up off the stone with a moan. He rumbled at the sound, the vibration riding up my legs and adding to the overwhelming tornado of *Kane*. As his lips reached my inner thigh, I trembled with desire, an orgasm already building even though he hadn't touched my core yet.

He paused, close enough that I could feel the heat of his breath, panting right over my pubic bone, fingertips trailing along the edges of the tiny bathing suit bottoms between his mouth and my soaking flesh.

"This is your last chance to tell me to stop, if that's what you want..."

Shocked, I levered myself up on my elbows. His face was deadly serious. Desire burned in the depths of his eyes, but I had no doubt he would respect my wishes if I asked him to stop, even this close.

"Don't you dare." A sexy-as-sin grin curled at the corners of his lips as his fingers hooked into the bikini bottoms. He kept eye contact with me as he peeled them down, oh so slowly, making my breath catch in my throat.

I was spread wide, and as he backed up to pull the bottoms down over my knees, I knew I was on display for him, my mate. Still he didn't look away, his wolf's eyes shining through. And there, on the edge of the pool, fully bare before him, my wolf reawakened. I gasped in shock at the sensation.

She'd never woken so quickly after a shift. Usually, it took *weeks* of emptiness before she was strong enough to return to me. But here in our mate's arms, I could feel this *siphoning* sensation between us, as if she knew he was near and was gaining strength from him, from our physical connection.

Kane growled, startling me.

"Your eyes... They're lovely."

"My wolf is back." Why did I sound so choked up?

He smiled again, more tenderly this time, and dropped a kiss to the inside of my knee, where he still held it.

"She didn't want to miss this next part."

"What?" My shock had thrown me off, and it took my brain several precious seconds to catch up to what I was seeing. He practically dove forward, sending a wave of warm water through the pool and crashing into my exposed skin as he hooked my knees back over his shoulders and arrowed straight to my center, hands spreading my thighs wide and holding them there.

I lost all thought as his mouth met my flesh, hot and wet and swirling as he lapped at my slick folds with his tongue. I sank back to his shirt, grateful he'd thought of it, and lost myself to his fervent kisses. And when his tongue connected with my clit a second later, I saw stars.

"Kane!" His name was a half gasp, half shout on my lips, and somehow, my hands were tangled in his short hair, holding him to my center as if he were going to vanish. Neither of my previous boyfriends had ever been willing to go down on me, so with them, it would have been a distinct possibility. But Kane? He growled low against my flesh, the vibrations ratcheting the pleasure up another notch as he licked and sucked and sent me reeling. Minutes ago, I'd been telling him why we couldn't do this, couldn't take that next physical step. Now? It felt like I'd die if he stopped.

I arched back again, the hard stones digging into my shoulder blades as I hooked my heels against his shoulders for leverage. His hands lifted and supported me, letting him dive in deeper to my dripping core.

"That's it's, baby, ride my face, take your pleasure. I want you to come all over me. Are you going to be a good she-wolf and scent mark me? Leave that delicious honey on my beard so *everybody* knows who this alpha belongs to."

The dirty words had me climbing higher, a possessive streak I didn't know I had rearing up in exultation at the idea of *marking* him, and then his lips fastened to my clit, tongue playing with the hood *just so* and the stars careening overhead blurred as I came, my entire body lit up like fireflies in June.

He didn't stop, though, his tongue gentling on me as the aftershocks rolled through, pushing them along until I lay there, completely spent in his arms.

"Kane that was..."

"Good?" he provided, and I couldn't help the indelicate snort that escaped.

Good? My college boyfriend never lasted more than five minutes, and that *included* the part where he was inside me.

"Incredible. *Almost* as incredible as you," I said. He gently lowered my legs from his shoulders to the warm water in the spring, leaning up and over me so he could look me in the eyes as we spoke, and I let my fingers play over his damp chest, content to lie there with him. There was a small sprinkling of black hair over his hard pecs, trailing down to disappear into the waistband of his boxers. He grunted when I let my nail tease one of his flat nipples.

"Just wait, my heart—that was only the beginning. I'm going to learn every single place on your body that makes you whimper, and it will be the greatest joy of my life to make you come screaming on my tongue every single night."

I moaned, unable to hold it back at the image he painted. Combined with the heat radiating off him, it was a heady combination. Something in my chest jerked, tugging me closer to him. Was this really my life? How did I get so damn lucky to get Kane as a mate? I owed the Goddess some sort of thank-you offering, STAT.

His erection, still trapped in the wet boxers, rubbed against my inner thigh in this position, and I realized that while I was lounging around like the Queen of Sheba waiting on my orgasm-fogged brain to clear, he hadn't even *asked* me to take care of his needs. My mouth watered at the idea of peeling him out of those boxers and tasting him.

I let the boldness take over and wrapped both arms around his neck and pulled him down flush to my chest.

He rumbled happily at the contact, so I reached up and snapped off the tie that held my bikini top in place. He froze as the cups came loose, as if he wasn't breathing, and I laughed lightly, teasing him.

"Never seen a pair of breasts before, big bad alpha?"

His much-larger hands enveloped mine, taking the straps from me and putting just enough distance between us that he could see me as he peeled them down my skin with painstaking slowness.

There wasn't a hint of laughter in his tone when he said, "I've never seen *your* breasts before, and I don't want to miss one single second." He'd started slowly, but I could see the spark in his eyes when he lost his patience and pulled my top free, flung it to the side, forgotten, as the last of me was revealed.

His groan sent a bolt of heat to my core, and suddenly, I was right back to the edge, all liquid need and *want*. How did he do that?

Romance books might like to talk about eighteen back-to-back orgasms, sure, but I was a perfectly content one-and-done girl, myself. Things were *sensitive* down there after, and I was easy enough to please.

Apparently, not with Kane. One groan, and I was about to beg him to touch me, take me. *Mark me*.

I didn't have to ask.

TWENTY-NINE

Kane

The sight of her took my breath away. I'd thought that saying was an exaggeration, but with Brielle? She stopped my heart in my chest and froze the air in my lungs. She was flawless: creamy, perfect skin, her breasts two mounds that were just more than a handful. Irresistible pink buds already stood at attention at the tips, waiting for my mouth.

I couldn't resist another second, or my dick was going to punch a hole through my boxers. I laved her left nipple with my tongue, cupping both sides in my hands, squeezing and rolling gently to see what she responded to, what she liked. But my little Texas firecracker? She was so responsive, it was like she was made for me. Every touch, every kiss, every nibble, and I don't even think she realized the effect she was having.

Soft sighs and deep groans had me throbbing, and her taste... Goddess. She was the finest honey I'd ever tasted, and I knew nothing else on the planet could satisfy me the way her sweetness did. She buzzed on my tongue, set me on fire, and I would never get enough, not if I lived another thousand years by her side. She was a goddess in the flesh, and I was duty bound to worship her. It would be the greatest glory of my life to love my mate the way she deserved, starting tonight.

She was right there with me, arching deeper into my mouth, practically purring under my fingertips, when I heard running footsteps. My wolf snarled, not pleased about being interrupted when we were *finally* where we wanted to be with our mate. Hot, ready, and willing to take our bond to the next level. *Trusting*. She was trusting me with herself, and with her past. And I wasn't going to take that honor lightly.

I ignored the footsteps at first, continuing to switch back and forth between sides as I nipped her quickly reddening nipples lightly, knowing that I had warned everyone away from this spot so we could have the entire night to ourselves if needed. There was nothing more important or precious than this time, building our bond. She was mine for life, and she deserved all that I had to give her.

Granted, I hadn't planned for the conversation to go *this* well, but I would never complain about having my mate's cream slick down my chin and neck. But the footsteps pounded closer, and I released her tightly furled nipple with a low growl, resting a warning hand on her shoulder as I looked up.

Gael's scent wafted to my nostrils a second before he would have rounded the corner.

"Stop!" My alpha command sent him skidding to a stop at the edge of the rocks that rimmed our hot spring oasis. I quickly raised a lust-dazed Brielle off the rocks and pulled her back into the hot springs. My wolf was not pleased to be interrupted, and her nudity was *mine*. The water lapped at her collarbone, and I checked to make sure she was steady before I climbed out of the water.

"What is it? Is something wrong?" she asked, her lovely brown eyes still glowing bright with her wolf as she tried to spin toward him.

"Come!" I barked, not bothering to soften my tone with my

second. I couldn't, really, with my wolf riding me as hard as he was to take our mate.

Gael stepped around the rocks, and the dank smell of *sorrow* rolled off him.

"Alpha, I'm so sorry. I wouldn't interrupt if it were anything less." His eyes never strayed from mine, politely ignoring my curious mate, my raging hard-on, and the perfume of her arousal I knew he could smell from where he stood.

"What is it?"

His face fell, and I immediately began searching the pack bonds. Someone was seriously hurt or injured, or else...

"I'm sorry, Kane, but your father... your father's been killed." My mind went white, blank as a sheet, as my lifelong friend and second-in-command dropped to both knees, his eyes locked with mine. "Long live the high alpha, Kane, son of Kosta, son of Konstantin, ruler of the nine great packs."

No.

No, it wasn't possible. My father had decades of ruling ahead of him. And my mother wasn't even here. She was back in Romania, and she was also—I reached out further, past Pack Blackwater, pressing for that familial pack bond, and where there had always been strength and comfort, the solid foundation I'd built my life on, I found... nothing.

Stark, cold emptiness.

They were gone.

I threw my head back and howled.

GAEL WAS TALKING, saying something. He'd stood back up and was trying to impress upon me what had happened, who was there, what Reed was doing, what the guard who found him said—I didn't hear any of it. My brain had shut down, moved into survival mode.

My father was gone. The man who'd taught me everything I knew about being a fair, strong leader. The man who'd played soccer with me every day after school behind the pack mansion in Romania was gone.

My mother, the one who'd sung me Romanian lullabies and kissed my scraped knees, who'd let me cry and never told a soul when my first girlfriend broke up with me was gone.

Every pack under my father's command save a handful had representatives on my pack lands, and he was gone. There was no high alpha, no one holding the reins of all the packs.

Except, it wasn't true. There was a high alpha. *Me*.

Pain seared through my heart like broken glass, but I shoved it aside, down and down and down. I would deal with all of it, but first I must see to my mate. Her safety was the only thing that mattered now, and all the rest would come after.

"Turn!" I barked at Gael again, and he fell gratefully silent when he turned his back on us, giving us a moment of privacy.

This wasn't how our first sexual encounter was supposed to end, but I couldn't ignore this, no matter how much I wanted to crawl into her arms and let her comfort me, take it all away. No, I knew what had to be done.

And so I moved with wooden efficiency, grabbing the towels that had been left here for us, gently pulling her from the water and patting her down carefully with the first towel.

Something jabbed into my chest and finally broke through the blank cotton haze I was operating in. I looked down, surprised to see her finger poking me.

"What?" I asked, genuinely confused.

"Kane, I can dry myself off. I feel fine now. After... umm..." She cast a glance at Gael, his back toward us, but scant feet away. "Not important. I'm fine. Please, get your clothes. We have to get back and see what's going on. I can't believe someone would poison your father, not *here*. It's awful, Kane. I'm so sorry.

But I'm here for you. Please, let me do this so we can get back quicker. Your wolves need you."

Poison? Had Gael said that? Had some bastard really taken the *coward's way* and poisoned my father, taking my mother in the process? Clearly, Brielle was processing more quickly than I was, because I hadn't heard a word Gael had said after *your father's been killed.*

The shaking started with my hands, went up through my arms, then my shoulders began to shake so hard, I knew I was about to shift whether I wanted to or not. I took a large step back from Brielle so I wouldn't hurt her when a massive wolf burst out of my skin, but she stepped forward aggressively, not letting me take that space.

"Kane! Stop!"

My entire body stilled, and her hands were on my chest again. I didn't know how she did it, stopping me midshift. I didn't really care, frankly, if it was more proof of her omeganess. All I knew was my mate was the only thing who made sense, who grounded me, who felt like home.

"This is awful, it's terrible, you're in shock, and it's going to be a long night. But you cannot do this, okay? You cannot break down, not right now. Your people don't need to see your wolf, they need *you*, the man. That's the sucky part of being Alpha, right? But you are the most alpha wolf I've ever met, and I know we can get through this. But how you respond *right now* sets the tone for the rest of your reign, so it needs to be right. Take a moment to settle yourself. It's okay not to be okay. He was your father. Your people don't need to see you like this."

She sucked in a deep breath through her nose, holding eye contact with me, both hands on my shoulders. I followed her, letting her wisdom guide me in this time of grief. She blew it out slowly between her lips, puffy and reddened from my kisses, and I knew without a doubt she was my true north. No matter how lost I felt, with the gaping hole where my connection to my parents used to be, she would never let me go astray.

"Excellent. Now, let's get dressed, and get back. We've got a murdering bastard to find."

The glint in her eyes told me that my peace-loving doctor would happily tear the guts out of whoever had done this, and something shifted in me again. She was right. I didn't have time to be shocked right now, and I had to be clear-headed. Somebody had murdered my parents, and that low-life scum was going to pay.

I grabbed my wrinkled and now semidamp shirt, tugging it quickly over her head. Her cover-up was basically nothing, and I didn't want her to catch a cold before we got back. I did pull on my sweats, and helped her step back into her bikini bottoms. She clutched the top in her fist as I scooped her up, ignoring her protests that she was fine.

"Let's go."

Gael moved instantly, but silently, giving me time to process as we ran through the now-dark forest. The sun had set while we made love, and I hadn't even noticed. But my wolf was on high alert, taking in everything around us now, from the deepening twilight bruising the sky above us, to the scent of the pine needles and the earth churning under our running feet, the lack of movement from the small animals around us, most likely scared off by my grief-stricken howl.

But at the center of it all was agony, like a serrated dagger rending me in half with what had been taken from me far too soon.

Nestled against my chest and warring against that raw ache, though, was Brielle. She could have used her own two feet, but selfishly, I wanted her close. And after her days of illness, I wasn't taking any chances that the only light left in my life would be snuffed out like my parents. I slowed as we thundered up the steps of the pack lodge, the usually comforting sconces glowed steadily, but I took no warmth from the familiarity.

Brielle rested her chilly fingers against my neck, just above my heart, and I sucked in another deep breath, steeling myself for what I was about to see, to experience.

"Do you want to put me down, Kane? I'm okay."

I squeezed tighter, unable to answer past the lump in my throat, and strode toward the door. Gael opened it with a bowed head, his powerful shoulders strained against his black tee.

The scent of death hit me before a sense of wrongness hanging in the air. It was indescribable to human senses, but my wolf's hackles were raised, his low snarl ripped from my own throat.

"Easy, Alpha. This way." Gael's words were gentle, but firm. He was my second for a reason; a less dominant wolf, and I'd have torn his head off for speaking when I was this close to the edge.

I knew without Gael's direction where my father—no, his *body*—was. Some sixth sense led me there, my feet traveling without my permission. But I didn't hesitate at this threshold, the sounds of low voices and furious growls reaching me as we turned the corner and arrived at his suite in the lodge. I tuned out the small crowd of my closest pack mates and my father's security, homing in on the scene, my wolf's keen senses looking for any clue of who did this.

The oversized sleigh bed, which I'd carved myself, stood steadfast against the wall, royal-blue covers undisturbed. Most of the room looked exactly as you'd expect. Fastidiously clean, nothing missing or torn to indicate this was theft driven. My stomach turned to curdled milk when I saw him, and I snarled again, overcome by the urge to *kill.*

To hunt and tear and rip to shreds whoever had dared strike down my father. Because nothing could ever prepare me for the sight of his body, on the floor in front of the wingback chairs under the reading lamp in the corner. His right hand was curled into his tunic, half-shifted, the wolf's claws keeping it there even in death, his face tinged with blue and his eyes glassy as they stared at nothing overhead. There was an open decanter of bourbon and a half-empty cut crystal glass on the small table between the chairs, and no blood or other obvious disturbance to the room.

Brielle made a soft sobbing sound, and it snapped me from my horrified staring. I turned and gently set her on her feet near the door, blocking the grisly view with my body. Gael was there in an instant, looming protectively.

"Take her to her friends, please. She's not to be left alone, not for a single minute."

"Kane, no. I'm not leaving you alone with this," she argued, but I ignored her.

This was no place for her, not now. My wolf was on the very edges of my control, and the drive to protect her had risen above anything else. I couldn't think clearly, not with her arousal-saturated scent permeating the air and our bond incomplete. It killed me to send her away, but I was likely to tear out someone else's throat if I didn't.

"Kane, I'm serious. I'm a doctor. Maybe I can help figure out—"

"No." She flinched back from my hard tone, but I didn't have room in my head or my heart to speak softly, not standing in the same room as my father's corpse.

"I understand, Alpha. I'll send my best men—"

"No," I snarled, my fangs lengthening in my mouth and making speech impossible. It took three ragged breaths to calm myself enough to pull them back. "You. Stay put on the door and check on her every fifteen minutes until I say otherwise."

"Yes, Alpha." He bowed his head deferentially, but I didn't miss the sorrowful look he cast toward the scene. I was sure he was itching to continue his investigation, but Brielle's safety was the most important. I wouldn't accept anyone less than my best man, not when there was a killer in our midst.

As the soft sounds of her footsteps trailed away, I turned back to the scene.

"Who found him?" The words were a whip cutting through the room, and everyone froze.

"Me, sire." Dimitri's voice was a low rumble, angst etching the simple words and making his accent thicken.

"Walk me through it. Tell me what happened."

"I was on post outside the door, as he'd said he needed to call your mother, update her on the day's progress." He swallowed hard but soldiered on. "He was only inside about fifteen minutes before I felt something sharp in the bond, and then I heard him fall. He didn't answer when I called for him, so I shouldered my way through the door."

He pointed, and I followed the direction of his fingertips to the door, which was indeed splintered as if hit by a freight train. It hung crookedly off one hinge, the other two dangling uselessly in the air.

"He was still breathing, and I called for Sergei to get the healer, but he faded in front of me, Alpha. It was seconds. Mihaela's name was on his lips when he passed."

My wolf was clawing angrily at my insides, raging to come out and shred this room with claws and fangs, but I locked him down with iron will.

"I want the Russo Alpha found and brought back immediately. This reeks of Russo cowardice. Send out three enforcers." I gave the order to no one in particular, but the sound of running footsteps assured me that it would be carried out.

I would kill the bastard who did this, and I wouldn't lose control a second before. My wolf would have his revenge, sate his bloodlust with his fangs in the throat of the man who dared strike the high alpha of Pack Blackwater.

THIRTY

Brielle

My hand shook on the knob to Shay and Leigh's bedroom. I shoved it open, not bothering to knock.

"Is that Brielle? I need all the details on your time at the hot springs!" Leigh practically purred from the bathroom, but I couldn't respond. I was in shock, and sad, and my head was spinning. It felt like I'd been strapped into a roller coaster of emotion tonight, and I was not in the least prepared for it.

The highs had been incredible, but the lows... I couldn't compute the lows yet. The look on his face when he saw his father's body and the moment when he pushed me away, sending me off like a kid with a scary babysitter were currently warring for *worst moments of my life*.

Shay stood from her spot huddled behind her Mac at the small desk tucked in the corner, worry creasing the skin between her eyebrows as she pulled her headphones off. "Brielle? What's wrong?"

The sobs came before the words, and she rushed to me, wrapping me in her arms as she called for Leigh.

"What? I told you she was going to come back smelling like sex and sin—" Leigh's whole demeanor changed when she came out of the bathroom, hair half-curled. "Oh my Goddess, if he hurt you, I'm going to *kill him*!" she snarled as she wrapped her arms around me too, right over Shay's. "You have to tell us what happened, sweetie. Did he hurt you? Push you? Try to make you bond with him before you were ready? I don't care who he is, I'm going to rip off every toenail and shove them up his nose before I take his asshole head off!"

I shook my head, trying to get her to stop. "No, Kane was amazing. It's Alpha Kosta. Somebody killed him."

Shay gasped, the sharp inhalation blowing against my damp hair and making me shiver in their arms. "That's terrible. What happened?"

"I don't know yet, but I didn't see any blood, so it didn't look like a physical attack. Maybe poison? There was an open drink on his side table, and no signs of an intruder, though I didn't look around long."

"What a coward's way out. Who else would poison the high alpha but someone who couldn't challenge him in a fair fight." Leigh was vibrating with anger. Wolves might have been natural-born hotheads, but we respected a fair fight. Strength led in the wolf world. She pulled back a few inches, studying my face, before urging me to the end of her bed.

"I don't know, I really don't. But whoever it was, they got away."

THREE DAYS. It had been *three days* since I'd seen Kane, and I was losing my mind. The three of us had been cooped up in this room, Gael and Reed perpetually on guard, with them being the only ones to bring us food or speak to us.

The announcement of Alpha Kosta's death had rocked the gathered wolves, howls tearing through the air the next morning, when word spread. The activities had been called off immediately, but no one had left, at least from the little Leigh had managed to wheedle from our guards. Gael seemed to have a soft spot for her, despite the fact that they fought like enemies. Or lovers, though Leigh would never admit if she was attracted to him. Right now, she was cussing him a blue streak after pounding on the door until he got tired of the racket and opened it.

"You can't just keep us locked in here! This is insane, and I want to speak to our Alpha!"

Gael stood solid and immovable in the doorframe, his shoulders filling it solidly and leaving no room for an escape attempt around his crossed arms and rock-hard chest.

Leigh was unimpressed, glaring at him as if she wanted to punch him in the throat. She had tried yesterday, but he deflected it with annoying ease, which only ticked her off more.

"I've told you this for three days now, and I'll tell you once more in the hope it gets through that thick skull of yours. I have orders from the Alpha himself that you three don't leave this room until I get word otherwise. Now are you going to accept that like a good she-wolf, or am I going to have to put a muzzle on you so you don't scream down the whole dorm?" His voice was all gravel on the words *good she-wolf,* and I wasn't sure if Leigh was going to self-combust or jump him.

Leigh gasped, and cocked back a hand like she was going to slap him across the face.

She's going to beat the brakes off him.

I moved faster than I thought possible, snatching her hand and pulling her back from Gael. It was hard, but I put myself between them and walked her back a few steps, rage blazing in her eyes. We didn't know this alpha well enough to push those buttons without there being serious consequences. While I'd like to believe my bond with Kane meant he would be respectful no matter what, I would have also liked to think that I wouldn't be locked in a room for three days.

So, taking a chance on Leigh losing it on Gael was a big fat *nope*.

"Give us a minute, Gael," I called over my shoulder, and was relieved when I heard the door click shut behind him.

"That arrogant son of a bitch!" She spat the words and paced away from me. Her shoulders were so tight, she could probably pop a kernel of popcorn between them.

"I know, Leigh, but he's following orders."

"Yeah, well, his orders suck. I can't stand being cooped up like this, and what's the point?"

"They haven't found the killer, Leigh, and you know that. This is for Brielle's safety." Shay's calm tone belied her own unease, though I could see it in the lines of her jaw, how stiffly she held herself now. She had a thing about enclosed spaces, and the charming room was beginning to close in on all of us.

Something had to give, and Leigh's rants weren't accomplishing anything because Gael was too loyal to Kane.

No, a change had to come from the top, which meant I had to put my foot down. I'd given him time to process, but I was his mate. His *fated* mate. Which meant he didn't get to shut me away and take away my decisions. We were partners, and I'd had enough.

I crossed to the door and rapped twice.

Gael opened it, an eyebrow lifting when he saw it was me, not Leigh come to cuss him again.

"Yes, Brielle. What can I do for you?"

"Take me to Kane."

He shook his head, about to argue, but I lifted one palm, cutting him off. "I need to see my mate, *now*." Command I didn't know I possessed laced the word, and he rocked back on his heels.

"Brielle, don't do this. He wants you safe right now, and he's barely holding on to his control."

"That's exactly why I need to see him. I'm the one who's supposed to help him with his control."

Gael sighed, scuffing his palm warily against the scruff on his jaw. "Fine. But you'll have to wait until Reed gets here to stay with the others."

I nodded, my heart starting to pound at the thought of seeing Kane again after so long. When had three days turned into eternity?

Reed arrived to take over guard duty quickly, but it felt like torture after waiting so long. Kane and I had been so close for a few sweet moments, and then he'd ripped us apart for *days*.

We'd only known each other for a little while, but the pull I felt toward him was inescapable. I craved him, his warm smile and his spicy orange scent, like nothing else. And I was done being told I should sit off to the side in safety. That was not where I belonged, and I intended to show him that.

GAEL'S KNOCK on Kane's door was met with a growl that sounded near feral and a *fuck off*. My speeding pulse might have been mistaken for fear if my panties didn't go damp at hearing his voice. Even if he was spitting mad, I still wanted him. I probably needed my head examined, but that could wait until after I'd had a taste of my alpha.

"Kane?" I called out, hoping my presence would change his response.

The sound of a chair scraping back roughly on the other side of the door was the only warning before he ripped the door open so hard, he nearly tore it from its hinges.

Gael stepped in front of me protectively with his hands raised, but not before I saw Kane's red-rimmed eyes, and claw-tipped fingers. He was wearing nothing but thin sweatpants, and his chest gleamed from a fine layer of sweat.

Gael had been telling the truth. Kane was nearly feral, and if I was wrong about what he needed, I might tip him over the edge. And an alpha as powerful as Kane... he could kill us all if he lost to the urge.

Yet somehow, it wasn't fear that guided my steps.

Lust, hot and searing, ripped through my belly at his proximity after so many days apart. Something primal in me recognized our mate and didn't care that he was on a hair trigger.

She just wanted him, claws and all.

I sidestepped Gael and, for the second time in the same night, moved with speed I didn't think I had, lunging for Kane's broad chest.

Gael reached to stop me, but he was too late, his fingers brushing the back of my shirt as my chest crashed into Kane's. He swiped Gael's hand back with a snarl that made the hair stand up on my arms and the back of my neck. I ignored it, wrapping myself around his broad frame like a spider monkey, clinging tight. I buried my nose in his neck, dragging in a deep lungful of his delicious scent, but finding the cinnamon smelled burned instead of its usual tantalizing spice.

"Alpha, with respect, your mate is fragile. Don't do anything you'll regret." Gael's words were pleading, and I heard him take a step forward, but Kane didn't respond. When I looked up, his eyes locked onto mine, pupils dilated nearly to blackness. He didn't break the eye contact as he stepped back into his room, and slammed the door shut in Gael's face.

His hands came down to grip my ass, clutching me tightly against his already impressive erection, but it seemed subconscious. His pupils were still blown, the wolf right there pressing against the man's boundaries.

"You're supposed to be in your room." The words were raspy, like he was hoarse.

"I was tired of being in my room. I wanted to see you. I've missed you." I opted for simple honesty, calmly staring back into his eyes, ignoring my pounding heart and the sweat slicking my palms where they were clasped behind his neck.

"You're *safe* in your room." He growled again and began pacing back and forth, still clutching me tightly to his chest. His room was half-destroyed, shredded bedding and splintered furniture littering the floor, gathering in the doorway to the bathroom, decorating the largest four-poster bed I'd ever seen. Had he been staying locked in here too?

What would get through to him? His wolf?

"I'm safe *here*, in my alpha's arms. This is where I belong, not locked away. No more, Kane. Promise me. Let me stay with you."

What began as a growl shifted into a rumble, the vibrations ratcheting up the need inside me, and I couldn't stop the moan bubbling up my throat. He was still pressing me close, and the vibrations of his chest against my already-hard nipples felt like an electric pulse straight to the clit. If he didn't stop rumbling and pacing, I was going to come apart in his arms, fully clothed. But I wasn't here to do that, and I needed to pull it back. I wanted to help him, console him, bring him *down* from this edge he was on.

I hadn't expected my body to take charge, though, and it was proving more difficult than expected.

He stopped and, to my mortification, sniffed. He could scent my arousal in the air, and the rumbles amped up to another level. I moaned again, this time dropping my head to his shoulder, the scent of him turning sweet again, oranges and sunshine and *alpha* as I fought for control.

"Kane?" I tried to ignore how breathless I sounded and focus on the goal.

He rumbled again, deeply, and moved my hips, rubbing me deliciously against his straining arousal, which was separated from my soaking center only by the thin fabric of his gray sweatpants. My skirt had rucked up when I wrapped myself around him, and my lace panties were a scrap of nothing against his intense heat.

Holy hell. Maybe he did know what he was doing to me, because that was *definitely* intentional.

"Kane, I didn't come here for this, though I'm glad to be close to you again after, ahh—" The sensible words died in my throat at the sensation of his teeth grazing the sensitive skin of my neck, the sharp edge of his lengthened canines scraping deliciously against tender flesh, the promise clear.

Mark. Mate.

My blood hummed in delight at the possibility, and I clutched his neck tighter, holding my breath. Should I have pulled away? Maybe. Could I have? Not if a hundred freight trains tried to drag me from his arms.

Would he do it, though? It wasn't traditional to mark your mate outside a full moon ceremony, but it had been done before. And I found myself... not hating the idea. The idea of solidifying this bond between us. Making the ties between us permanent, irrevocable.

Claiming him, never being alone again. Protected, cherished.

I craned a bit farther to the side, giving him easier access to my neck.

But after a soft nip, his lips took over where the delicious promise of fang had been, and I was lost to Kane. His scent, his heat, his strength enveloped me, pulled me into his orbit, promising to never let me go again.

Somehow, he held me up with one arm and divested me of my favorite T-shirt, the soft cotton whispering to the floor, landing among bits of fluff from his shredded comforter. I barely noticed, though, as he wasted no time stripping off the lacy bra underneath, and lifting me higher so that my breasts were bare before his seeking mouth.

As he worshipped my nipples with his talented tongue, all

my resolve to talk him out of his feral state faded. He kissed and nipped the skin between my breasts, trailing lazily between them and leaving a wave of longing everywhere he touched. Maybe he didn't need words. He just needed *me.* When the realization struck, I grabbed hold of it with both hands.

"Bed, Kane. I need you, now."

He went stock-still and lifted his head, eyes glowing, his wolf painfully close to the surface.

"I don't want to hurt you, Brielle. I'm not... I'm not myself right now." The gravel in his tone underlaid the truth in those words, but I didn't care.

I let my hand slide down from the back of his neck and around to rest on his jaw, feeling the tightness of his control there. He was on the edge, but I had never been more certain that he wouldn't hurt me. *Couldn't* hurt me.

"Is that why you've locked me away, like some fairy-tale maiden in a tower?" I murmured the words, watching his face closely for clues.

The petulant glint in his eyes told the truth, even when his lips wouldn't.

"Am I your mate or not? Are you rejecting me, Kane?"

"Never, Brielle. You belong to *me.*"

"Prove it. Take me, Kane. Own me. Love me. Make me yours like no one else ever has."

A pained expression crossed his face, and he dropped his forehead to my chest, his lips absently dropping soft kisses on my belly for a moment before he answered.

"I need you to be safe, Bri. You're my whole world, and if I lost you like I lost my father, my mother—"

"Hey, hey— Stop. Stop that right now. You think there's anywhere else in this world that I'm safer than *here*, in my alpha's arms? No. I *am* safe. I have never felt so safe as I do right now, wrapped up in you, loving you. Kane. Look at me." I tugged on his jaw, forcing wary eyes up to mine. "I am safe with you, and your wolf. Your wolf doesn't want to hurt me, any more than the man. You know that. Look down. What does he want?"

He sank his teeth into his bottom lip as he held my gaze, and the sight of fang tips peeking out had heat pooling in my belly anew.

"He wants to please you. Mark you." One of his hands left its grip on my thigh and caressed my belly softly. "Put our pups right here."

I shuddered at the words, unable to stop my body's reaction to the primal way he spoke about his wolf's desires.

Because deep down, that's what we were. Primal.

And I wanted every second of it with him.

"Yes."

His eyes sharpened, but he didn't move. "You can't—"

"I can, and I am. *Yes.*"

THIRTY-ONE

Kane

Something inside me snapped. Being anywhere but inside her was no longer acceptable. I leapt for her lips, those perfect, plump, kiss-reddened lips, as I scooped her off the wall and turned for the bed. They were mine, and I took them. Part of me warned that I should slow down, wait for my head to clear, but the wolf was in charge. His mate said *yes*. Yes to love and marking and family. And there was nothing I wanted more than all that, with my stunning Brielle.

I regretted shredding it, now that I wanted to use it, but I was able to keep her up with one arm while sweeping the ruined comforter and most of the fluff off the end, exposing bare sheets, which were mercifully untouched. I laid her back gently, letting my eyes feast on her flushed skin, the way she gleamed in the soft lamplight.

And then she whimpered, and I dropped to my knees. My mate needed me, and she was never going to be left wanting again. I took my time spreading her knees, shredding her lace panties to expose her glistening pussy and inhaling her perfume, ignoring the need pulsing in my dick as it tried to punch a hole in my sweats. She came first.

I leaned in close and startled her with one long lick from the bottom of her seam all the way to the top, stopping briefly to circle her needy little clit, the perfect bud practically crying for attention. But I didn't—couldn't—hold myself back like last time. This time, she needed all of me, and I had to get her ready.

She was so small and fragile, my mate. I sank two fingers deep inside her, and she arched off the bed, putting her exquisite round tits on display for me. I growled my appreciation against her clit, but didn't stop moving.

"Oh Goddess, when you growl it's, it's—"

I did it again, pressing harder with my tongue and curling my fingers inside her, finding that hidden sweet spot. If I focused on her, I could pretend I wasn't dogging the line of my self-control, wasn't a bastard for taking her when I was half-wild with the moon lust.

She screamed her release, and her walls milked my fingers so good, it was criminal. I couldn't wait to feel her strangle my cock. I kept rubbing, easing back a little as she rode it out, but not stopping. She was panting under me, so beautiful in letting go. Goddess, what had I done to deserve her? I didn't know, but I'd get on my knees every day and worship her, body and soul, to keep her.

I pulled back and added a third finger, stretching her wider, and she let out a moan.

"Kane, I want the real thing. Don't tease me. Please, please, please." She was writhing again, though, and those needy little *pleases* meant my mate was going to come again before I gave her my cock.

I stood, kicking off my sweats in one simple move, never stopping my fingers pumping in her tight channel as I leaned over her, catching her eyes. My wolf craved them, deep pools of gorgeous brown, so expressive, so liquid.

"Look at me, Brielle. You want my dick? Hmm? Want to squeeze me while you come?"

"Yes, Kane. Yes. That's what I want, please—" Her hips surged up, impaling herself harder on my fingers, drenching me with every clamp of her inner walls, making me groan.

"I want that too, but you're still too tight. I need you to come again for me, like the good mate you are. Do you want that?"

"Kane..." Her eyes fluttered shut, hands fisted in the sheets as I worked her relentlessly. My wolf pushed again, growing restless to be inside her, to claim her.

"Bare your neck."

She didn't hesitate, craning her head away from me, exposing her creamy throat, and I rumbled, the desire to please her driving me forward. Dragging my nose up her neck, I stopped at her ear. When I nipped the lobe with my tongue, her whole body jerked under me.

"So responsive, mate. You were made for me. Are you ready to take me?"

"Yes, yes, yes."

I licked and kissed down the length of her neck, feasting on her whimpers of need, right to the pulse point where her neck met her shoulder. When I bit her, she screamed again, going rigid as her pussy locked down on my fingers in a wave of bliss. It was torture, not letting my fangs pierce her, mark her, but I wanted to do everything right with Brielle. She deserved the most beautiful full-moon ceremony for her mating, and that was what she'd have. But for now, I could give her this small taste of what it would be like between us. And I couldn't wait a second longer to sink inside her.

She stifled a sob when I pulled my fingers free. "No, Kane, please, I need more, I need—"

I pulled my hips back and nudged her entrance with the head of my cock. She was so slick, I nearly slid in with the barest pressure. The desire to piston all the way in was strong, but I didn't want to hurt her. Gripping both hips, I slowly guided myself in, mesmerized by the sight of her pussy sucking me in inch by inch and the feel of her heat. She was heaven, and I never wanted to leave.

She moaned low and long, sending tingling heat to the base of my spine.

I took it slow, trying desperately not to completely lose it as her perfect pussy gripped me, her jasmine perfume going to my head and trying to send me into a full-on rut, but it was our first time. I needed to make it mind-blowing for her.

I started to pull back, continue the slow easing, but she lifted her hips and slammed against me, driving me the rest of the way home in one hard stroke, and my eyes rolled back in my head at the feel of her.

The rest of the world faded away as I lost myself in her and finally let go. I plunged deeper and faster, and she took me, matching me stroke for stroke and saying little nonsense words of encouragement. She clung to my shoulders, scratching her nails over my chest and back until finally, she flung her head back in bliss, locking down on my cock and pulling me over the edge right along with her. After, as I gathered her to my chest and buried my nose in her apple-scented hair, I felt the tether between us solidify further, the whole world tilting on its axis, as she owned her place at the center of my universe.

THIRTY-TWO

Brielle

I was deliciously sore when I woke up, and comfier than I'd ever been in my life, wrapped in a pair of big, strong arms that smelled tantalizingly of cinnamon. His scent was all warm spice this morning in the aftermath of our first time, and it made me ridiculously happy. The way he'd let go and trusted me to handle all of him, the wolf and the man. He'd loved me without restraint, without holding anything back.

And today, I'd have to wrap every second of that around me like a cloak to get through his father's funeral at his side. But for now, I wanted to bask in the best afterglow of my life.

As he sensed my awareness, the hand that had been firmly planted on my ribs began to travel, setting a wake of goose bumps to life as he trailed his calloused fingertips over my sensitive stomach. They were drawing little circles on my hip when I realized we were covered in the softest blanket I'd ever felt, which definitely hadn't been here when we'd fallen asleep, legs tangled together like teenagers in the massive bed.

"Where did this come from? Did you have it tucked away in a closet?" I lifted the edges of the deep-blue fabric and gasped when I saw the perfect, tiny stars sprinkled over the surface.

The background faded between blue and black and purple, a work of art and the mirror image of a beautiful night sky.

"It's from one of your chests. From my mother."

"Umm, what?"

He propped himself up on his elbow, watching my fascination with the beautiful blanket. "Your pack doesn't have this tradition? The bride gifts?" One sculpted eyebrow arched in question. I let myself trace it, my fingers falling down his scruffy cheek to land on his perfect lips. They twisted into a wicked smile beneath my fingers, and he nipped the digit playfully.

The simple tease had me blushing, which was ridiculous given all we'd done last night. Three times we'd come together in the night, one of us stirring and reaching for the other on instinct. It was glorious, uninhibited, and I knew that the feel and the taste of him was forever imprinted on my being. The last time was slow and tender, the final evidence of the wolf fading from his eyes after. He was back—my calm, intelligent alpha.

"I mean, there are regular mating gifts. The whole pack brings a little something, but what do you mean *chests*?"

"In my father's pack, and in Pack Blackwater, also, it's customary for the male's family to assemble a chest of gifts for the new mate, to welcome her into the family. My mom started assembling things when I was fifteen, and she never did anything halfway. She always looked forward to eventually having a daughter to spoil. So, she started early. Every year or two, she'd ship me another to put with the rest."

"This was something she chose for her future daughter-in-law?"

"Yes. If it's not to your taste, there are many more spread through the chests that you can choose from. I chose this one because it matched your starry T-shirt. It's the only thing I've seen you wear twice since you've been here."

"No, I absolutely love it. It's the most beautiful blanket I've ever seen." I was floored, and my throat clogged with emotion. His mother, whom I'd never met, had put together this amazing gift for me? To welcome me?

"What's wrong? Why are you crying, baby?"

I hurriedly swiped away the traitorous tear that leaked down my cheek. "I'm sorry, it's stupid. It's just so nice. And I— My mom has been gone so long, it just really sucks that yours did this amazing thing for me, and now I'll never get to meet her. To thank her for the chests, but also for raising such an amazing son."

I looked up and the warmth and love in his eyes took my breath away. He flipped me over, pulling me on top of his chest, and enveloped me in another hug. I relished the comfort, soaking it up like a long-dry sponge, never wanting it to end.

"She would have loved you more than you know," he said, the words soft against my hair.

An insistent knock on the door interrupted our bubble.

"Fuck off," Kane growled, but there was no heat to it, not like last night.

Reed's response was dry. "Fine, but I have a dress for your mate, and unless you want her to attend the funeral naked, you should open up. Her friends insisted on proof of life after she didn't come back last night."

I reluctantly slipped off Kane's chest, wrapping the inky blanket around myself while Kane pulled on last night's discarded sweats. A big chunk of stuffing was stuck to his butt, and I giggled as he crossed to the door. He cast me a suspicious glance as he opened it.

Leigh swept past him a split second later, barging in with Shay hot on her heels, though she at least paused, waiting for Kane to nod her into the room.

"You scared us to death! You didn't take your phone, your hot alpha-hole apparently *destroyed* his at some point, and you didn't come back! You better explain yourself, missy." She paused, surveying the room's destruction as her eyes grew wide. "Better yet, give me the play-by-play in excruciating detail. I want to know every. Last. Bit."

A growl erupted behind her, and I spotted Gael brooding behind Reed, still respecting the doorjamb's boundary and keeping his eyes pointedly clear of my blanket-clad form. But while Reed and Kane spoke in low tones, his attention was riveted to Leigh.

"I don't think that would go over so well."

She snorted, coming to sit on the edge of the bed beside me, and spread a dress bag carefully over what had once been the arm of a wingback chair. "Is your alpha really *that* overbearing?"

"No, but it looks like yours is." I nodded toward Gael, and she stiffened.

Her tone was icy when she answered, and definitely loud enough for the men to hear. "I don't *have* an alpha, and if I did, he'd know I wasn't up for repressive caveman behavior. Now, are you going to try to get ready in this war zone, or can you come back to our room to get spruced up? We've barely got an hour, and you've got major JHU hair."

"JHU hair?" I patted it self-consciously.

"Just-hooked-up hair, duh." She shimmied her shoulders playfully, ignoring Gael's possessive growl.

There was *definitely* something going on there, and she was either completely blind or pointedly ignoring it. Shay and I shared a questioning glance, but Leigh just shrugged. I'd have to ask her what was going on later.

SHAY AND LEIGH worked their bestie magic, turning me from a just-hooked-up mess into a studious, proper mate in a mourning gown in record time. For the finishing touch, Leigh sashayed over in her four-inch black heels and pinched my cheeks, hard.

"Voilà! Now he'll be so distracted by how utterly fuckable you are that he won't remember to be so sad."

"Leigh! Really?" Shay jabbed her with an elbow and shook her head at me. "You *do* look stunning, Brielle, but we'll keep our inappropriate jokes to ourselves today." She shot a narrow-eyed glare at Leigh, who just grinned.

"Look, I've got to get them out now, or else they'll slip out later at an inappropriate time."

"It's fine. I'm sure Alpha Kosta was lovely, but I didn't know him, and right now, I'm mostly worried about Kane." I picked at the cap sleeve of my little black dress, even though it was flawless, and Leigh swatted it away. My hands weren't used to being idle, and funerals... well, they brought back my own parents' funeral, and it was one of the worst days of my life.

So, yeah. I was going to fidget.

A staid rap on the door broke up our not-fight, and I rose slowly to answer it before Leigh could. She was still smirking and whispering something—which I would bet my medical degree was an inappropriate joke—to Shay.

I didn't mind, though. Where I fidgeted and Shay retreated into her music, Leigh used humor to deal with her hurts. And while no one might guess to look at her, she had plenty of hurts in her life to hide from.

The sight of Kane in a finely tailored black suit on the other side of the door sent my heart skittering in my chest. He was tragically handsome. His solemn eyes and freshly shaved jaw definitely shouldn't have sent a jolt of electricity to the apex of my thighs today, but they still did.

He stiffened, and I knew he scented my arousal when his pupils blew wide.

"You look stunning, mate."

"You look fantastic too. I'm sorry for the occasion, though. I didn't tell you last night, but I really am sorry for your loss, Kane. I know how it feels, and I wouldn't wish it on anyone." I placed a hand on his chest, his solid warmth radiating through the layers of finery and calming my wolf.

Such a simple touch, and yet she settled in my chest, content.

"Thank you. Having you at my side today means the world to me. If I hadn't found you yet..." He trailed off, the words ending in a dark question.

Would he have gone feral? Torn apart all the gathered packs and decimated the wolf shifter world?

I froze, my blood like ice in my veins. Had that been why someone had done it? Were they trying to wipe out our entire *species*?

"What is it?" He stepped into my personal space, cupping my elbows in his hands and gathering me to his chest.

I couldn't answer him, my thoughts moving too fast for words. Every wolf wasn't here, but many powerful Alphas were, and if Kane had flipped and taken them out... wolf kind would have been left unprotected, vulnerable to attack.

"I just had a thought—"

"Alpha, you're needed at the head of the procession. It was supposed to start five minutes ago, and people are getting antsy." Reed's head was respectfully ducked, but his tone brooked no arguments.

There was a funeral happening, and we weren't dragging it out further. *Especially* not for my completely unfounded suspicions. I pasted on a supportive smile and patted Kane's chest.

"Let's go, Kane. Reed's right, we shouldn't keep everyone waiting."

Shay squeezed my shoulder lightly as he released me and offered his arm. I slipped mine through, hanging on to his forearm like a lifeline. From the memories, as much as from the day to come.

THIRTY-THREE

Kane

I watched in stony silence as the last of my father's body turned to ash, and floated away on the breeze. His pyre was the biggest I'd ever seen, as befitted the high alpha of all wolves.

I didn't let myself think about how large my pyre would one day be, or about my mother's, burning together with my father from halfway around the world. I couldn't, because then I'd start sliding back into the darkness, the angry red clawing at my vision and sucking me into mindless rage. No, I wouldn't think about that.

For now, I needed to make an announcement to the packs. Move forward, solidify Brielle's position as my mate, and let everyone know that I wasn't an unmated weakling, easy to challenge and topple. Hotheads would still challenge me, of course, and I'd be forced to end them, as was wolf custom. But hopefully not today.

The red rage was right there, beckoning me like a lover, and the only lover I wanted from now on was the stunning brunette clasping my hand tightly in hers as if to stop me from blowing away with my father.

As if I'd leave her side while I still breathed. Never. I'd had three days of that, and I never wanted to spend another night without her in my arms, in my bed. She made me whole, and focusing on her light kept me from sliding into that endless pit of rage.

I gestured to Reed, and he nodded, knowing the signal to round up the packs for my announcement.

"What's happening?" Brielle whispered close to my ear, and I rumbled. My wolf sensed her unease, and had to soothe it, regardless of the crowd.

"I need to address the packs now that I'm high alpha. It shouldn't take long, and then we can retire for a private reception."

"Ahh. I hate that you have to work minutes after saying goodbye to your father. Nobody should have to do that, not even the high alpha."

I shrugged. It was not that I was indifferent to my father's death—no, *murder*; I would never forget that someone had taken the coward's way and stolen him from me—far from it. But he'd raised me to put the packs first. My duty came first, to my mate, to my wolves, and then to the packs. My grief would be there for many years to come, whether I did my duty or not. So, I would do my duty.

And then I would seek justice. My parents' killer could not be allowed to roam unpunished.

We trailed toward a raised stage, which had been intended to share announcements regarding the pack gathering, new mates and bonds forged between the packs. I felt hollowed out inside as I released Brielle and climbed the steps to address the heads of all packs, now my wolves to rule and protect.

They were nearly silent for a group so large, their somber moods fitting the occasion. I appreciated their respect. I couldn't say what I felt as I looked over them, their upturned faces underlining the weight of what I was about to take on for the rest of my life. I glanced at Brielle, each of her hands clasped by Leigh and Shay, their eyes trained on me. She gave me an encouraging nod, and I started to speak.

"My father was a good man and Alpha, fair and wise to all he protected. His death was unexpected, and yet, he didn't leave me unprepared. My entire life, he has been training me. Grooming me for this worst of all days, when he would no longer be here to offer a word of guidance, to lead the packs. And while I may never be as great a man as he, I stand before you ready and willing to accept the pack bonds.

"I, Kane, son of Kosta, son of Konstantin, accept the pack bonds, and all that is entailed therein."

With that done, I stepped forward to the edge of the stage and waited.

There was a long moment of silence, and then wolves began to move, streaming toward the stage. Gael was first, and he bowed his head as he dropped to one knee.

"I, Gael, of Pack Blackwater, accept this bond and covenant. I pledge my life to your service. Long live Kane, high alpha of the wolves."

He rose and clapped a hand over his heart before stepping aside, turning his back to the stage to monitor for threats. Ever vigilant, ever my second.

Reed was next, repeating the oaths. When he rose he pointed up to me, then returned to stand at Brielle's back, protecting my heart.

Next came the other Alphas. One by one, they dropped to a knee and took the oaths. With every one, a new pack bond flared to life in my chest. For through the Alphas, I felt the packs.

By the time the tenth had knelt and pledged, my chest was a nuclear reactor of power. Had my father carried this all with him daily? He'd never acted like it bothered him, but if I gave in to the urge to go feral now, I might wipe out the entire continent. I let my gaze flicker back to Brielle. She was still there, chin high and eyes fixed on me. There was a proud smile on her face as she watched me, and it was like electricity charging my control. I could do this, so long as she was there smiling at me like that.

Sweat beaded on my brow as the line of Alphas dwindled, but I managed to accept pack after pack without crumbling, without combusting.

When no more Alphas stepped forward, I moved back to the center of the stage to make my next announcement.

"Your loyalty and trust mean more to me than you could ever know, and I will do all in my power to earn it over the decades. I am pleased to announce that I will not be ruling alone."

A ripple of shock rolled through the crowd, murmurs and gasps reaching my sensitive ears all the way from the back row.

"Much to my father's joy and intent for this gathering, I've found my fated mate." I waved for Brielle to join me on the stage, and she paled, but stepped forward, all eyes in the crowd turning toward her for the first time, sizing her up.

"We have not yet completed the bond, but will do so as soon as is appropriate after completing the mourning rites." Hopefully, she'd forgive me for announcing that without discussing it with her, but I couldn't wait a day longer than necessary to have her, and I didn't want anyone getting the idea that I was unsure, or that they might slip in and steal me from her. She smiled at me, a private smile, telling me she agreed and causing a burst of joy in my chest.

"I challenge for mating rights to High Alpha Kane!" The shout rose from the back of the crowd, and everyone froze for a half second before chaos broke out. Gael moved to stand in front of Brielle, putting himself between her and the crowd, as a snarl ripped from my throat. I couldn't identify who'd spoken at first, but the crowd began to part as a tall, muscular she-wolf pushed forward.

She stopped at the foot of the dais, staring up at me defiantly before turning a withering glare on Brielle, fully a foot shorter than she was.

"Who are you to defy my fated mate?" The words were thick in my mouth, and I realized my fangs had descended at the threat to Brielle. My wolf was close to the surface, and this woman didn't realize how fine a grip I had on my control right now, how close she stood to death incarnate.

She lifted her chin and spoke loudly enough for all to hear. "I am Jasline, of the Northern Territories Pack, and I challenge for mating rights, as outlined in the wolf accords. If any high alpha is appointed without a completed mating bond, it is written that the strongest she-wolf can battle for mating rights."

I snarled, seething and about to deny her ridiculous challenge, when Brielle shoved out from behind Gael. "I accept your challenge." Her gaze was pure steel as she faced down the much more powerful wolf, but my grip on my wolf was wearing thin. He wouldn't accept a challenge to our mate, not when she didn't have the safety of our bite.

"One week, here, in fur. You may name your second." Jasline was calm, unworried by the sight of Brielle.

Brielle paused, looking over her shoulder at her two best friends as if unsure who to choose.

"Shay of the Johnson City pack will act as my second."

Jasline nodded in acceptance, *winked* at me, and then turned her back and left the gathering, the crowd once again parting for her to leave.

THIRTY-FOUR

Brielle

"No!" Kane snarled as soon as the door shut behind our small group of six.

"No, what?" I spun to face him, hands crossed over my chest.

"No, you cannot accept Jasline's challenge. I'll not risk you, not against a stronger she-wolf. I won't lose anyone else. *No.*"

The Alpha command made me flinch back, my knees wobbling at the forcefulness of it, his wolf's eyes glowing green, even in the strong light of his office.

As the words sank in, hurt flooded me.

"So you're saying I'll lose? You don't have any faith in me at all, do you?" I snapped, trying not to cry at what felt like a knife jutting from my chest.

"Brielle, I have nothing but faith in you, but your health… You weren't able to maintain your last shift, let alone *fight* in your wolf form! It's suicide, and I can't stand by and watch you die. You *have to* reject the challenge."

"No. I'm not doing it, and you can't make me. I'm the only one who can withdraw it. Those are the rules of a challenge."

"I'm high alpha. I'll change the rules!"

"Put yourself in my shoes, Kane. If Reed challenged you for the right to mate with me, would you just stand by and watch, or would you accept the challenge?" I saw Reed stiffen out of the corner of my eye, the four others with us primarily standing to the side and letting us scream it out.

I wished one of them would talk some sense into Kane, but apparently, they'd decided I could fend for myself. That had to break some sort of best-friend code, but that was a problem for another time, when my fated-mate bond wasn't on the line.

"I'd tear out his throat and bathe in his blood." His fangs lengthened, and I took a pointed step to the side, intercepting his glare at Reed.

"Yeah, well, *Reed* isn't challenging you. Jasline is challenging *me*, and I can't stand by and watch her take you any more than you could watch someone else take me. I will stand for the challenge, and you can either help me, or get out of my way. But I'm not backing down, and I'm hurt that you'd ask me to. That you'd just assume she's stronger."

"She's alpha! Of course she's stronger!" He rammed a hand into his short hair and began to pace angrily back and forth, making the large office feel tiny. "This is why alphas are supposed to mate with other alphas," he growled under his breath, but I heard him.

The knife in my chest twisted as I stared at him, and I blurted out another question. "Do you want to mate with her?"

"What? No!" He lunged forward, grabbing me around the waist with his stupid-fast shifter reflexes before I could bolt. My wolf and I had to have a talk about her showing up more when I needed to evade assholish alphas, because seriously, I should be able to *dodge* as fast as he was able to *grab*.

"Look at me, Brielle. *Never* could I want anyone besides you. But to lose you would rip my heart out of my chest, and I can't handle that right now. I barely have a grip on all the new pack bonds in my chest. I need *you* to steady me, and I can't live without you."

"So you think I can?" My voice cracked, the pain finally leaking through. "You think I can step aside and watch you *mate someone else,* just because she's an alpha and I'm not?" My voice shook, but I couldn't stop it if I tried, pride or no pride. He was seriously trampling all over my heart, not to mention my self-esteem.

"I would never, Brielle. We'll mate tonight. Once the rites are complete and you wear my bite, our bond can never be challenged again." His grip on me tightened to near pain, a frantic determination in his eyes.

"You can't do that, Kane." Gael was the one who finally stepped forward, a hand raised in a peacemaking gesture.

"Why the hell not?" His voice grew gravelly with his wolf's urging.

"Because if a challenge for mating rights is accepted and then one of the challengers attempts to circumvent it by completing the bond, it's an instant forfeiture of their life. You'd be signing her death warrant. For better or worse, she accepted the challenge in front of hundreds of witnesses, and she has to go through with it. All we can do now is help her win."

You could have heard a pin drop in that office, and I'm pretty sure no one breathed for at least a minute as the weight of what he'd said sank in. I was in it, and there was no way out but through the fight. Fangs and claws and blood. It was the wolf way.

"No. I'm the high alpha. I'll not let my defenseless mate be torn apart by some alpha she-wolf with something to prove just because some dusty old law says so. *No.*"

Defenseless.

Was that how he saw me? His poor, defenseless not-alpha mate. Couldn't do anything for herself, let alone earn her place at his strong, capable side.

My heart was like a paper crane, crushed under his harsh words. It wanted to crumple up and die, hide away from the unflattering truth.

But that wouldn't solve anything, and I wasn't a quitter. You didn't make it through life as a wolf who couldn't shift by being a quitter. You didn't make it through med school—with no family or pack support—as a quitter.

I had been dealt plenty of shitty hands in my life, and every single one, I'd overcome. I could do it again. He thought I was some weakling? I'd just have to prove him wrong. *Prove* that there was more to strength than simply being an alpha.

Drawing myself up a little straighter, I leveled a no-nonsense look on Gael and then on my hurtful mate. "As I said, I accepted the challenge, and I will be competing in it. I'm definitely not going to waste any more time talking about how weak and defenseless I am, just because I wasn't *blessed* to be born alpha. Leigh, Shay—take me back to our room, please."

My besties surged forward, bracketing me and lending their support.

"Let's do it to it, bestie," Leigh said, looking down her nose at Kane.

Shay didn't speak, but she shook her head sadly at him.

And then we walked out, three slack-jawed alpha males staring after us.

"I'M JUST SAYING, if you're not one-hundred-percent sure he's the one, I'll happily murder him for you for being a douche canoe, and then we can pretend that none of this ugliness ever happened," Leigh offered again.

I couldn't hide my groan as I slathered on my nighttime lotion in the bathroom mirror.

"Leigh, give it a rest. You're just mad she named me her

second," Shay grumbled.

"No, I'm not. I know *why*. I mean, I've never spent an entire year of my life furry, so, yeah. I get it. You've got the wolf mode on lock, and you're the obvious choice. Doesn't mean I can't mess that *asshole's* pretty face up just a little for talking down to my girl."

"Yes, it does. She wants him to stay pretty so he's worth the trouble."

Leigh cackled. "Okay, touché. Can I beat his ass? That's not pretty, right?"

"Wrong," I called again. "Please don't beat any part of him. I intend to do all the beating myself."

Leigh appeared in the bathroom doorway, rubbing her hands together like a black-and-white cartoon villain ready to strap a helpless alpha male to the train tracks. Rather than run off and harass Kane, though, she threw both arms around me and squeezed. "I knew you had it in you. I'll hold him down, you teach him a lesson."

I rolled my eyes and hugged her back. Dang, she was burning up. "You okay? You feel feverish. Hang on, let me get my thermometer out of my bag, and I'll check—"

"Uh-uh, no way, Bri-se! You're not changing the subject. I feel fine, and you're not playing the *I went to med school, you have to listen to me card tonight*. We've got bigger fish to fry, capiche?"

"I have never said that."

She squinted her eyes suspiciously at me.

"Okay, once. I said that *once*, and you were bleeding all over my favorite rug. I was right then too."

She snorted, and then guided me out of the bathroom by my shoulders and deposited me on the end of the bed. "I drop one barbell on my bare foot, and you'll never let me live it down. But that's old news. Right now, we need to know how you plan to execute operation TABAL."

"Operation what?" Shay asked, slipping her laptop into its sleeve and tucking away the headphones for the night.

"Duh, Operation: Teach Alpha Barbie A Lesson."

"Oh Lord, I'm never going to remember that." Now it was Shay's turn to roll her eyes. We loved Leigh to death, but when she got on a roll? There was no stopping her. We'd be memorizing her code name or we'd never hear the end of it.

"Hence the acronym. Operation T-A-B-A-L."

"It sounds like you just don't know how to spell table."

"I know you didn't just make a blonde joke when I've already been denied one beatdown tonight. You might be the second, but in skin, I can take your scrawny behind out like yesterday's paper."

"Ladies! Enough. I don't think anyone even reads real newspapers anymore, Leigh. And the truth is, I don't have a set plan, per se. I know there were defense classes on the docket for this gathering, so, my thought was I could see who the teacher was and ask for one-on-one tutoring between now and next week."

"I like, I like." Leigh gave me a thumbs-up.

"I have a schedule right here and... oh. Umm, Gael was supposed to lead those sessions." Shay passed me the fluorescent blue paper.

"Good. Then we know he knows what he's doing." I nodded once, trying not to let my trepidation show. Now that my hurt feelings at Kane had faded into the background, I had absolutely no idea how I was going to accomplish this. Jasline may as well have been Goliath and me a little Jewish boy with a slingshot for as even a pairing as we were.

Good thing David kicked ass. I just had to find my slingshot.

"Right, but... what about the part where you faint every time you shift? Got any ideas for that one?" Leigh asked, sounding a bit guilty for pointing out my Achilles' heel.

I dropped back to the bed, letting my arms starfish out to the sides. "Not a damn clue."

THIRTY-FIVE

Kane

"Kane, your knuckles are bleeding, and I'm pretty sure you've broken several of the little bones in your hand. If only we knew a doctor who could confirm that. Oh, wait." Reed's droll tone wasn't enough to convince me he wasn't concerned, but I didn't give a fuck.

"I said, another! I didn't ask for your medical assessment, Doctor *Chef*."

He curled a lip at my jab, but braced his feet and held up another board for me to smash, nonetheless.

"You know, you've got a mate now. She's not going to sit home and play obedient housewife. You're going to have to learn to talk about your feelings soon, or else there won't be any trees left in this forest, and it would be a shame to take down hardwoods that have stood for centuries just because you can't control your temper."

I snarled as the board gave under my fist. "Shut. *Up*. Another."

"If you wanted somebody silent, you chose the wrong wolf. Gael's your man for brooding, and I'm your man for common sense. You know this, I know this. So, you know deep down that you're here for more than just bodily harm and self-flagellation. Why don't we dispense with the karate routine and get to the bottom of this, hmm?"

He held up another board, but the challenge in his eyes was pissing me off. Looking me in the eye right now wasn't just stupid, it was a death wish. I turned my back on him and paced across the quiet barn to one of the nearby support beams. The wood was rough cut, and splinters dug into my forearms as I rested my head on them, on the beam. But I didn't care. I craved the pain.

The physical pain couldn't ever cut as deep as Brielle walking out on me with that look in her eye like she'd chosen wrong. Like fate had handed her a big, steaming pile of shit instead of the love of her life.

And could I blame her?

I'd gone full caveman and tried to force her to see things my way. I couldn't help it, though. Rationality wasn't my strong suit when my mate's life was on the line. I'd *never* be okay with her risking her life. Not for me, not for anything. She was too precious. She was my whole world, and somehow, instead of telling her *that*, I'd told her she was too weak to win.

Reed had been right, though. I hadn't called him here just to help me beat myself into submission. No, I needed his brain. A way to get Brielle out of this unscathed. What I needed was a loophole.

"How do we get her out of this, without forcing me to mate with a she-wolf I find repugnant and devastating my true mate?" I ground out the words, communication difficult when all I wanted was to lose myself in the physical.

But I'd already done that instead of thinking after the initial investigation into my father's death was done, and look where that'd left me and Brielle. In trouble.

It was a mistake I couldn't afford to make a second time, even if I felt helpless again.

There was nothing worse in the world for an alpha than being helpless. We were made to protect, to fix, to guard. Not... to sit around and watch those we protected risk themselves. And for what? A match that would result in three miserable wolves?

"I don't know, Kane. I've been racking my brain the whole time you tried to dislocate my shoulders through those boards."

I snorted and cast a rueful look at him. He *was* rubbing his shoulder, but he was a shifter. He'd be fine in an hour. Besides, Reed might have been the sophisticated one, but I knew he hid a massive beast beneath those polished suits.

"We could make Jasline disappear. If *she* doesn't show for the challenge, it's considered an immediate forfeit."

I cringed briefly at the thought. It was dishonorable, and that rubbed my fur the wrong way. But how honorable was it to challenge a fated mate for bonding rites?

"I know, I don't like it either."

Apparently, I'd spoken aloud.

"But it's the only thing I've got that doesn't result in bloodshed. Tricky thing is, though, *you* can't be involved. If you—as the object of the challenge—are found tampering with the results, it also results in forfeiture. Of whichever opponent you tried to help. Meaning, you'd end up mated to Jasline, and Brielle wouldn't even have a chance to stop it."

My hackles rose, and my wolf howled his distaste in my mind.

"Let's keep it in our back pockets. We have a week before the challenge. Maybe we can find something—an exception in the rules or some way to call off a challenge in the case of a fated mate bond."

"I'll make it top priority, Alpha."

I nodded and began scraping the splinters out of my forearms as we walked out of the barn, shoulder to shoulder.

A week wasn't much time to deal with a problem of this magnitude, but one thing was for sure. At the end of it, I wouldn't be mating anyone except Brielle, no matter what the old laws said.

THIRTY-SIX

Brielle

Dear Goddess, what have I gotten myself into? Flat on my back, I stared up at the undersides of tree limbs overhead, trying to suck in a wheezing breath. Unfortunately, my lungs had decided that now was the ideal moment to take a vacation.

My life had taken a serious left turn since that one little note arrived announcing the mandatory pack gathering. Back then, I'd been happy and safe, if a little overly timid, tucked in my little office-slash-lab researching wolf shifter maladies and genetics. Trying to solve my mother's case. *My* case.

No one had ever tried to tear me limb from limb back then. And I couldn't lie, in that moment, I might have given anything to go back to that life. That perceived safety.

But had I really been safe? Had I really been happy? There was nothing wrong with my life, but this disease had still been coming for me. And I hadn't had a mate, that soul-deep connection that burned in my chest, after spending two days away from Kane. Back then, I hadn't known what I was missing, but now I felt the ache of his absence, and my wolf sulked in the back of my mind.

"Any time now, princess. You only have five days left, and we can't afford for you to spend them on your back. You've got an alpha for that, right? Is he not giving you enough attention?"

Anger rose like a tidal wave surging through me at Gael's taunts. He could go screw himself if he thought it was funny to pick on the fact that Kane and I weren't speaking—let alone doing anything that involved being on my back—at the moment.

I levered myself up with one elbow, lungs burning, to give him a pissed-off glare. "Go. Screw. 'Rself." I huffed and puffed, but the words still had no real venom. Venom required oxygen, which I was severely lacking.

Collapsing back to the earth, I screwed my eyes shut. This was hopeless. Gael was more likely to break my will to live than get me ready to face Jasline in the five days we had left. The first forty-eight hours had resulted in plenty of bruises, chafing, and intense muscle soreness... but no measurable increase in skill. I was a doctor, not a fighter. If only I weren't too exhausted every night to treat myself for my thousand aches and pains beyond taking a few burdock root capsules.

"You know, that's a real childish thing to taunt her with," Leigh snapped at Gael. "You know as well as the rest of us that this has caused a rift between the two of them. You could at least have some sensitivity."

Shay's face appeared above mine a split second before she hoisted me up by the armpits. "There you go. Next time, come in lower, okay? You're getting close to a takedown."

I grunted, still unable to talk. I wasn't so injured, though, that I didn't get an eyeful of Gael and Leigh facing off *again*. The two were like angry, magnetized hornets. They couldn't stay away, yet all they wanted to do was sting, sting, sting.

Or have sex. It was a fine line.

"You think I'm blind? *Sensitivity* isn't going to get her mad enough to get up and go another ten rounds. *Sensitivity* won't keep your BFF alive. You realize her being the last one standing at the end of this is more important than her feelings, right?"

She lifted her hands off her hips to gesture angrily. "Of course I do! But you can motivate her without poking at the biggest sore spot—"

"I'll tell you what—if you think you know how to motivate someone so well, why don't you show me how it's done? Get her to last more than sixty seconds and I won't say another word about her mate for the rest of our days of training."

"Maybe I will. You better be prepared to keep your end of the bargain, though, because I know my girl." She pointed two fingers at her eyes, then accusingly back at his.

Unimpressed, he tightly crossed his arms over his chest and waited for her to work her magic.

Much as I hated to let one of my besties down, I didn't see how she planned to keep me in the ring any longer. Shay was a friggin' girl beast, and sixty seconds was a generous estimate for how long I was lasting. We hadn't tried shifting to fight yet, since that could potentially knock me on my butt for days that I didn't have to recover.

No, shifting was going to be a day-of, last-ditch effort not to die.

"Shay, get over here."

Leigh stood at the center of the mulched circle, her personal-trainer face on.

I hated her personal-trainer face. Usually, it meant she was going to try to get me to put less creamer in my coffee and run before dawn. *No, thank you, ma'am.* I was very comfortable with my extra ten pounds. I'd named them, they were part of the family, and coffee without creamer tasted disgusting, anyway.

"Do you know who this is?" She snapped me out of my delusional rabbit hole with a finger pointed at Shay.

"Umm, yes. I didn't hit my head *that* hard." I was doing self-concussion checks every hour, just to be safe.

"Who is she?"

"Shay."

"No, this isn't Shay. This? This is the hussy who wants to *steal your man*."

I froze, anger shooting up my spine like a lick of flame.

"Ahh, I see we struck a nerve. You want to just hand her Kane on a silver platter? She's coming for you. This bitch wants to knock you on your ass in front of half the wolves in the damn world and *humiliate you* and then *take your mate*. Is that what you want?"

"*No*," I snarled, surprised at the heat in my words.

"She thinks you're a weakling. An *easy* win. Can you believe that? She's never even met you, but she thinks designation rules all. What do you think, Shay? Does designation mean our Bri-Bri is going to get her pelt shaved in front of everybody that the werecat dragged in?"

Shay shook her head, but didn't answer. She was intensely focused on me, weight balanced on the balls of her feet and her brows drawn down in concentration.

"See, I disagree. You know what I heard? I heard she wants a public claiming. Can you believe that? It's not enough she wants to steal him, she wants everybody under the moon to watch him bite her, then, while his fangs are *still in her neck*, he'll take her. Right there, with all those witnesses. Because—"

I didn't hear the reason. Somewhere between the image of Kane's fangs in someone else's neck and the idea of her fucking him under the moonlight before my body was even cold, a haze of red descended over my vision.

I charged Shay, running faster than I ever had before. She moved as if to sidestep my frontal assault, but my wolf was riding me hard, her predator's instincts spotting the evasive maneuver a mile off, and I adjusted just before dropping my shoulder and ramming it straight into Shay's gut.

She fell like she'd been hit by a Mack truck, not by a slightly chubby she-wolf with chipped nail polish. But I didn't stop there. I jumped on top of her, grappling with her until I got control of her arms, pinning them overhead. My fangs were bared, the haze urging me to bite, *rip*, when two arms like steel bands connected around my rib cage, lifting me off her as if I were no bigger than a pup.

"Let me go!" The words weren't recognizable as mine, there was so much gravel in my tone. "Nobody takes what's mine! I'll tear her to shreds!"

"Nobody is going to touch me, mate. Just you. If you'll ever forgive me for being pigheaded and deign to touch me again, that is. A man can dream."

My heart hammered in my temples, my throat. My pulse was erratic, violence urging me to ignore him, ignore that honeyed tongue, and finish what I'd started. Nobody threatened my mate, my bond, and lived to try again.

Until he rumbled. The sound was like flipping a light switch, the soothing calm of cool water dousing me, sucking away the red, hazy heat, and leaving me limp. He turned me in his arms, cradling me to his chest. "There she is, my sweet mate. Are you all right? Did Leigh push you too far?"

I shook my head, too busy sucking in deep lungfuls of his scent—Goddess, how I'd missed his particular bouquet of oranges, cinnamon, and male musk. I wanted to bathe in it.

No, I wanted to roll around in the sheets with him until that scent was so far embedded in my skin, it was oozing from my pores. Somewhere around the fourth lungful, realization that I was rubbing up against him like a wolf in heat clicked into place, and I froze. I was still mad at him.

More than mad. *Hurt*.

"What are you doing here, Kane? You made it very clear how you feel about all this. And I was very clear in asking *you* to trust me, which you clearly don't."

"I sensed through the pack bond that things were getting... interesting."

I curled my lip at the vague answer and pinned Gael with an accusatory glare.

"Don't blame Gael. He can't keep his thoughts from me when his emotions are high, and his distress at the idea of you killing your friend instead of the true opponent burst through the bond."

I turned back toward Kane, awareness of our less-than-PG embrace sinking in alongside his words. There was a thick, hot erection pulsing against my inner thigh, my breasts were smashed into his chest, and I was practically high on his scent. If I didn't put some space between us immediately, I was going to do something I regretted in the morning.

Namely, ride him down to the ground, tear his clothes off with my teeth, and have my way with him right here, regardless of who was standing around watching.

"Put me down, Kane."

"Baby, you needed me. Shay was in real danger, and I knew you'd never forgive yourself if you actually hurt her."

"All I need right now is to be standing on my own two feet and to have a mate who doesn't believe I'm a lost cause and too weak to stand by his side."

He jerked back as if I'd physically hit him and loosened his grip enough for me to slide down his tantalizing body to the ground.

"Shay, are you okay?" I asked, never letting my eyes leave Kane's. There was turmoil there, and I sensed we weren't done with this conversation.

"I'm fine, Bri. But Leigh's not allowed to talk any more while we spar. I think you cracked a couple of my ribs."

Leigh snickered from somewhere behind me, not the least bit concerned about taking things too far.

"I could never think you're a lost cause, Brielle. How could you think that?"

"How could I think that? Are you kidding me? You flat-out said that alphas are supposed to mate with alphas. That I didn't have a chance at beating her. That doesn't sound like a lost cause to you?"

He stepped forward, reaching for me again, but I stepped out of reach, jerking my chin up as I stared him down. Awkward when he was so much taller than me.

"I was angry and afraid, and I said things I didn't mean." His tone was so even. A small part of me thought I should give in, accept his apology. But the other part of me? The wild part deep down? She wanted to stomp out that train of thought completely. Make him see that we weren't weak. We were his perfect mates, and that meant we were strong enough for whatever his position, his title, his designation threw at us.

"That's not how it works, Kane. Deep down, you believed every word you said. When emotions are high, that's when the truth comes out. You might think you're okay with me being psi—or even omega—but when the rubber meets the road, you're not." He tried to interject, but I held up a hand, and he bit his bottom lip. "You're *not*. But you're wrong about something. My designation isn't a flaw, it isn't a problem. It's *who I am*, but it's not all that I am. I can be strong and omega. I can be fierce and protective and fight at your side—and still not be alpha. Because I have so much more deep down than you've taken the time to see, Kane. And if this challenge is what it takes to prove that to you, then I'm glad it happened. Because I can't mate with someone who sees me as weak."

The muscles in his jaw flexed, and his next words were slow, measured. "Are you rejecting our bond?"

"No. I'm proving that I'm your equal first."

He stepped forward again, a half step, as if I were a terrified elk calf and he the big bad wolf. "You're wrong about that,

Brielle. You're not my equal. You're so much more. You're kind and intelligent. You treat everyone as if they're worthwhile. You're stunningly beautiful. And you... you're my other half. The one my wolf has chosen. And I'm so sorry that I made you feel less than. It was never my intention. I wanted to protect you, keep you safe at my side. I never meant to put you into danger."

His eyes were anguished as he continued. "I'm the one who's supposed to take all the danger, be the protector, your safe space. The fact that this she-wolf is challenging you simply because you're my mate..."

"Hey, stop that. You did a crappy thing. Said some things that were hurtful, absolutely. But, Kane, you can't take responsibility for someone else's actions. You announced what should have been good news, and she took advantage of *my* weakness. It's no secret to any of the wolves gathered here that I can't hold my shift. If I'm honest... I can see why strong wolves like her might not see me as fit to be mate to the high alpha."

"They're wrong." Goose bumps rose on my arms, my chest tightening at his words. There was so much conviction there, and he gripped me by the back of the neck and peered into my eyes as he spoke again, "You are everything. They just can't see it yet." His thumb stroking the tender skin of my cheek had tears pooling in my eyes.

This was my mate, my heart. The man I loved. I sucked in a breath through my nose at the realization.

"You said I can be omega... Do you think it's true? Have you accepted the possibility?" Had I? His words nearly knocked me on my ass.

Something was different with Kane around. I didn't know what, but I was changing. I felt stronger, and I'd been able to do things—hold power—that I hadn't before. And somewhere, deep inside, it felt right, even though it made no sense.

"I think it's a possibility, but I have no idea how," I admitted.

He nodded, eyes serious as they held mine. "I do too. We'll find out. There has to be someone out there who knows, and we'll find them."

It was a big risk for him to knowingly flout the anti-Omega laws. One he took without question, for me. I loved him. It had only been days, but I knew he was mine. Now, I just had to prove it to the rest of the packs.

THE WORDS WERE on the tip of my tongue, when the sounds of a wolf arrowing toward us through the woods had us all spinning in case of a threat.

The wolf was short and fast, steel gray around the muzzle, with vibrant blue eyes and thick, gray-and-black mottled fur.

Kane squeezed my nape lightly in reassurance before releasing me.

"Julius, what is it?" He turned toward the wolf, clearly familiar with him.

He whined low in his throat, and then jerked his head toward the main lodge.

"Julius is one of the wolves I sent to hunt down the Russo Alpha for questioning."

I sucked in a startled breath, and Kane turned back to me. "You think they had something to do with your father..."

He lifted one shoulder in a shrug. "We'll turn over every stone until we find the truth. For now, I need to go with him, see what they've found. Stay safe, my beautiful mate. I'll be back as quickly as I can."

He pressed a chaste kiss to my lips and then, as easily as breathing, melted into his stunning wolf. I ran my hands tenderly over his soft head, letting my fingertips dance over the lighter gray fur around his muzzle in a wordless goodbye. For the wolf, touch would always be more powerful.

"All right," Gael called with a clap. "Let's get back to work.

This time, don't try to rip your friend's throat out, but I like the energy. Instead of a shoulder tackle, we're going to work on a takedown where you get your arm behind her thigh, like this."

I blew out a breath and watched as he demonstrated the move on Shay. Leigh watched at my side, growling low in her throat whenever Gael made contact with Shay.

"You okay, Leigh? You seem... off."

"I'm fine. He just rubs me the wrong way." She waved off my concern. "This isn't about me. We have to keep you alive, and then I can stay far, far away from Marine Corps Ken."

I snorted. If she still had her sense of humor, things couldn't be too bad.

"You're up, Brielle. Keep the focus, and let's see you do it."

Crap. I hadn't seen the second half of the move, distracted by Leigh. Gael was going to be *so* pleased with his star student.

THIRTY-SEVEN

Kane

The Russo Alpha was bound and bruised, his right eye swollen shut and blood oozing from a gash above his ear. They'd placed him in the equipment shed, the farthest outbuilding we had from the dormitories, which were still full.

While a few packs had stayed true to their plans to leave immediately after the funeral and the oath binding, more than half had opted to stay to see the results of the challenge.

As soon as it ended, I intended to politely invite them all to get the fuck off my pack lands and give us some time to settle in and enjoy our bonding ceremony in peace. Assuming my men had finished questioning everyone about the murder by then. But first, I had to deal with this piece-of-shit alpha and find out if he'd had anything to do with killing my father.

I paced to a stop in front of him, his good eye tracking my every movement. I'd intended to let him sweat for a few minutes, but my wolf was pushing me to get this over with and be one step closer to an answer.

"Tell me what you know about my father's death."

"Is that what this is about? I had nothing to do with that! My pack was halfway to Vancouver when your little bitch brigade caught up to us." He spat, the bloody glob landing two inches from the toe of my boot.

I stared down at the offensive bodily fluids, then looked back up coolly. "You're lucky that you have piss-poor aim. And my enforcers had no trouble bringing you in—from the middle of your entire pack, no less—so I guess that makes you worse than a bitch. Stop circling, Shane, and tell me what you know. If you do, we'll fly you to Vancouver unharmed on the pack jet to meet up with your pack."

"You call this unharmed? One of your enforcers broke my arm!"

I looked over at Julius, who'd now shifted back to his human form and stood nude a few feet to my left.

"He resisted." He shrugged, the gesture one of boredom.

A man of few words, as usual. But he always got the job done. Since Dirge had turned feral, he was my best enforcer outside my top three. He was mated and had been for centuries, so the likelihood of him falling into the same trap was blessedly slim. Not that we knew what had sent Dirge over the edge, a fact which Reed was unable to come to grips with.

"He can break the other, as well, if you don't feel like talking yet. Or, I can have our healer bring out the wolfsbane. Whichever you prefer."

He froze, terror rolling in his good eye at the prospect. Wolfsbane was anathema to shifters. It dulled our connection to the wolf and, in high enough doses, could sever the connection altogether if not treated.

"I don't know anything, I swear on my wolf." His panicked eye was wide, pupil dilated as he snatched against the bonds.

"If only you had a scrap of honor, I might believe that. Somehow, I don't. Try again." Without looking over my shoulder, I added, "And someone go get John Henry."

"Don't do that. You don't want to do that. My pack will take that as an act of war, Kane, and high alpha or no, you don't want to."

"I think I do." I wordlessly extended a hand toward Julius, and he pressed a wicked-looking Damascus buck knife into it. The back of the blade curved elegantly, a work of art by a master crafter. I held it up, catching a ray of summer sun with it, letting it lazily cast a beam back and forth over the floor of the barn.

"You see, I am high alpha now. And there is *nothing* I want more than justice for my father's death." I lifted the tip of the blade, tracing it lightly over the skin on my fingertip. "And I think"—I let the blade trail down, across my palm—"that you just need a little more motivation to tell the truth." I skated the blade up to the pad of my thumb and let it dig in just enough to start a fat drop of blood welling there. I grinned and held up the bead for him to see, then began walking toward him.

He bucked against his restraints, his boot-clad feet scrabbling uselessly against the loose shavings coating the floor, doing nothing but kicking up dust as the acrid scent of his fear billowed around him.

He better not piss himself in my chair.

Julius beat me to him, locking his leg down in a vise grip to still him for my approach. I planted my bloody thumb on his forehead, just above his eye, smearing it into his skin. He tried to jerk back, his breaths growing ragged through his nose, but I flicked the blade up and over my shoulder, letting it bury itself in the wall of the barn, and clutched his jaw in my other fist. His bones squealed under the pressure as I let my thumb shift, the wolf's claw pricking his skin as my blood smeared against him.

"Are you ready to swear fealty to your new high alpha, or do I need my healer to administer the wolfsbane?"

"I'll do it! I'll swear fealty! Please! Just not the wolfsbane, you crazy fucker!"

I paused, not lifting my razor-like claw from his flesh, waiting for the words that bound him under my authority.

"I, Shane, of Pack Russo..." I squeezed, and his jaw creaked again. He hurried to finish the oath. "I—I accept your bond and covenant. I pledge my life to your service." He glared up at me sullenly, but I didn't let go until he finished it, every last word. "Long live Kane, high alpha of the wolves."

I released my grip on his jaw and watched as he worked it slowly up and down to erase the feeling of my hand on his flesh. "Now, let's try that again. What do you know about my father's death?"

"Nothing, I swear."

The burgeoning pack bond to Pack Russo was an angry red beacon in my chest, a hint of green around the fringes. He was lying, but now I had visceral confirmation. I also had an alpha blood bond he wasn't aware of, courtesy of my already-healed thumb.

"Ahh, but Shane. I know you're lying now." I tapped my chest and looked over my shoulder at John Henry's approaching footsteps. Strangely, Reed walked at his side. He gave me a weighty look, but kept silent as he stopped just inside the open barn doors.

"Thank you for joining us, John. Our guest is going to get one last chance to tell the truth, and if he doesn't answer every single question truthfully, you're going to dose him with wolfsbane to loosen his tongue."

John Henry nodded and dug a syringe and vial of murky, green-tinted fluid from his healer's bag.

"Please, don't do this. I don't know anything!"

I shook my head sadly at the mess of a wolf. "You do. Now we just need to know what. Are you ready, John?"

"Yes, Alpha."

"Shane Russo, did you or any member of Pack Russo kill my father?"

"No! I swear it!"

The green tinge faded from the bond, showing he was telling the truth. Damn.

"Do you know who did?"

"No!" Still clear. "I've been telling you, I don't know anything!" The green tinge returned, showing his lie.

"You don't know who killed him, but you know something. What is it?"

He ground his teeth and began kicking uselessly again and snatching at his restraints.

"Okay, John, you know the drill. Julius, hold his head, please."

Julius held his shoulder and shoved his head to the side, the tendons in Shane's neck standing out as John Henry approached with the vile wolfsbane. I waved my hand behind my back for him to slow down, take his time.

Even I didn't like to see wolfsbane used, and if the anticipation would get him to talk, I'd be equally happy.

John Henry approached Shane's side and pressed a cold alcohol wipe to his skin, rubbing it in a practiced circle over his jugular. The acrid stench of Shane's piss filled the air as John Henry disposed of the wipe.

As he lowered the needle toward Shane's neck, I stopped him with a question. "How long will I have left to question him before he passes out from the poison?"

He paused, rubbing his chin as he considered it. "Probably a good hour. Three more after that, give or take, before the bond begins to sever. He's pretty banged up already, so maybe less." With one last bored shrug, John Henry inserted the needle.

"Okay! Okay, stop! I'll tell you what I know, please! Just don't give me the wolfsbane!"

I waved my healer back.

"I'm listening."

"Alpha Varga sent the tip to the Omega Defense League. He was trying to stir up trouble for your father, but I don't know of any murder plots!"

The green tinge from the pack bond disappeared once again, the angry red settling into a dusky yellow. Fear, but honesty.

Interesting.

Was Russo in bed with the Hungarian, all the way from Virginia?

"Varga was one of my father's long-term allies. Why would he want to cause trouble?"

"I don't know, I swear to the Goddess. Please. I don't know anything else!"

There was no change to the bonds, and I knew he'd told me all he knew. It wasn't much, but it was something. Julius met my eyes, and I nodded that he could let go of the Russo Alpha.

"John, see his bones are set. Julius, load him onto the pack jet as soon as he's done, and take your enforcers to drop him with his pack in Vancouver. Reed, walk with me." With that, I turned on my heel and left, his screams echoing against the airy rafters of the barn as John Henry rebroke his bones to set them.

"That was something else," Reed said, nonplussed as we walked side by side away from the carnage.

"He's despicable, but not a murderer."

"This time," Reed amended.

"This time," I agreed. "What do you have for me?"

"Inuksuk is ready to meet you and Brielle. I mentioned that we would be having a bonding ceremony come the full moon, and he wishes to extend hospitality the week after. I assume you're amenable to that, and I can confirm?"

Relief washed through me. The shaman was our best bet of finding out what was going on with Brielle's magic, and I'd move heaven and earth to get her there. Find out the truth about her omega status.

"Yes, do it."

"Consider it done." He clapped me on the shoulder and headed off toward the lodge. My mind had already moved on, though, as I paced toward the woods for a run to think.

Alpha Varga of the Hungarian pack.

I had some digging to do.

THIRTY-EIGHT

Brielle

I lay in my shared bed, Leigh's even breaths beside me lulling me toward sleep myself. My muscles were sore, my body exhausted, but I still couldn't sleep. It was evasive, slipping repeatedly through my fingers. Tomorrow was the challenge, and I kept replaying the dozens of strategies I'd practiced in the past six days. I was by no means an alpha, in strength or dominance, but I still felt like I had a shot.

When my wolf pressed forward, she helped me hit like a freight train, and I knew Jasline wouldn't be expecting that.

Which was why Gael's suggestion was that I strike fast and strike first. And when I had her pinned, to shift and go for her throat. The idea of ripping out another wolf's throat left me numb, but I didn't have another choice. She would be going for mine.

If I made the mistake of shifting before the crucial moment, I'd be the one dead. Or worse, alive, and when I woke up, my mate would be gone, and I'd be left alone to watch him live out his life at another's side.

A lump rose in my throat at the awful thought of never feeling his arms around me again, and for the hundredth time,

I second-guessed my decision not to spend the night in his bed. But I shook the thought away. I wanted *all* the nights with him, damn it, not one last one before he was torn away.

I would win the challenge in the morning, or I'd die trying. There was no third option.

Pounding on my door had me jackknifing upright and off the bed in surprise, Leigh and Shay right behind me.

"Brielle! It's Reed. We need you. Gracelyn's baby is coming, and she's not doing well. John Henry asked that you come and assist."

Oh, Goddess. Not Gracelyn. Not the baby.

I bolted for my medical supply bag without bothering to turn on the lights, fear crawling through my veins like ants. I jammed my feet into tennis shoes, cursing myself the whole time for not bringing a more extensive medical kit.

In a minute flat, I was yanking the door open on a worried Reed, Gael right behind with his arms crossed. Any other time, I'd have been embarrassed by my bedhead and pajamas, but in an emergency, I didn't give a flying flip how I looked. I had a mother and baby to help.

"Where is she?"

"Their cottage, the same one we took you to last time. I know it's awful timing, but—"

"Don't say another word. There is no way I'm not helping. Let's go." I stepped out of the room, and Reed nodded and held out an arm to lead the way.

"Us too," Leigh said, standing next to Shay in the doorway.

Gael held up a hand to stop them. "No. You two are still on lockdown, and we don't need to draw more attention to the fact that Brielle isn't here. The last thing we need is an attack on their cabin while Gracelyn's in distress."

Shay worried her bottom lip between her teeth, looking pleadingly at me to step in. Before I could, Leigh got into Gael's personal space, both hands on his chest as she shoved him back.

He barely rocked on his feet, despite how strong she was. "You listen here—we can help. We might not be doctors, but we *always* go with her to attend rough births. Do you know how exhausting it is? How much can go wrong? She needs help she's comfortable with, and we won't get in the way. You can try to stop me, but I swear to the Goddess, I will not be locked in this room another second."

He growled, the sound reverberating in the empty hallway, the alpha dominance making me shift back on my heels.

"What's going on here?" Kane's words were like ice, cutting through the tension and making every head snap his direction.

"Leigh is trying to defy your orders to stay in the room."

"Shay and I *assist* Brielle with births back in Texas. She needs us, if this is a bad one. Don't deny Gracelyn help right now for a threat that's not even aimed at us."

"Let them come. Whatever will save Gracelyn and the baby."

Gael stepped back, but he didn't take his eyes off Leigh, not for a second, and I would swear I saw flames in his eyes.

Those two are going to burn the place down if they don't work out their differences soon.

I ran down the hall, leaving Reed behind as I caught up with Kane. He kissed me briefly on the temple, but we didn't stop for a lengthy reunion. He took my bag, and then we jogged down the stairs, everyone else hot on our heels.

GRACELYN'S WAIL of pain cracked through the night before we even saw the cabin through the trees, and I bolted toward the sound. Something was very wrong if she sounded like that.

I didn't stop to knock or wait to be invited in, I just flew through the door, where I spotted John Henry, pacing with a devastated look on his face.

I skidded to a stop at his side. "What's going on? What's wrong?"

"I'm not sure, honestly. She was doing okay, in early labor, and then she started screaming. The pup's fighting it, and her blood pressure is low. I'm worried there's a bleed, but I don't know where or how to stop it."

"Shit. I'll see what I can do."

Following the sounds of pain, I let myself into the bedroom. Shay was on my heels, Leigh right behind her as I cracked open the door. "Gracelyn? I'm here. Can I come in and help you?"

"Nobody can help me! I'm dying, I'm dying." She sobbed, curled sideways on the bed and clutching her stomach.

"Please help her." Adam's voice was hoarse, his face pale and haggard as he knelt on the edge of the bed, looking helpless.

"We're coming in. You're not dying on my watch, you hear me? I'm not a quitter, and I didn't think you were either. Where does it hurt?"

"*Everywhere*. It hurts everywhere."

Her desperate voice cut me to the quick.

"I know, I'm sorry. Can you take a few deep breaths for me and uncurl a bit so I can see how close you are?"

She sniffled, but I heard her breathing change as she dragged a long breath in through her nose.

"Good girl," Leigh crooned, sinking to her knees at Gracelyn's side. "You're going to be just fine. Brielle is the best. She's *never* lost a mom or baby, and we've done this a lot of times."

"Really?" she asked, her voice watery and edged with pain.

"Really," Leigh promised, squeezing both of her hands. "You just hang on to me and look in my eyes. Do I look scared?"

"No."

"That's right. And you don't have to be either. We can help you do this. You're not alone."

I scrubbed my hands in the bathroom and slipped on a pair of gloves while Leigh calmed her and Shay found a place for my bag. To my relief, there was already a delivery kit spread out neatly on a dresser, a sterile pad underneath.

"Okay, Gracelyn, I'm going to check and see what we're dealing with. Are you okay with that?"

"Yes." She was still staring into Leigh's baby blues, breathing in time with her. Leigh was an amazing anchor person, while Shay helped me with the babies. We were a good team, but I was concerned. In my home pack, I was always called as soon as labor started. Gracelyn appeared to have been in distress awhile.

I gestured to Adam as I gently felt to see how dilated she was.

He crossed to my side, worry hanging in the air around him, turning his scent bitter.

"How long has she been like this?"

"I'm pretty sure she's been in labor all day, but she seemed okay until around midnight, which is when I called John Henry. She started screaming about forty-five minutes ago."

"Okay, thank you. We're about eight centimeters, but the head isn't dropping." I withdrew my glove, my own nerves ratcheting up a degree at the amount of glossy, dark blood coating it. Something was wrong.

I peeled off the gloves and accepted the stethoscope Shay held out for me.

"Okay, time to listen to the little one's heart. Everyone stay quiet for me." I pressed the diaphragm of the stethoscope to her belly gently, moving it around until I found the best spot. It was steady, but a little slower than I'd like. Not distress yet, but not ideal either.

Next I checked her blood pressure, and my heart sank. It

was low, dangerously so, and we didn't have much time to figure out what was going on.

Without more medical equipment, though, I was flying blind.

"How far is the nearest hospital?" I asked Adam quietly, and his jaw clenched.

"More than an hour by seaplane."

"Go tell them we might need the plane."

He nodded, his expression bleak as he left the room. I took the cuff off her arm, handing it to Shay and running through my best next steps in my head as a sudden urge overtook me to drop my hands to her belly.

"Leigh, can you give me a little room?"

She looked up, confused at the deviation in our usual method, but scooched as far to the right as she could, giving me access to Gracelyn's stomach.

I placed a knee on her bed and let instinct guide me. One hand went to the top of her stomach, the other lower, near the baby's head. Unsure what I was looking for, I closed my eyes to concentrate.

Magic like I'd never experienced before surged under my palms, and I sucked in a breath as my wolf pushed forward. Gracelyn was right, something was very wrong. There was a tear in the lining of her uterus, and for some reason, her wolf wasn't healing it as quickly as she should have been. It wasn't a complete rupture, but if she continued to struggle and strain...

My eyes flew open, and I turned away from the bed, crossing to where Shay waited.

"She has a tear," I said under my breath.

"What? How do you know?" Her eyes were tight, tension leaking into her usually calm demeanor.

"I don't know, I just do. My wolf can see... something changed. I don't know."

"Can you fix it?" she whispered, trying not to alarm Gracelyn.

"I don't know that either," I whispered, trying to stay calm and not alarm Adam, who'd just hurried back in and resumed his haunted vigil at her side. "Normally, this would be cause for an emergency C-section. But the hospital is an hour away, and I'm not equipped for that here."

"If your magic can diagnose it, maybe you can help heal it too."

"I don't know how to do that!" I tried to stay calm, but panic was clawing its way up my throat at the thought of losing Gracelyn and maybe the baby too. I'd come to care about them already, and I would be devastated.

Shay reached up and slapped me lightly on the cheek, shocking me back into the moment. "Try. Whatever you did to find it, go do it again. And this time, concentrate on *fixing* it. Now. We don't have much time. *She* doesn't have much time."

"You're right, okay. Okay." I spun back to the bed, settling my shaking hands back onto Gracelyn. Her forehead was coated in a sheen of sweat, and she was looking paler than when we'd walked in. Shay was right. There wasn't much time left, and if she ruptured...

I let my eyelids fall shut again, feeling for the small tear. I found it more quickly the second time, and panic tried to strangle me again when I realized it had doubled in size.

Goddess, no. I can't let her slip away from us. How do I help her? I don't know what to do!

Entreaties to the Goddess fell from my mind like raindrops, and I never expected an answer. Which was why I nearly fell over when I heard gentle words, like soothing balm, whispered into my mind.

Your wolf knows. Let her guide you.

Let my wolf guide me. Let my wolf guide me? How? I didn't

know how to call her, work with her. She rarely made herself known, and lately, it had only been with Kane—

My eyes flew open, and I bolted from the room.

"Kane! I need you, now."

He was at my side in an instant, and I ran back to Gracelyn's side, putting my hands back in place. "Touch my skin somewhere. My wolf needs your strength."

He didn't question, simply slid one hand to my waist, rucking up the bottom of my nightshirt so he could press his palm flush against my abdomen, the other hand snaking up and twining around the top of my arm, holding me gently and with ease.

My wolf pressed forward immediately, and magic surged beneath my fingertips again, stronger than before.

Heal her. Fix the tear, I urged, unsure what else to do. To my utter relief, the magic rushed to the injury, and I could feel it knitting back together, until there was nothing left but strong, smooth muscle.

Gracelyn moaned lightly, her hand fluttering up weakly to the side of her belly. I didn't move, willing the magic to search out what else was wrong, if there were any other issues. All I found was some blood loss, so I urged it to work with her to create new blood cells, boost her wolf's natural healing.

I don't know how long we stood there, Kane pressed to my back, holding me steady while I urged the magic to move, to work, to heal, but when my wolf finally pulled back, I swayed in Kane's arms. Gracelyn's color had returned, and she was napping peacefully on the bed.

"Baby, you've done too much. You need to sit."

"I'm okay, just... drained. That was a lot."

"What just happened, Bri?" Leigh asked quietly, still holding Gracelyn's hands, currently limp with sleep. "I've never seen you do... whatever that was before."

"My wolf healed her. I don't know how, I don't know why.

But Gracelyn had a uterine tear, nearing a full rupture, and she fixed it. I fixed it." I was babbling, exhaustion making me loopy as Kane lowered me into his lap on a chair tucked into the corner of the cozy room.

"Shay, can you take her blood pressure again? I don't want to wake her up, but I need to check... I just need to check."

It went against all my medical training to trust that she was just *better* somehow. Her blood pressure would be visceral proof that she was on the mend. Though, she looked *so* much better, it was like a different woman lay on the bed. Her forehead was smooth in sleep, her color high and rosy, and a half smile curved her lips. Her hand rested easily on her belly, and the pain that had been tearing her in two had clearly gone.

"One-twenty over eighty. It's perfect." Shay gently undid the cuff and put it away, never waking Gracelyn.

A small, relieved sob escaped my lips, and my head dropped to Kane's shoulder.

I didn't know how, I didn't know why, but I'd done it. The Goddess herself had spoken to *me,* and I'd saved Gracelyn's life, with the help of my wolf.

I turned my attention inward. *Thank you. You were magnificent.* My wolf preened at the praise before curling up contentedly and tucking her nose under her tail, eyes drifting shut. Mine fell shut moments later, and I couldn't have stopped them if I tried.

THE REST of Gracelyn's labor was smooth, and her little girl was born just before dawn to raucous cheers, and joyful tears from everyone hunkered down inside the cabin. She was tiny and perfect, with dark, curling hair and the wisest of blue eyes.

Something about a newborn baby made you step back and examine life, the wonder and beauty of it, and this time was no different. We left them tucked up in their bed, glowing with joy as a new family of three, blissfully unaware of how close they'd been to the edge, to death. Or at least, I liked to think so.

When I staggered from the cabin at Kane's side, the sun was peeking over the treetops, and I didn't want anything more than my bed—no, *his* bed—and to sleep for a week.

We were halfway there when the same gray-and-black mottled wolf came running up. This time, though, he shifted into a salt-and-pepper-haired man. I averted my eyes from his nakedness.

"Alpha, they're preparing the field. The challenge starts in one hour."

THIRTY-NINE

Kane

A snarl ripped from my throat that had Julius taking a wary step back. She couldn't compete *now*. She'd spent the entire night awake and expending considerable energy on saving Gracelyn's and her daughter's lives. I owed her a life debt, and I wasn't going to repay her for saving my pack mate by letting her go out to her own death, weak and exhausted.

"No. There are extenuating circumstances. She's been up all night saving Gracelyn and the baby. The challenge has to be postponed."

"No!" She jerked out of my arms, putting her hands on my hips. "You know as well as I do that there is no postponing. I fight, or I forfeit. And there's *no way* I'm giving you up. No. I'll be there. I just need to change out of my pajamas and splash some cold water on my face. Cup of coffee. I'll be fine. Tell them I'm coming."

She leveled a determined look at Julius, and he shifted back, bolting before I had a chance to argue or skin his hide. She turned slowly, seeing the darkness lurking in my eyes.

"You can't do this, Brielle. Please, don't do this to me. Don't make me watch you fight today. Not after what you did for my pack. You were excellent, utter perfection. And it will rip my heart out of my chest to watch you risk yourself for me."

She placed a whisper-soft palm on my cheek, stroking with her thumb, making my wolf howl in despair. "Kane, son of Kosta, son of Konstantin, high alpha of wolves... I love you. I love you, I choose you, I will fight this fight to claim you, and *I will not lose.*"

She pressed up on her toes and sealed her lips to mine, the effect instantaneous. Every cell of my body wanted her, so I wove my fingers into her hair, tipping her head back. I deepened the kiss, parting her luscious lips and delving deep. She gave so sweetly, everything she had, holding nothing back, and a rumble rattled free of my chest as my blood heated and I resisted the urge to take her down to the ground and claim her right here.

When the kiss was done, she pulled back, a sadness in her eyes that struck me like a knife to my chest. I couldn't breathe when she looked at me that way. Without another word, she turned and jogged off toward the dormitories. She left me standing alone in the too-still forest, watching her take my heart away with her.

THE GROUND WAS PREPARED, the crowd gathered. The large earthen circle was ringed with spectators already, though neither challenger was yet present. The quiet, constant murmur mixed with the energy of so many wolves in the air had my teeth on edge.

"High alpha! We've got a place for you here."

Vance, Alpha of the Northern Territories pack, was smiling, *jovial*, at the thought of a challenge today. While I knew it would be awful diplomacy to do it, in that moment, it was only my iron control that kept me from eviscerating him. My mate was not to be used for *sport*, wolf way or not.

Alpha Todd of Johnson City stood scowling at his side, his mood much more closely resembling mine. As I approached, he shoved forward, stepping in front of the other male.

"I would like to formally contest that this challenge *not* be to the death, on behalf of Brielle of the Johnson City pack."

I nodded solemnly, as if I were considering the request and hadn't already arranged every one of my enforcers around the circle in plain clothes. Each and every one had orders to step in before a killing blow against Brielle could be struck, or sooner if she fainted out of her wolf form.

I knew the law. I knew the old ways, that I would be expected to bond and mate Jasline. But I wouldn't, not when I knew what fate had for me. She could issue the challenge, and I might have to see it through, but I could and would still reject her. There was no wolf alive or dead that had the power to force my teeth into her neck.

"I accept your request. The challenge will be to submission."

Vance growled, joviality gone in an instant. "You expect Jasline to live and lead at your side with one eye over her shoulder? No! A challenge is to the death. You can't change the terms now. I won't stand for it."

I turned ice-cold eyes on him and stepped up to his chest. He was a good four inches shorter than I, and craned his neck back, looking up at me. He met my eyes in rank defiance of the differences of our position.

"If you find my decision flawed, you are more than welcome to issue a challenge of your own, and we will use this circle for a death match. The she-wolves can fight another day." Normally, I had to hold in my dominance, pull back on the alpha power that rode me so heavily, but for once, I let it all out to hang in the air like a cloak.

Gael was at my side, adding menace to the threat as the weaker alpha choked and grabbed his throat.

He waved a hand and backed away as he lowered his gaze. When I eased up just enough so the man could breathe again, he finally gasped an answer. "No, High Alpha. I do not wish to issue a challenge. We will accept the modified terms of submission."

"As it should be. Tell your wolves that if *any* should cross me or defy my decree, I will put the offender to death by my own hand."

"Yes, Alpha."

Todd and Vance both nodded in grim acceptance, and I pulled back the dominance another notch. I'd gotten what I wanted, and I couldn't afford to keep letting my wolf out of control, or I'd lose it as soon as Jasline took the first swipe at Brielle.

And no matter what, I had to maintain control. If I went feral over my mate, not even Gael could stop me.

I declined the prepared seat, turning my back to it as I stood at the edge of the circle, flanked by the two packs' Alphas as was customary.

That was when I felt her. My wolf perked up, the first delicate notes of her jasmine-and-apple scent reaching me over the muddled chaos of the crowd. The mass of bodies parted, making a clear path for her to the circle. She was radiant, though I spotted the dark circles under her eyes. Her silky brunette hair was tied back in a braid and pinned close to her scalp, leaving nothing for an opponent to grab or use against her. She wore all-black stretchy athletic pants and a sports bra that I wanted to peel her out of with my teeth when this was over.

It had been more than a week since I'd been inside her, and my wolf needed to claim her again, love her again. After this, I would demand that we never spend another night apart.

She loved me.

I couldn't believe she'd said the words, but I wanted to hold them close to my chest, use them as a shield to protect her from the whole world, if she'd let me.

But my mate was strong and stubborn, and I knew she wouldn't. All I could do was watch her spread her wings and wait and catch her when she fell.

Because I would *always* catch her when she fell.

FORTY

Brielle

Jasline stepped into the ring, and the noise of the wolves around us rose to a fever pitch. She was grinning, but the expression was so sharp, I could see her already-shifted fangs. She was practically feral at the idea of ripping me to pieces, and a cold tingle ran down my spine. I didn't flinch, though. Didn't let myself show the fear that tried to worm its way through me.

I was Kane's fated mate. No amount of choking dominance rolling off her would change that, and no amount of fear would change what I was here to do. I was here to claim my mate, and nothing and nobody would stop me. She began to pace around the circle, staking the claim on her space. I followed the motion, pacing in the opposite direction so that we stayed squared off.

Kane's scent hit me, and I allowed myself a single second to drink in the delicious sight of him, standing there brooding at the head of the ring. He was dark and dangerous, and I wanted to climb him like an oak tree when this was over.

Because I *would* win. Shay and Leigh had pumped me full of coffee and some weird runner's goo for energy—gross, but whatever worked at this point—and helped me into my *badass uniform* as Leigh had dubbed it. She insisted psychology was half the battle.

Jasline was expecting an easy win, and if I could do anything—big or small—to disabuse her of that notion, that surprise might be the window I needed to knock her flat and end this in my favor.

"Pack mates and friends!" A thunderous clap rolled over the field, Jasline's Alpha stepping up to toe the chalk line that made the boundary as he addressed us all.

Everyone froze, except Jasline. She kept circling like some kind of feral land shark, so I did too.

"We are here today to oversee a challenge for mating rights to Kane, son of Kosta, son of Konstantin, high alpha of the greatest shifters in the world!" He raised a fist at the end of his proclamation, and the onlookers as one went wild.

It was history in the making; I understood that, but it was so much more to me. It was my *life*, and I started to get angry.

The flush started at my chest and slowly rose up my neck. I was probably turning red, my scent sharpening in the air, but I didn't care. These people acted like this was a freaking game of football, when I might *die* today.

I let myself lock eyes with Kane when I was across the circle from him. He held my gaze, and I could see the fury burning at the edges of him. He looked relaxed, but his hands told the story. One was clenched, the other half-shifted. It was subtle, but I knew in that moment that we were in sync. Already, we were bonded. Already, we were mates.

This fight was just details. Proof for those who'd question me.

I snapped my attention back to Jasline, as her Alpha droned on.

"—a time-honored tradition. The rules are simple. Two

competitors. One match. There are no breaks, and winner gets bonding rights. Seconds are allowed, but discouraged."

I glanced at Shay, who was furious, but calm. Ready. She bounced on the balls of her feet, giving me a nod. We'd discussed it over the last week, and while she did *not* want to bond with Kane, she'd agreed that if I lost, she would dive in and finish Jasline. She'd insisted, actually.

Even if I lost today, Jasline still wouldn't get my alpha.

It was as backup to a backup, but I was glad to know this power-hungry bitch wouldn't lay a single finger on Kane.

"No interference is allowed, except from seconds if a challenger loses. And per the challengee's Alpha's request, today's match will be to submission. This challenge is *not* to proceed to death, and you will accept a submission, or your own life and that of your pack will be forfeit."

Jasline took a lunging step toward him—apparently, something *could* rattle her—and he held up both hands. I didn't know how to feel about the fact that it wasn't to the death. Grateful, I supposed? But if I lost, wouldn't they all put up a vicious fight about us being allowed to mate?

"It is at High Alpha Kane's insistence."

She snarled and whirled back toward me, shoulders taut as a bowstring.

"You may begin!" he shouted, and she charged. There was no hesitation, not a breath of oxygen between the *-in* and her motion.

She was fluid and graceful, her fangs already protruding from her mouth, and I did the only thing I could think of. I charged straight back at her.

I couldn't stay at the edge, not with her running that fast, or she'd knock me out of the ring, and I'd lose.

A second before we collided, I lowered my shoulder and grabbed for her right arm. She wasn't expecting it, and I managed to semisuccessfully toss her over my shoulder, lessening the brunt of the impact from our bodies meeting at full speed.

She landed on her feet, though, and charged toward my exposed back before I was completely turned to face her. This time, her attack landed, and she drove me into the ground like a pile driver. There was dirt and grass in my mouth, and I had to blink back shock, but there wasn't time.

She was trying to flip me over, expose my belly and throat, and end it. *No.*

Using every bit of strength I possessed, I wedged my legs between us and pushed, bucking her off me. One of her hands shifted, and I felt a searing pain as she flew free, one of her clawed hands dragging through the tender flesh of my side.

Blood was flowing freely as I staggered back to my feet, and time slowed around me as the shock kicked in. My hands felt disjointed from my body as one fluttered up and clasped my gaping flesh, the wet ooze of blood between my fingers making the gorge rise in the back of my throat.

I heard a distant howl and realized that she'd stopped to *celebrate* drawing first blood, completely unafraid as she threw back her head. Fists clenched with rapture, her back was to me as members of her pack howled back, praising her.

Assuming her victory.

If I didn't pull it together, it *would* be her victory. The cold reality of blood loss meant I wouldn't have much time left, if I didn't act right now.

I spared a glance for Kane and saw his teeth were bared, fangs dripping with rage as he watched my blood begin to puddle at my feet. His alpha dominance hung so heavily in the air, the wolves around him had formed a three-foot perimeter, backing away from him on instinct, even as they watched the ring.

It didn't choke me, though. It called to me, like a siren's song or a lover's caress.

The Goddess's words echoed in my head, *Your wolf knows. Let her guide you.*

Help me! I cried to her, still reaching for Kane's raw power, caressing me like his skilled fingers down my inner thigh.

Something snapped inside me, and instead of caressing me, Kane's power, his essence, his *dominance* began to pour into me, filling me up. It was heady and wild, urging me to fight, attack, *kill the bitch*.

Wound forgotten, everything around me grew sharper, crisper. I could feel her arrogance, smell the putrid stench of vanity, like rotting flowers left too long in a vase.

But none of that mattered. A red haze dropped over everything, and I attacked her unguarded back. Whether she heard me coming or someone warned her to watch her back, I couldn't say. The world narrowed to me and her, and I could no longer see or hear anything but the pounding heart in her chest, the drumbeat of blood pulsing in her arteries.

Blood I was about to spill.

For only the second time in my life, my fangs descended in human form. My fingers were tipped with claws, and as she turned to face me, I slashed.

She caught the blow on her forearm, but my claws split her flesh like a hot knife through butter, and I caught a glimpse of white bone before she dropped it with a hiss. I didn't stop, barreling into her like a locomotive.

She kept her feet, dancing back toward the boundary line before twisting out of my reach. I followed, pursuing her like she was fresh meat and I was a wolf starved. I *was* starved. Starved for justice. For revenge. For my mate.

She stopped and spun, sweeping out a kick, but I leapt into the air, over her leg, and made full contact with her torso as I tackled her to the ground.

Clawed hands scrabbled underneath me, and I felt a few hot slices make it through, but my target was one thing: the throbbing pulse in her throat. Once I controlled her neck, she'd be forced to submit. Gael had shown me a way to incapacitate someone with a choke hold that would cause them to pass out, but I was on top of her, and I didn't know how to accomplish that hold from this position.

My knees dug into her stomach, and her breath came in shallow pants as my hands closed around her bare flesh.

"Submit." The words weren't recognizable as mine.

She thrashed, shaking her head and trying to dislodge me, but I squeezed tighter, cutting off her air.

"Submit!" I snarled again, not giving her an inch. Not a second's reprieve.

Her face was fading from red to purple when she finally stopped scrabbling beneath me. One arm went weakly out to the side, and she patted the ground three times.

"Let her go! Brielle, she's tapped! You won!" Leigh's voice was the loudest, reaching me above the cacophony, but it was Kane's power, stroking me, and his voice that broke through the bloodlust that had consumed me.

"Well done, mate. Let her go and come kiss me."

I released her, and she grabbed her bruised throat to suck in air. I left her there, turning my back to greet my mate, my love, my other half.

Pride glowed from his eyes, and he held both arms out for my approach. I absentmindedly saw a worried-looking John Henry right behind him with his medical kit.

I looked down, shocked to see dozens of cuts littering my body. The largest had partially closed up, but my black clothing clung to me with sticky blood. How much of it was mine or hers, I couldn't say.

Any other time, I'd be horrified, but right now all I felt was triumph as I moved to plant my lips on Kane's and claim him as *mine*. For good.

The sound of clothes shredding reached me when I was

halfway across the ring. She'd been wounded and would probably shift to speed the healing.

I didn't have that option, but hopefully, my wounds were superficial enough to heal without a shift.

"Brielle, look out!" Kane's words were harsh, guttural, and he lunged forward, but he wasn't close enough to stop me from being bowled over, eating a mouthful of dirt *again* as a crushing weight landed on top of me. Claws dug into my back, and a vicious howl ripped from the wolf on top of me.

Jasline.

The shift came over me in a flash, my wolf springing free and rolling to defend. We gnashed with teeth and tried to shred her belly with our back claws, but only got in one good swipe before a honey-and-coffee-brown wolf slammed into her side, knocking the cheating bitch free.

Shay's wolf had no mercy, pinning her by the throat and dragging her razor-sharp claws across her tender belly, sending fur and blood spraying into the air like twisted confetti. She held her, pinned and dying, as Kane reached us.

"Jasline of the Northern Territories! You have broken the rules of a fair challenge. In front of the Goddess and in front of these witnesses, I declare your life forfeit!"

I didn't turn my head away as Shay ripped out her throat, or as her body stuttered one last time and went still, the life gone from her eyes.

Shay stepped back almost daintily and crossed to stand in front of me, both of us still in wolf form. I'd managed to stagger to my feet as Kane spoke, and our wolves stood nose to nose now.

I reached forward and licked her muzzle, accepting her help, thanking her for her loyalty. She threw back her head and howled, so I joined in. The feeling was unfamiliar but right, as every member of my pack—and Kane's, a moment later—

howled their approval to the Goddess. It was otherworldly, and it was a feeling I'd never forget.

Shay bowed, dropping her forelegs down and tucking her head until I yipped gently for her to get back up. She leaned against me, shoulder to shoulder, and watched the crowd with a ferocity that dared someone else to try. I was shocked as Leigh joined us, her tawny fur and greater height pressing in from the other side as Kane and the healer tried to get to me.

"Let's take her to your rooms, Alpha. There will be more room to tend her there, and we can put security on the door."

Kane looked down, meeting my wolf's eyes. "Can you hang on for two more minutes?"

I bobbed my head.

"On this day, you've borne witness to the challenge for my bonding rights. As the result of this challenge, I hereby claim Brielle of the Johnson City pack as my mate. We have been fated and bear bonding marks."

He lifted off his black T-shirt in a fluid motion, showing the royal-blue ink adorning his chest and side.

"I will accept no further challenges, as I will not scorn this gift the Fates have bestowed upon me. We will be mated during the next full moon ceremony, in three days' time. Any further challenges to Brielle will be met by *me*, on the spot. I will not suffer repeated attacks on my fated mate." He spun as he spoke, letting his heavy gaze drive each and every wolf back a step, his full alpha dominance let out to play.

"If anyone tries to exact retribution for the death of Jasline, I will remind you that she submitted and then showed her dishonor by attacking my mate after the challenge had ended, which is a crime against the old ways. Her death was honorably enacted by my mate's second, and any who seek to challenge *her* will face *my* second. Are we clear?"

"Yes, High Alpha," hundreds of wolves droned as one, many

falling to their knees at the weight of his power crackling in the clearing.

"I want every wolf who is not part of the Johnson City pack or Pack Blackwater to be off this territory within twelve hours, or you will be removed by my enforcers."

At that proclamation, no fewer than two dozen wolves threw back their heads and howled, each placed around the ring, already protecting us and pushing back the lingering crowd.

"We need to get her to your suite. She's fading, Alpha."

John Henry's concerned words were the last I heard before I blacked out, crumpling into the dirt between my best friends and my fated mate.

FORTY-ONE

Brielle

The bridal suite inside the pack lodge was stunning, with an enormous picture window taking up almost one whole wall. It looked out over the pristine forest where the nearest snowcapped mountains jutted up into the wide twilight sky. Leigh was curling Shay's hair, so I'd finally escaped her clutches to stand at the window and just *breathe* for a moment.

Gracelyn stood outside, and I could see her from here, a bright, flamingo-pink, stretchy wrap strapping little Dawn to her chest as she barked orders at the wolves running to and fro with flowers, candles, and Goddess knew what else she'd pulled together on such short notice. She was fully healed from the birth and back where she liked to be: in charge.

She was also wildly relieved that the Omega Defense League had checked little Dawn and declared her beta, meaning not a threat. They'd promptly left the state, or so I'd been told. I'd still been unconscious when they did the check.

Bonding ceremonies often took more than six months to plan, with elaborate guest lists and extravagant food brought from all over.

But we agreed we didn't want to wait. He already held the other half of my soul; waiting any longer would just be painful.

The full moon was tonight, which meant Kane and I would be bonded in just a few short hours, amid both of our packs, surrounded by the beauty of his lands and the love of our closest friends. I didn't need anything else, and he didn't either.

The small, persistent ache in my chest wouldn't let me forget that my parents weren't here and wouldn't get to see this. My mother would be proud I'd found my fated mate. My father would be proud I'd kicked Jasline's ass. Even if they couldn't be here in the flesh, I knew they were here with me in spirit.

They had to be for me to have made it this far on my own.

No, not on my own.

I turned my back to the stunning view and masterfully orchestrated preparations and gazed lovingly at my two best friends. They each wore a cocktail dress, in colors that complemented their natural skin tones.

Shay's was a dazzling gold, the tight slip underneath hitting her just above the knee, while the full skirt flowed down to the floor. Two slits from her waist to the floor showed off her long, toned legs and beautiful brown skin.

Leigh's was nearly opposite, the winking bronze material sculpted to her every fit curve, her gold-spun hair and bronze eye makeup making her look like a fairy. Well, maybe a *sinful* fairy. The hem of the dress barely covered her butt, making her legs look a mile and a half long of creamy perfection.

Those two were going to have alphas drooling over them all night.

I, however, had dressed for one alpha and one alone. The dress was customary for a bonding, backless and with no shoulder straps, so my neck and shoulders were fully bare for Kane's bite. It had a modern edge, though, with low-slung straps over my biceps and a deep cut down the front, nearly to my navel. The lines were clean and crisp, and it shone in sapphire blue and white crystal, offsetting my natural complexion. It fell to the floor in a soft tumble of smooth satin, with a risqué slit all the way to my right hip, so I could move freely. Leigh had highlighted my cheeks, so I looked rosy and fresh, while Shay had helped me with the bombshell, tousled curls. Clipped to kiss only one shoulder, so the other would be free.

If I knew Kane, though, he would be carefully removing each and every one of those precisely placed pins and picking whichever shoulder he wanted.

I was okay with it. A shudder ran through me, and my scent must have spiked, because Leigh wrinkled her nose at me.

"I'm just saying, I know it's the big night. But Brielle will forgive you if you can't make it. She's a *doctor*, for Goddess's sake!" Shay was using her stern voice, which was very rare for our reserved bestie.

"What's wrong? Why wouldn't she be able to come tonight?" I turned the question on Shay, because Leigh was too stubborn to ever admit a weakness, even if it was so we could help her.

I wasn't proud of the feeling of panic that threatened to seal my throat shut at the idea of not having Leigh's strong, brash presence at my back tonight as *everyone* watched the public portion of the claiming under the moon. It might be worse than facing down Jasline. Or Gael, and he was *far* more intimidating than any she-wolf I'd ever met. What if I forgot the words? She was the one who was supposed to know them all and whisper them in my ear if my mind went blank!

"Look at her! She's panicked. A little fever isn't going to keep me from showing up for my bestie. I *am* coming, so stop looking like that," she chided me gently.

"Okay, but only if you let her check you out. You really are burning up, Leigh."

She rolled her eyes, but didn't back away when I very unscientifically held my wrist up to her forehead. Shay groaned.

"What? I don't have my medical kit, but she shouldn't be much hotter than either of us. It's a decent method. And you're right, she's scalding. Are you sure you feel okay?"

"I'm *fine*." There was a small growl behind the words, and I squinted at her. My usually jovial bestie had been snapping and snarling a *lot* the last week.

She couldn't be going into heat, could she? It would be unusual for an unmated female to go into heat, unless her bond mate was close by. As far as I knew, Leigh wasn't vibing with anyone here, and most of the single male wolves had left at Kane's orders. Unless someone in one of our packs was triggering her? It couldn't be anyone from Johnson City, or else she'd have found him ages ago. But we hadn't spent much time with anyone outside the inner circle of Kane's pack.

She-wolves had fairly light and regular periods, until they were bonded. And then, once or twice per year we went into heat, meaning we were fertile and able to get pregnant with our mates. I'd never experienced one, and I didn't think Leigh or Shay had either.

It would be strange, given that most heats weren't triggered until *after* a mating bite, but it wasn't impossible. There were stories of she-wolves being triggered early and finding their mates through the heat craze. Stranger things had happened in the last two weeks.

"When was your last—"

"Ladies!" The bridal suite's door flew open with a bang, Gracelyn on the other side. "It's time to head down to the clearing. Ohhh, you all look *gorgeous*! Lucky, lucky males tonight! Oh, I can't wait. I bet at least one of you two starts a fistfight." She clapped with glee, the baby sleeping peacefully snuggled on her chest completely unbothered by her noisy mother's excitement, even though she had her *mom voice* on lock.

I stepped forward, drawn to baby Dawn like a magnet.

"May I?" I whispered, gesturing to her downy little head poking out of the wrap.

"Girl, for you I'd *wake her up*. I don't know how you did it, but I *know* you saved my life. Our lives." She dropped a hand to the baby's back, and I heard a tiny sniffle.

I gave her a warm smile and let my fingers dance lightly over the baby's soft, dark hair. She was perfection, her little rosebud lips suckling lightly in her sleep. "Don't cry on me now, Gracelyn. Somebody's got to hold it together, or this ceremony is going to fall to pieces."

She straightened, propping her hands on her hips. "Don't even think about jinxing this! I have pulled off a *miracle*, and tonight's going to be perfect. Assuming we're not all late. Let's go!" She spun to the door and stopped. "Wait! Feet!"

We all rolled our eyes, but stuck out a foot so she could see our bare toes.

Apparently, Kane's pack had a tradition that you bonded in bare feet, to better access the earth's magic. I'd never heard of such a thing, but after our time here... maybe I did believe the magic was a bit stronger, a bit more primal than back home in Texas.

So, bare toed I went to meet my mate, my love. My heart beat a little faster as I stepped out the door and toward the rest of my life.

A GENTLE HUMMING melody and the heady scent of jasmine greeted me as we approached the ceremonial clearing, twilight finally sinking into full night like its lost lover's arms.

"Okay, you three wait here. I've got to get in place, and then you walk in when the music kicks up. Remember, Brielle is first, chin tucked, and you two flank her. Blackwater pack is *very* traditional, ceremonial keeper etiquette included." She shot a pointed glance to Leigh, whose color was high.

She didn't snap back, though. She just nodded and took up her position behind my right shoulder, while Shay took the left.

Gracelyn slipped down the path with a double thumbs-up, and we waited, nothing but the sounds of our own beating hearts and the gentle hum to show there was anything special happening tonight.

It wasn't long before the humming turned to gentle singing, which rose and wove through the tree limbs like magic. I didn't know the words; apparently, they were Romanian. Gracelyn had assured me that they were a beautiful tradition in the home country... and that Shay could be in charge of the music at the after-party.

Not that I would *be* at the after-party. I would be in the bonding cottage, with Kane. I shivered, even though I felt hot with nerves. The cool night air on my shoulders was a blessing from the Goddess.

The Goddess, who was really listening. Yeah. That was going to take some getting used to.

"I think that's our cue, Brielle. Are you ready?" Shay's words were soft, nonjudgmental. Just like my bestie.

I blew out a shaking breath and started walking down the path. The ground under my feet was surprisingly soft, strewn with real flowers that we crushed under every step, adding to the thick perfume in the air.

It was only a minute, and the path widened to reveal the large clearing. The trees around the edges were old, older than time if you believed Pack Blackwater's stories, and seemed lit from within as they towered over our pack mates. They gathered in loose groups on both sides of the clearing, but my eyes weren't on them.

I couldn't look anywhere but at Kane, standing with his hands clasped behind his back in the middle of the clearing, inside a circle of mounded flower blossoms in every color, his eyes glued to mine. He was a vision of masculinity, his jaw hard and clean shaven, his lush lips curved into a soft smile, and his dark hair swept back smoothly from his forehead. He wore a pair of black slacks over bare feet, with a sapphire-blue button-up that matched my dress exactly, unbuttoned at the throat. That little expanse of tanned skin hit different when I saw it here, now.

In just a little while, I'd be peeling him out of that shirt and leaving my mating mark there, binding us together for the rest of our lives. I shivered again, nothing to do with the crisp night air now. Now it was all liquid heat, pooling in my belly at the thought of me and Kane, *alone*.

I walked a little faster as I covered the last of the distance, and a few chuckles reached me from the watching wolves. I didn't care what they thought. I was eager to be in the arms of my love.

I stopped a foot from him, inside the circle of flowers. We swayed toward each other, like magnets trying to click into place. But we couldn't, not yet.

Gael and Reed stood at his shoulders, and I knew Shay and Leigh bracketed mine.

Reed stepped up first, a large, antique golden key in his outstretched hand. He laid it at my feet. "For prosperity," he said, voice raised for all to hear, before stepping back behind Kane.

Next was Leigh's turn.

"For fertility," she said, dropping to her knees between us and sprinkling scented water from a jar on our bare feet and ankles.

"For passion." Shay surprised me when she stepped up, boldly saying her part despite the many males surrounding us.

Perhaps my shy bestie is starting to crack open her hard shell, after all this time?

She dabbed the insides of my wrists and the spot behind my ears with a perfume stick I knew was heavily laced with lovelace, a known aphrodisiac for shifters. She repeated the action, dabbing Kane efficiently before stepping back into her place.

Gael was the last, holding up a pair of shining rings. He pressed one first into Kane's hand and then the other into mine. "For eternity."

When he stepped back, Kane stepped forward, bracketing me in his arms, at long last. Typically a father or relative would marry us, but since we had none, Adam stepped forward to complete the ceremony. His eyes gleamed with happiness as he looked at the two of us, clasped together like nothing would ever peel us apart.

"Kane and Brielle, we gather here under the Goddess's moon to bind you two together as mates. It is a lifelong bond, unable to be broken, even in death. Alpha Kane, what do you offer this woman to prove that you are worthy of her love?"

He met my eyes, the gentle smile I knew he reserved only for me sending butterflies swooping around my belly. His nostrils flared, and my scent had to be spiking, as the low heat of arousal since I'd spotted him built into a raging inferno of heat and want. I wouldn't care if he offered me a shiny rock like a crow. If it came from him, I'd treasure it.

"For my first gift, I've begun converting one of the larger rooms on the ground floor of the pack lodge into a lab for you. I didn't know exactly what equipment you had, but Alpha Todd graciously provided me with an inventory of your lab back home in Johnson City. With help from a few of my pack mates, we placed rush orders for brand-new equipment, to match everything that you had back home, as well as a few new pieces the sales rep assured me you'd be happy with. It's all been delivered, and tomorrow I'll be at your beck and call to install it all to your satisfaction."

I was floored. He was building me a lab? For my medical research. It was the most thoughtful thing anyone had ever done for me. He wasn't just making space for me in his heart, but in his home as well. For my dreams, my ambitions.

"Brielle, do you accept this first gift?"

Tears prickled the corners of my eyes, and I had to swallow hard to be able to answer Adam. "Yes, I do."

"Excellent. The second, Kane?"

"I would like to offer my second gift in private, if Brielle will accept that."

Confused, I nodded. "I accept." What *else* could he possibly have chosen as a bonding gift that he wouldn't present it here? A lab was *more* than extravagant enough. It would have cost thousands of dollars to purchase everything I'd had back home, and none of it had been new, top-of-the-line models.

Adam nodded solemnly. "You may exchange your rings."

Kane held my trembling hand in his much steadier one and slid the stunning, jewel-studded ring onto my finger. It looked antique, with clustered diamonds around a blue stone that perfectly matched the color of our mating marks. The ring itself was carved with leaves and wolves, and every part of it was beautiful to look at.

He offered his hand, and I took it, carefully sliding the band onto his ring finger, letting my fingertips graze his palm underneath. Heat flared in his eyes as it settled into place. His was heavier, a masculine cut with a square stone sunken into the carved gold. It appeared to be from the same era as mine, and I wondered who in his family these rings had belonged to.

"The bond between mates is completed with a bite. It is customary for this to be done privately and must be completed before the moon disappears from the night sky. In the eyes of the Goddess and these witnesses, I bless this joining. Go forth, and claim your mate."

Kane's lips fell to mine, and he ravished them like it was the only kiss we'd ever share again. Whoops and hollers rose around us, mixed with howls as a few wolves shifted to run under the full moon. Heat surged in my veins as I clung to him, my fangs dropping dangerously low in my mouth. I must have nicked his lip, because when he pulled back to rest his forehead against mine, the bow shape of his lower lip glinted with blood in the moonlight.

When he leaned down, I thought he was going to kiss me again, but instead, he dropped his lips next to my ear, his voice a whisper too low for anyone else to hear over the cheering.

"Are you ready for me to chase you, little mate?"

A jolt of excitement shot through me. The hunt.

He'd asked yesterday if I was okay with upholding *that* particular piece of the Old World tradition, and I'd said yes.

I grinned up at him as I stepped back, leaving his warm embrace... just for a little longer. Without another word, I lifted the hem of my billowing dress, and I bolted.

The path to the bonding cottage was lit with fairy lights, and I ran for all I was worth. To fulfill the ancient rites, he would have to fight his way past his ceremonial keepers and then catch me before I could latch the cottage door. If he wasn't able to capture me, the Goddess was said to have deemed him unworthy, and he would have to repeat the ritual under the next full moon to earn bonding rites.

I didn't know how far away it was, but I had *zero* doubts he'd catch me quickly. Still, I wasn't going to make it easy on him. I whooped with glee as I ran, the soft grass and moss squishing underfoot, and the cool night air blowing against my overheated cheeks. The path twisted and turned gently, but I never lost sight of the twinkling lights, and before long, the lovely, ivy-covered cottage came into view. The front door was propped open, a warm light inviting me in. I could just see the corner of a soft and thick mattress, piled high with pillows and blankets in the back room.

I craned my neck to see more as I ran up the smooth cobblestone walkway, and that was when Kane's arms crashed around my waist, locking me to his chest.

I laughed, nearly breathless with adrenaline from the run and the heady scent of him, as he scooped me up and carried me over the threshold, my long dress trailing underneath us like that of some fairy-tale princess of old.

When we stepped inside, Kane pulled the front door shut and turned the lock with a soft click.

FORTY-TWO

Kane

I stalked forward until I once again caught her, my mischievous mate, and pinned her hands to the cottage door above her head.

She shivered delicately, and the motion sent her breasts rubbing against my chest. I couldn't feel the peaks of her nipples through the double-layered fabric of her gown, but it slipped and slid easily, like a waterfall of heat between us.

I would do my best not to ruin it when I took her out of it, but I made no promises. If I knew anything about my mate, it was that she would forgive me for any blunders. I wouldn't even mind the groveling, so long as I got to make it up to her sweet, honeyed pussy. Besides, I'd buy her a thousand dresses if I got to take her out of them at the end of the night.

Her jasmine-and-apple perfume rose around us in a thick cloud, her pupils blown wide as I bent down to lave kisses up the column of her throat.

Her little whimper almost took me out at the knees, and I hadn't even peeled her out of her gown yet.

"You look good enough to eat in this dress. The whole time I was chasing you, you caught the lights and shone as brightly as my own personal star." I let my fangs scrape lightly over the skin of her shoulder. Not enough to break it, only enough to tease. To *promise*.

But first, I owed her another bonding gift before we completed the blood bond. Forcing my lips away from her was like trying to stop the Yukon, but I managed, just long enough to lead her through the bedroom and attached bathroom. It was oversized compared to the rest of the cabin, but given its purpose, it was perfectly suited.

The shower had three heads, a steam enclosure, and the separate tub was big enough for two. A mirror stretched from the top of the long, marble counter up to the ceiling, reflecting our flushed faces back to us. Her gown was askew from her flight through the woods, but I liked it. She looked wild, like my own personal forest sprite. The way her breasts pressed temptingly against the deep blue fabric urged me to *hurry up already and taste her*.

Now that I'd had the flavor of her on my tongue, I was ruined for any other dessert. She was finer than the finest wines, and sweeter than any cream a pastry chef could dream up.

Patience, Kane.

I turned the tap on the tub, letting warm water flow and adding a generous pour of lavender-scented bubbles underneath the stream.

"You want to take a bath, first? I kind of thought we might just..." Her cheeks turned adorably pink, and I leaned forward to kiss the tip of her nose.

"My darling, I get the feeling you're trying to get me into bed." I gave her my most scandalized expression, and she giggled.

My brilliant, stunning doctor. Giggling like a teenager. I liked every side of her, and I coveted them all.

"I thought you might like to bathe after. There will be

blood, and I want you to be able to get comfortable, if you're sore."

"Oh. That's incredibly thoughtful of you. Is this the gift? I accept." She pressed a kiss to my cheek, and I held her close, breathing in the scent of her hair. So sweet, so innocent. Everything I never knew I so desperately needed.

"No, this isn't the gift. This is just me loving my mate. Seeing to her *every* need."

She caught her breath at the words, and I ran my fingertips over her parted lips. Damn, she made it hard to concentrate.

"What is it?"

"You said loving... you just haven't said the words yet. I know it's been fast, but..." She bit her bottom lip, worrying it between her teeth in a *very* distracting manner.

"I thought I'd shown you, my heart. You are everything to me. The air I breathe, the blood in my veins. Without you, there is no me. *Of course* I love you, more than life itself."

Tears gathered on her thick, dark lashes, and in that moment, I realized the gravest mistake I'd made yet. In all the ways I'd *shown* her I cared, I hadn't understood that she needed to hear the words.

"I love you," I murmured, pressing a kiss to the top of her head. "I love you," I said again, dropping down to sear a kiss to her clavicle.

"I love you today," I whispered to the creamy flesh of the tops of her breasts, my hands coming to the laces at the back of the dress, pulling them slowly. "I'll love you even more tomorrow." I nibbled her ear as the dress began to gape away from her perfect breasts.

I lifted her easily, setting her on the counter, and began peeling the dress down with slow, measured movements, letting it puddle at her waist. She wore a matching blue corset underneath, her breasts high and needy, pressing against the lacy fabric and begging for my touch, my tongue.

Letting my finger trail down, I traced the edge of the fabric, reveling in the feel of her silky-smooth perfection.

"I will love you every day, every minute, every *second* of eternity."

She gasped, and I let both hands come forward, cupping her stunning breasts in my hands, lifting them free for my mouth. I played with one nipple lightly with my fingertips while I lavished attention on the other with my tongue.

Brielle moaned and leaned back, letting her bare shoulders press into the mirror. Her eyes fell closed, her knees spread wide to make room for me. I took every inch, loving the way her warmth enveloped me, consumed me.

Her arousal was thick in the air, and I quickly peeled the dress the rest of the way off her, leaving it in a pile on the bathroom floor. She helped me with the corset, pulling once, and an entire row of hidden clips came free, leaving her bare for me.

Goddess, she was perfection. I trailed down her flat belly to her mound, covered only by a thin scrap of blue silk. It matched her mate marks. The sight would stay with me for the rest of my days. Her curls were wild from my hands, her eyes desperate for more, and the wanton way she opened for me... How did I get so lucky?

I shredded the lacy thong, tossing it aside and pushing her thighs wide, giving myself full access to her gleaming wet pussy.

FORTY-THREE

Brielle

I arched and moaned when his mouth hit my overheated flesh. Goddess, the man was so skilled, he knew what I needed before I did. The sight of him bowed before me, his broad shoulders under my thighs as he devoured me was intense, but I didn't close my eyes. I wanted to hold on to every second, sear it into my memory.

Then his tongue circled my clit, and my eyes fell closed, my shoulders digging into the cool, smooth mirror behind me. The scent of lavender from the bubble bath faded, overwhelmed by the spicy, delicious scent of his cinnamon and citrus as he nipped and kissed and pulled me into oblivion. The world around us narrowed to a point, just him and me, here in this moment.

"Kane, I need more... I need—" Words failed me as he looked up, his eyes burning brightly with his wolf.

He never took his mouth off me, but slid his fingers up, working me on his fingers as he sucked harder.

The orgasm overtook me in an unexpected rush. I screamed, his name a one-word chant on my lips as he continued working me with one hand. When my eyes opened, he was there, bracing himself over me with the other hand, and his chin glistening with my arousal.

"You milk my fingers so good, sweet girl. Are you ready to milk my cock like that?"

I whimpered, clinging to his shoulders and pressing hot, openmouthed kisses along his throat until I hit the collar of his shirt. How was he still fully dressed when I was a naked mess? That wouldn't do.

I snatched the collar open, sending a couple of buttons flying free. His chuckle was dark and pleased, and he took over unbuttoning the rest as I fastened myself back to the side of his throat. When I reached the pulse point where his neck met his shoulder, I sucked hard, letting my fangs scrape over his skin.

He growled, low and teasing, and the vibrations on my nipples nearly pushed me into another orgasm.

"Don't stop. I like the feel of your teeth on me." His voice was all gravel, and I loved knowing that *I* did that to him. I was the one unraveling him, breaking down his carefully crafted alpha facade, one thread at a time.

He pulled the shirt off, and I let my nails run over the corded muscles of his shoulders. He was golden perfection, and the urge to mark him, bite him, rose up so quickly, I swayed back.

"What's wrong?" he murmured, nibbling my ear.

"The urge to bite you, just..."

"Mmmm... Are you ready?"

I nodded, feeling strangely shy. We both knew what was coming, but my wolf was riding me hard, wanting me to take the first step.

He scooped me off the counter with ease, turning the tub's tap off with one hand as he carried me to the massive bed.

Kane set me down gently, reverently, at the edge. I noticed a bowl of still-warm water and a stack of small towels next to the bed, to take care of the bites. Someone had really thought of everything. But to do it, to bite...I'd have to let my wolf take control. What if I fainted? That would be the worst bonding night ever.

Nerves had me pausing, gripping his waist, as I stared into his eyes.

Somehow he knew, because his touches turned light, giving me a moment to breathe. He stroked my mating marks reverently as he spoke, tracing the swirling patterns with blunt fingertips.

"My gorgeous mate, I would like to present you with your second gift."

I nodded, too nervous to speak.

"I've found a high shaman, of a nearby Athabascan pack of wolves. Their histories are older, deeper than ours. He is ancient and wasn't here for the great pack gathering. However, I've secured his promise to let us visit on their pack lands. While I don't know what's happening to your magic, I know that he *will*. He has agreed to assess and direct us on how to heal your magic. He thinks there might be something hindering your connection to the wolf, and that it's reversible. He may also be able to finally confirm for us that you're omega."

My jaw dropped open, shock displacing my fear. "He... he might be able to fix it?"

"That is my hope. He'll see us next week, and I've already arranged a private seaplane for the six of us. I assumed you would want to bring your friends along. I promise to spend the rest of my days pursuing this. We will see you whole and healthy and happy. I will not rest until your future is secure at my side. Your burdens are mine, and mine are yours. Together, we can solve any problem."

Tears hit me in a wave. I quickly scrubbed at my eyes to dash them away, relief and hope and so many emotions I couldn't identify warring for dominance. "But what about your parents' killer? We still have to find him. It feels wrong to ask you to take time away from something so important. You need that closure."

"I do, and I will find him. But your safety comes first, always. Once I know you're secure, I can go after the bastard with all my attention. But until then... you're always going to come first for me." He trailed gentle fingers down the column of my throat, ending with a small, delicious swoop over my collarbone that had me shuddering with want.

"I accept your gift." The words were barely a whisper, but I knew he heard them just the same.

He smiled lazily, but his eyes were concerned as he watched the tears I couldn't quite dash away. He reached up with his thumb, catching one I'd missed. "Don't cry, my love. Tonight is for joy, for passion. For us to become one."

His tone was gentle, but the reminder lit that spark again, bringing my wolf's instincts charging back to the front. My hand dropped to my lips, the feeling of my fangs descending one I might never get used to.

His lips quirked up into a smile at one corner, as if he knew exactly what I was thinking. "Are you ready?"

I nodded, talking surprisingly awkward with fangs. He stood and quickly stripped off his pants and black boxer briefs, my mouth watering for different reasons as his cock bobbed free. It was long and thick, and if I didn't have fangs taking up half my mouth, I'd have licked it from root to tip. *There's always after*.

Naked now, he dropped back to his knees, kneeling in front of me and wrapping his arms around my waist. With me perched on the edge of the bed, I could feel his warm abs pressed against my core, my slick coating him.

He groaned and dropped his head to my chest. "I want you to take your time, but it's hard to hold still when I can feel your juices dripping down my front. I'm going to smell like you for days." He playfully nipped my left breast, and I moaned, the sensation zipping right to my clit and sparking a fresh wave of heat.

"Good. I want you to smell like me forever."

He grinned, the look half wolf, half devil. "Then bite me, mate. Bite me and claim me, so every wolf knows who I belong to."

I patted the bed beside me, and he rose from the floor before sinking down next to me on the mattress with a curious expression. I tossed my leg over his lap, and his eyes heated, boring into mine as I slowly lowered myself, impaling myself on his cock inch by inch. This time, he was the one moaning, dropping his head back in ecstasy. And Goddess, the feeling of him was perfection. The way he stretched me...I tried not to lose myself to it completely, letting myself play with the hair at the back of his neck as I adjusted to the intrusion.

I took a moment just to feel the connection there, to hold him tight and fist him with my inner walls, with his bare chest pressed to mine. He grunted, jerking when I locked down.

That's when I bit him. My fangs were ready, so I opened wide and sank them into the muscle next to his pulse.

He shouted my name and grabbed my hips, grinding himself up into my pussy as I sucked on his shoulder. To my surprise, he tasted sweet, like cinnamon rolls.

"Yes, Brielle, yes. Just like that." His words were reverent, the cords standing out in his neck as I let my fangs sink just a bit deeper.

After a few seconds I leaned back, careful not to move too much as I let my fangs slide free. The urge to lick him was overwhelming, so I did, carefully covering the wound with my tongue. It began to close up almost immediately, only a few rivulets of blood escaping to run down his chest and back.

The bonding magic would keep the scar there permanently. I licked it one more time, and he moaned again.

"If you don't stop, I'm going to come right now, and you're far too coherent for that. I need you screaming my name, making a mess of my cock before I come with my fangs in your neck."

I shivered, the words sending heat racing up the back of my neck and making my breasts tingle when I pulled back from the bite.

He didn't waste a second, flipping our positions without leaving my center. When I was stretched out in the middle of the bed with him over me, he began to move again, slowly at first, stopping at the end of each stroke to grind against my clit.

"Kane... If you keep doing that..." I panted, unable to finish the sentence.

"That's right, baby. I want your orgasm, right here, right now. What do you need from me? You need it harder, softer?" He held my hands overhead, pinning them into the mattress as he pumped in and out, never letting me come down from the growing high, that impending cliff of ecstasy I could feel building dangerously high.

"I want everything. Let your wolf go. Claim me." I looked up into his glowing eyes as I said the last words, and it was like I could see the switch flip.

Reserved Alpha Kane was gone, replaced by his wolf. He let my hands go, pulling out for the briefest second to flip me onto my hands and knees, and then he was back, so deep the head of his cock bottomed out with every stroke. The friction and heat were phenomenal, stars winking behind my eyes as I held on to the comforter for dear life.

He didn't let me stay there long, though. After a few pounding strokes, he banded an arm around my chest and lifted me, so I was impaled on his cock and stretched, his chest pressed against my back, sending delicious friction over all my sensitive skin. His hand traveled to my breast, and then in one swift motion, he pinched my nipple at the same time his other hand pinched my clit.

I broke into a thousand pieces, shattered like stars in the sky, with nothing to hold me together but his arms. He roared and sank his fangs into my neck as he came, sending me immediately into a second peak.

I was a being of light and love and lust. There was nothing left between us, and as he finished pumping his release into me, I felt the mental bond settle into place. It was like feathers falling from a torn pillow, bringing warmth and closeness.

He licked the mating bond with tenderness, each touch sending a jolt of pleasure straight to my core. I gripped his hand tightly, the sensations overwhelming... but at the same time, bringing a level of *wholeness* I'd never experience before.

The other half of my soul, my fated mate, was a blinding bright thread in my chest, tying us together, forever.

He lowered us to the mattress with great tenderness, nuzzling his nose against my neck and breathing me in deeply, like he still couldn't get enough.

Brielle? Can you hear me?

Yes! It happened fast. I... This is so weird.

Weird? I was going to say wonderful. *You don't like it?*

I felt a wave of disappointment from him.

No! I didn't say that. I do. It's just so different. I can tell what you're feeling now. I don't have to wonder anymore.

Yes. It's perfection. He pushed his hips forward, his semistiff cock still inside me and scraping along my G-spot at this angle. I arched into his arms, letting out a low moan. This many orgasms deep, everything was sensitive.

Why do I have a feeling that your new favorite thing is going to be to spy on my feelings when we have sex?

Because you're a brilliant doctor, and I'm a horny alpha who can't get enough of his bond mate.

His fingertips skated over my clit again, gently circling. I felt a wave of heat and desire from him, his cock already fully hard again.

Why don't you show me, then?

Oh, I will gladly show you as many times as you'd like, tonight and every night. And in the day, and after breakfast. With your pussy for dessert.

With an offer like that, how could a girl refuse? So I didn't.

Epilogue - Shay

Pack Blackwater took the full moon *very* seriously. We were inside the main lodge, a huge open room that they used for pack celebrations. Some of the wolves had run off in fur as soon as Brielle and Kane left the clearing, but most had come back here, to dance and drink first. A few had even snuck off to semiprivate corners, and I was pretty sure at least three couples were having sex right now.

I averted my eyes from the grabbing hands and undulating hips, focusing on the music. That was where I always hid, and I wasn't about to change that now. My laptop was hooked up to the room's surround system, and right now, dance music was blasting over the speakers.

"You look like you could use a drink." Reed startled me by appearing at my side, offering me a fresh cup of punch. I carefully lowered my headphones so I wouldn't undo all the work Leigh had put into my hair earlier in the evening.

"Thank you," I half yelled to be heard over the speakers. It *was* warm in here with so many people dancing, and the blood-red punch went down smoothly. Maybe *too* smoothly. I was on my third—fourth?—cup, and had a happy buzz humming in my veins.

Leigh, on the other hand, was crushed up against a hot beta wolf from back home with a bottle of Jack Daniels clutched in one fist. *Clearly, her mystery fever isn't keeping her down.* I didn't think there was anything serious between them. For all her sex positivity, Leigh never slept around. She was a one-wolf kind of gal, and always had been. Maybe it would be good for her to get it out of her system. We only had three days left until we left for the Athabascan pack's lands. Reed had let me know about the trip as soon as the ceremony ended, and I was glad Brielle was finally going to get some more information about why she had such trouble with her wolf. Hopefully, three days would be enough.

It was taking her so long to get over Marcus. It was always hard losing a relationship, but the salt in the wound when he'd left because he found his fated mate? Yeah... Even my ebullient bestie was taking time bouncing back from that, and it killed me.

Though things might *get* serious if they kept dancing like that. His thigh was pressed between hers, his hands wandering a bit too far for the dance floor—but given what was going on in the booths along the walls and the corners of the room, they weren't that bad—and her head was thrown back wantonly as he kissed her neck.

"Would you like to dance, Shay?" Reed drew my attention away from Leigh.

Would I like to dance? Maybe. But with Reed? I perused him more closely than I usually did. He was handsome; there was no doubting that. I'm sure most women would be happy to spin around the floor with him in his three-piece suit, and perfectly styled hair. It was long enough to dig your fingers into, something most of the wolves around here didn't bother with.

But my wolf was *not* interested. She huffed a low sound of disapproval before curling up with her head propped on her front feet.

I shook my head no, and he accepted gracefully. He did *everything* gracefully. Even if I was into him, I'd feel awkward all the time. I was not fancy, not like him. He exuded wealth, and I lived in beat-up sneakers and hoodies.

"Oh, shit. If you'll excuse me, I need to prevent a fistfight." He strode off toward the dance floor, and I snapped my eyes around to look for whatever danger he'd spotted.

Oh shit is right. Gael had left his position brooding against the wall and was cutting a swath through the dance floor toward Leigh, whose beta had now dropped both hands to her ass and was kneading it through the shiny fabric of her dress.

Leigh and Gael were such a contradiction. She always seemed ready to rip his throat out, but the vibes they gave off had definite *fuck buddies* energy.

I wasn't an expert at romance—unlike my two besties, I'd had exactly zero boyfriends since joining the Johnson City pack—but I had a feeling they were either going to get together or kill each other. There was no in-between.

Unless you counted Gael ripping the beta's arms off and beating him with them, which it looked like he was about to do.

I quickly switched over to my premade playlist, and leapt down from the small platform stage where my DJ booth was set up to help Reed play referee.

"Where do you get off! I swear, a girl can't even have a little fun now without the ball-busting brigade showing up. Is that what this is? You're just morally opposed to the idea of me getting laid now?"

"Lower your voice," Gael growled, his eyes sharp enough to cut glass.

Leigh, more than a little tipsy if the smell wafting off her was any indication, leaned her head back and cupped her mouth to amplify her next shout. "You're not my alpha! I'll dance with whoever I want to." She dropped the hand megaphone and leaned in close to whisper something in his ear. Even my shifter hearing couldn't pick it up above the pounding music, but whatever it was, she might as well have dropped a stick of dynamite.

He snarled, grabbing her around the shoulders and half pushing, half carrying her off the dance floor.

"Gael! Let me take over." Reed stepped up, arms out and ready to take Leigh. "She's clearly had a bit too much to drink. I'll escort her back to her room."

"I can take her, Reed. We share a room," I argued, stepping up next to my bestie in the hope of steering her away from Gael. He looked on the murderous side at the moment, and while my wolf was strong, I didn't know if we'd come out on top if I had to shift and fight him to keep him off her.

"He doesn't want that. Do you, Gael?" Leigh's words were surprisingly unslurred, and the challenge was clear.

He snarled, his eyes glowing and no words coming out.

"I can't hear you. I told you, I've got an itch in *desperate* need of scratching. If you won't let me scratch it with JP, well, I'll have to find another volunteer." She practically purred, reaching out a hand toward Reed's tie, as if to reel him in closer.

Gael shoved Reed back, stepping up chest to chest with Leigh.

"You will *not* scratch your itches with my pack mate."

"No? Who will it be, then, Mr. Caveman? I'm sure I can find a volunteer in this crowd."

"Leigh," I protested, worried for my friend. Maybe the fever *was* getting to her. This was not like her. She was a joker and loved sex, sure. But to advertise it loudly in front of all these wolves like she'd take anybody back to bed? Not so much.

"I volunteer." The words were low, dangerous, and all predator. I froze on instinct, eyes going wide as I took in Gael, his green eyes sparking with challenge.

"Finally," Leigh rumbled again, and then they were all over each other. Lips clashed, hands wandered, and I found myself blushing.

"Leigh! Stop!" I tried to get her attention, but she was trying to peel Gael out of his shirt right here at the edge of the dance floor, and people were staring.

Reed placed a hand on Gael's shoulder, and he snapped. He moved in a blur of speed, dropping Leigh and spinning, putting himself between her and Reed.

"Whoa, hang on. I'm not trying to touch her." Reed held up both hands placatingly.

Gael's only response was a snarl, nothing like the composed alpha-hole we regularly saw as our guard.

"Leigh, are you sober enough for this? How much have you had to drink?" I stepped into her personal space, and she snorted.

"This stuff tastes like shit for some reason. I've barely had any. I'm just horny, okay? I don't know what's gotten into me, but I know what I'd *like* to get into me." She shot a sultry look at Gael, who was still snarling at Reed. "Tonight. It'll get him out of my system."

She *sounded* levelheaded, if a bit more brazen than usual. She passed me the bottle of whiskey, and she was right. She'd barely touched it. Her eyes were clear, but she'd already lost interest in me, her eyes homed in on Gael's broad shoulders.

"If you're sure."

"I've never been more sure about anything in my life." She brushed past me, running her hand temptingly over his shoulders. He turned back to face her, bracketing her arms with his, pulling her close, possessive.

"Take me back to your room," she demanded.

He growled and picked her up by the backs of her thighs, and her long blonde hair hung down his back like silk. In seconds, they'd gone from fighting to wrapped up like vines, tangled beyond recognition. He carried her across the room, her arms already twined around his neck, lips locked. He kicked the door open, and it banged shut behind them.

"Well, this is royally awkward," Reed said with a laugh, running his fingers through his hair. "Do I need to get ten guys and go try to pry him off her? Do you think she's okay?"

I shrugged, holding up the bottle of whiskey. "She seemed weirdly clear, and she didn't drink much of this."

"Yeah, her metabolism has probably already burned that off. Well… They're both consenting adults. They might wake up with regrets tomorrow, but if they're not drunk…"

I shrugged. I wouldn't have let her leave with *anybody* if I weren't sure she was sober and clear. "Maybe this was the push they needed to stop fighting…" *or to spark something new.*

I would be happy for her, if so. She'd taken it so hard when her ex Marcus had left.

He shook his head slowly. "Want me to take that back to the bar?"

"Sure." He took the bottle and headed across the floor, so I delved into the dancing crowd to take back my position as DJ, where I was safely out of the sea of pheromones that was the dance floor.

I was almost through when somebody screamed.

"Look out!"

"What the hell!"

"He's feral! Somebody get the enforcers!"

Something twanged in my chest an instant before a massive black wolf with blood-red eyes burst through the crowd, arrowing straight toward me. I tried to dive out of the way, but he mirrored my movements. Dancers bailed away from him in every direction, but he ignored them all, skidding to a stop in front of me, head lowered as if he was about to attack.

Screams and shouts continued to ricochet off the walls as people ran, but I couldn't move a muscle. Something about this wolf called to me, and my own wolf pressed forward. I could feel her, my eyes shining into his. Goddess, they were *red*. That could only mean one thing, and it wasn't good. So why couldn't I move? Why wasn't I running?

The trance holding us broke when the music died and the sound of running boots thundered toward us.

He snarled and spun, putting his back toward me and edging me backward toward the nearest wall. I let him herd me, unsure what else to do in this situation. A stream of black-clad enforcers poured into the room past the escaping partygoers, weapons drawn as they ran at us. No, at *him*.

They formed up in a semicircle, trapping us against an open wall.

"Let the girl go, or we'll shoot!"

The wolf snarled and leapt toward the speaker, but then jumped back, refusing to get more than a few feet from me.

Was he scared they were going to hurt me?

"You have to the count of three or we're going to put you down. One!" a gray-haired man who seemed to be the leader barked. His alpha dominance grated over my skin, and I couldn't help a whimper under the onslaught. They were all so angry, it was suffocating.

The black wolf snarled at them again, but took another step back until his side was pressed tightly against my legs, as if to be a physical shield between me and the others. I buried my fingers into his thick fur, hanging on to him like he was my anchor.

What a weird thought.

"Can he even understand you? He's feral." One of the other enforcers took a step forward, but the leader held up a hand.

"Two!"

The wolf snarled, pressing me even tighter against the wall.

"It's okay, they're not trying to hurt me. They're afraid." I murmured the words, and his pitch-black ear twitched back toward me, but still, he didn't shift into his human form, didn't move. "Please, they're going to hurt you. Don't do this."

Why did I care? I should have been terrified. This wolf was feral, and he'd targeted me for some unknown reason, and yet—*no.*

I sucked in a breath. Everything happened at once.

"Three!" The leader raised his gun, zeroing in on the wolf's broad chest.

"Stop! Don't shoot! That's Dirge!" Reed's desperate plea rang out as he shoved into the leader, knocking into him as he fired.

Mate. My wolf rumbled in my chest. I didn't think, I didn't breathe, I didn't question. I threw myself on top of the black wolf as the sound of the gun firing echoed in my ears.

Thank you so much for reading Fated to the Wolf Prince! If you loved the book and have time to drop some stars or leave a review, I'd appreciate it! Reviews are make-or-break for new authors.

I'm so excited for us to find out more about Brielle's past and how it shapes her future as we continue through the series. Not to mention, *dying* to see what heats up between Shay and Dirge in book two, Fated to the Feral Wolf!

Scan to order Fated to the Feral Wolf, Coming July 2024:

Can't get enough of Kane & Brielle? Me either. Join my newsletter here (https://dl.bookfunnel.com/g2vc070qw5) for a bonus scene. You can also hang out in my fan discord channel, here (https://discord.com/invite/dWCFbYGZFz).

Also by April L. Moon

The Hunted Omegas Series

Fated to the Wolf Prince

Fated to the Feral Wolf

Fated to the Wolf Warrior (coming soon!)

Made in United States
North Haven, CT
03 May 2024